Meeting the Pieman

The John Day Company · New York

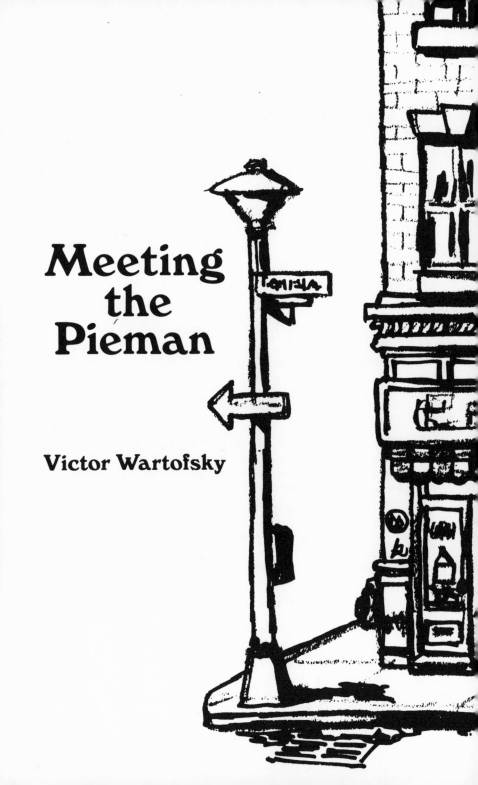

Meeting the Pieman

Victor Wartofsky

The John Day Company, 257 Park Avenue South, New York N.Y. 10010
an Intext publisher

Published on the same day in Canada by Longmans Canada Limited.

Library of Congress Catalogue Card Number: 77-125571
Printed in the United States of America
Designed by The Etheredges

Meeting the Pieman

The call persisted, but it was just too cold to urinate. Even if he took off his gloves and made it through the overalls, trousers, and long johns, it would be brutal to coax and then drag it out with freezing fingers from its relatively warm surroundings. He smiled to himself. How do Eskimos manage?

The urine congealed as it hit the ground. Had the temperature been a few degrees colder, the liquid might have been frozen stiff into a golden arched rainbow from source to snow. Of course, he couldn't tell Sarah that the men said it was piss-freezing cold. She didn't like that kind of language. He'd just tell her that it was pretty cold.

1

"This ain't no toilet, mister. Why don't you use the john?"

Simon Farber looked up. A tall, wiry man with clipboard in hand, and with a young face made red and raw by the wind, glared at him from sunken eyes. From a laborer's description Farber recognized him as the foreman.

"I didn't know where it was," Farber said, and then, casting his eyes downward, as if requesting something unreasonable, added, "I'm looking for work. Carpenter. You got anything?"

The foreman examined Farber closely. "You're an inside man, ain't you?"

"Jamb beams, windows, baseboards, anything."

"Got nothing like that now. Got a roof section needs work. Four dollars a hour."

"That's not union," Farber said.

"Crap on the union. Take it or leave it."

"Where do I go?"

Moments later, with fresh instructions, Farber picked up his toolcase by its strap and threaded his way on the frozen mud, rising like brown, naked hills, a corroded and scarred landscape in miniature. Piles of planks, piping, wires, and cinderblocks, almost animated in their huddles of frozen companionship, were scattered around him. Concrete mixers and wheelbarrows, layered with ice, stood still and unattended. He noted the absence of bricklayers, plasterers, and painters, and reminded himself that they couldn't work in this kind of weather. Only carpenters and floorlayers on the job could, and maybe inside plumbers.

[2]

He was lucky to find work, he thought, entering the skeleton of an apartment building. Like most buildings under construction, the inside elevator was inoperable while the temporary outside lift was prohibited to men and personal items. He dropped the toolcase and looked up ten floors to the roof, where in his mind he saw a network of rafters and joists waiting for him.

Farber mumbled that he was an inside man, and then quickly glanced around to see if anybody had heard his protest. The foreman stood in the distance, watching him.

"Okay, mister," Farber whispered, pulling his woolen hat down to cover his ears. "I'm going."

With one movement, he hoisted the toolcase onto his shoulder. Although a corner of the case, like a cat seeking a favorite nook, inclined snugly into an occupational depression of his shoulder, he grunted anew under the always surprisingly heavy load. Slowly, carefully, he began climbing the steps, each covered in spots with a film of ice, and nails, and cast-off pieces of wood. No baluster or hand-rails provided aid or a barrier against a sudden fall over the side to floors below. He knew that if he slipped, he'd have to fall forward, or against the recently plastered, white staircase wall.

To hell with the plasterers, he thought, commanding his legs to move faster. He wanted to get to the roof in plenty of time to fulfill a quota he knew the foreman had silently set. If Farber met it, he stood a good chance of being kept on.

For twenty-three years he had carried the eighty-pound chest, with its hammers and saws, chisel, level, sharpening stone, screwdrivers, hatchet, files, crowbar, and other tools for boring, leveling, slicing, cutting, measuring. He had trudged with it everywhere, carrying and caring for it like a mother an infant, looking for jobs and finding them, yet not daring to leave it overnight wherever he worked for fear that it might be stolen. One hundred dollars' worth of tools, it was an investment he began after the war with the purchase of a hammer.

The bulky case was a problem on the subway. The haughty looks of suited men were bad enough, but more disturbing to him were the hostile glances of young girls who grudgingly allowed his tools to deprive them of needed standing space.

Look, he wanted to say to them, don't do me no favors. Secretaries! Clerks! I make five dollars and seventy-five cents an hour. Match that.

Despite the cold, perspiration covered his body. He breathed deeply as he felt the load increasing and digging into his shoulder.

"You're getting heavier. Don't let me down, now."

Four dollars an hour. Goddamn crooks. I can't tell the union. The union can't find me another job, anyway.

Sweat now prickled on his forehead, chilling it, while the breath rasped in his throat. His legs shook with fatigue and weakness. Driving himself on, not daring to stop and rest, he made himself listen to the tools clattering in the case to take his mind off the climb. He played a game, trying to match the sound with the tool. He warned himself not to put the hammer so close to the measuring level, with its delicate, glass-sealed bubble in liquid.

[4]

Twenty-three years ago he had bought his first hammer for four dollars. It was a cast-steel claw hammer, stolen from him shortly after, but it had started him as a carpenter's helper. Just out of the army, he had been young then, so young and strong that now it hurt him to think of it, and of the ambitions he had had. Night school and a higher education lasted but a few months when he found that hard work and good pay only made him drift off to sleep in the classroom or home, studying. He was determined not to let the same thing happen to Allan.

The image of Allan came to Farber. He saw his son smiling and showing white and even teeth. Eleven hundred dollars. The orthodontist finished the job and removed the braces and only the bill remained. Where in the world was he going to get the money to pay? Certainly not from Sarah's part-time job in the dress shop.

Coming to a landing, he jerked the case from his shoulder and sat down on it to rest. He had gone only five flights. Five more to go.

Five dollars and seventy-five cents an hour. That's when I work, and when there's plenty of work needed to be done so contractors have to hire at union scale or else get nobody. A carpenter is king in spring, summer, and fall.

Don't complain. Think how tough it is finding a steady job in winter. Now I got a few days' work while other guys are collecting pennies from unemployment.

Thoughts of his luck gave him renewed energy to continue the ascent despite pain raking his lungs and jabbing like an ice pick the shoulder holding the case. Puffs of vapor riding on short gasps from his lips eddied and quickly

[5]

disappeared in a frigid draft sweeping the staircase.

Hurry, hurry, hurry. A couple more to go. You're not an old man yet. The nerve of that guy, calling me Pop. Forty-eight isn't old. But already contractors are asking, How old? Sure, a man over forty doesn't produce like one who's twenty. He slows down but he knows tricks to cut corners, save time, and keep up with the young guys. Worse than not being hired was being fired by a contractor who'd say, Sorry, we've carried you long enough.

As long as I don't get sick I'll be all right. In another fifteen years I could retire. Eight dollars a week union pension and thirty more from social security. Who could live on that? Maybe Allan would be something and take care of me and Sarah. You don't mind asking a son. He's not like a brother. Not that I really got anything against Benny. I don't ask and I don't take.

The top flight came into view. Moments later he stepped onto the roof, crisscrossed with scaffolding and piles of rafters, joists, planks, and joist bridges. Although only a one-story drop to the subflooring below, he carefully balanced himself, each foot on a joist. The timbers were spaced seventeen inches apart. Wide enough to let a man slip through, he thought as he walked on one, tightrope style, cradling the case in front of him with two arms and fighting the slippery wood and the gusts of wind slapping his back.

Situating himself, he gathered an armful of joist bridges and then removed his gloves. He knew they would slow him down when his hands would sweat and the freezing would stick skin to gloves, and gloves to metal nails and

[6]

tools. Besides, you couldn't drive a good, straight nail wearing them, he thought, a glow of pride filling him.

He blew on his hands and rubbed them together before wiping some hard spittle which hung like stalactites from his lip. For a moment he looked at his hands, thick and chapped raw with trickles of blood peeping through cracks in the skin. He knew that hands were important in judging a person's position, and he always tried to hide them, the symbol of his manual toil, whenever he and Sarah dressed to go out.

Only he among his relatives or Sarah's kin was a blue-collar worker. They were all professional people or businessmen who had started as plumbers and electricians but who later established their own firms and now had others doing the hand labor for them.

Farber swung the hammer. "Simple Simon," he said aloud, knowing that was the name his relatives called him behind his back. Sitting hidden in a rest-room cubicle, he had once overheard Benny and Benny's son Michael. It had been at a bar mitzvah reception. He'd never forget that they had called him Simple Simon and had laughed at his appearance.

After they had left he regarded himself wistfully in the mirror as he washed his calloused hands, and then slicked back his sandy hair with wet fingers. True, he didn't look sophisticated or distinguished with his ruddy face, he realized, stepping backward for a fuller view. His old suit had short sleeves which made his arms appear longer, while the tightness of the jacket accentuated massive shoulders. Heredity had given him a barrel chest, the same as Benny, but physical labor with hammer and lumber had packed muscle on Farber's torso and arms. His legs, unaffected by carpenter's toil, were hard but not bulky.

Benny's few years as a clothing salesman, his marriage to money and rapid amassment of more wealth through selective swallowing of competition by buying other clothing stores had made him shine in clothes and company. The chain stores of *Benny's Clothes* established his standing in the community of the wealthy, while guile and good luck ensured his remaining there.

Farber thought of how Benny had asked him many times to come into the business. Farber knew it wouldn't work out. He didn't want to be a charity case, or a figurehead, or a high-paid errand boy as useful as one of the dummies in Benny's windows. Besides, he didn't know anything about business.

Well, neither did Morris, Farber thought, envying his carpenter friend who had quit the job to enter the hardware business. Morris had the right idea. Sell hardware, don't use it.

Content with his thoughts, he pounded nails until they disappeared to unite wood with wood. He gripped the handle rigidly and braced himself against each recoil of the hammer, yet blows rebounded to jar his body and seemingly to rattle his bones. Vibrating aches struck his wrists and ran up his arm to deposit pain at elbow and shoulder. His grip loosened as his joints ground in anguished rebellion against holding hammer and wood. Eight-penny nails dropped from fingers unable to pinch.

Not now, goddamn it. That's all I need, another attack.

Trauma and cold could trigger an attack, the doctor had explained. It'll flare up now and then. Your joints will swell and your muscles will knot and go into spasms.

There's nothing I could take?

Just aspirin. There's no cure. It may get worse, even reach the crippling stage if you're not careful.

How can I be careful?

Find an easier job.

But carpenter work is all I know.

The doctor had shrugged his shoulders.

Crippling arthritis. Farber had no choice but to continue working. The attacks became more frequent, more painful. Until a remission came, he suffered silently, his botched work the only evidence of his misery. Unsteady hands with stiff, swollen joints wielded a hammer which continually struck off nails, bending them and denting the trim. Grip failing, it had been impossible for him to start a nail, using only one hand. The first trick an apprentice learned, it involved palming a hammer sideways while outstretched fingers of the same hand supported a nail, thus freeing the other hand to hold the wood evenly. But all Farber could do was to curse his hands.

Now, with the same frustrated bitterness, he cast his eyes about and wondered what to do before the foreman came. The joists. He could install them in the meantime, and then maybe get back to the more exacting bridges in the morning if he'd be all right.

[9]

He worked at a frenzied pace, ignoring a whistle sounding the half hour lunch. Several times his grip weakened and the timber slammed to the floor below. Up and down he went to retrieve the joists and lug them back to set and nail them against the beams. His pain became more intense, forcing him to stop working and look for aspirin in the toolcase.

With a few minutes left before the end of lunch, he also snatched his food pail from the case and sought escape from the wind. He found a half-finished room with wall studs sticking out like bony ribs and a cement floor brushed clean, ready for the floorlayers. Later, they would come with parquet blocks and hot, smelly tar which they spread over the floor with blackened brushes and brooms. Already he could smell the tar, cooking in a portable cylindrical vat on another floor of the building. Even on breezy days, the stench was almost enough to choke workers who came within a few yards of the vat.

Smoke spewed up the stairs and into the room. He moved closer to a glassless window from which he saw men outside standing dangerously close to a fire burning in a huge metal barrel. Some began to shuffle back to work without waiting for the whistle, and Farber knew they did so because they didn't like to be ordered like dogs by one man and a whistle.

Next he saw the foreman put the whistle to lips and blow. The rebellion of the rest of the men took the form of sluggish movement toward their jobs. One man, a laborer, stayed behind to tend the fire.

I should have gone down and warmed my hands. It

might have helped a little. It's too cold to work. Morris, he's smart. He couldn't even read a blueprint and look where he is. I can, and look what it got me. I should be running some business somewhere.

Now he saw himself in a warm store, wearing a clean, white apron, smiling at customers, and selling them something, an item hazy in his mind. The store was as good as Florida. It was warm and his hands didn't hurt him.

He sat down by the window and bit deeply into the cheese sandwich, prepared by Sarah last night. In order to accommodate the space and movement needed for the large bite, he kept his mouth half open while he chewed hurriedly, anxious to return to work.

"Around here we get back to work after the whistle."

Farber's head jerked toward the voice. He tried to reply, but the food in his mouth hindered coherence. At first he wanted to explain how he had worked through the half hour, but then realized that the foreman might think Farber had to, because he was so slow, or incompetent. Finally, with mouth clearer, but with scalp and stomach squeezing tightly, he said, "How did you get up here so fast? I just saw you on the ground a minute ago."

The foreman's face twisted into a gap-toothed smile he didn't want to smile. "Pop, you ain't doing so good."

"I'm sorry, I'm just a few minutes on company time."

"It ain't just that. I mean the bridges. Bad. Sloppy."

"The joists," Farber protested, "did you see them?"

"I *heard* them when everyone else was eating. You banged hell out that floor."

"I'm an inside man. I do a good job on trim and

[11]

doors." Farber's voice lost itself in the echoes of the empty room.

"Hell. You should a been able to handle that stuff one hand tied behind you." The foreman paused, looking at his watch, knowing full well the exact time, yet wishing to allow Farber seconds to realize a penalty was coming. "We'll pay you half a day."

Farber jumped up, anger showing on his face. "Goddamn it, mister! You didn't give me a chance."

The foreman pouted, shook his head, and left, the scrunch of his steps on building debris providing the only reply.

Downward now Farber stamped, the case unbearably heavy, but giving him ballast and gravitational assistance on the stairway. He stepped quickly, not caring if he would fall. In the back of his mind he hoped he would get hurt, if only to smother the sandpaperlike friction of his joints. He wished for a pain that would render him insensible. He wanted to punish his body for a disease which was ruining his livelihood, which, in turn, would destroy his body.

Outside, the whine of a buzzsaw tearing into lumber caught his attention. As the blade cut its way forward, its voice seemed to sharpen and rise to a wail of despair mingled with fury. He paused, transfixed by the saw whose sound penetrated his marrow. A man with back toward Farber fed the plank slowly into the blade's teeth, ripping along a crayon-marked line.

Staring at the saw, and strangely lulled by it, he thought of how he'd tell Sarah that he had had a job but

[12]

then had lost it. Again. Relief in telling would come to him immediately, but her tight and terrible silence would continue for days, reinfecting him and making his existence one of quiet sadness.

The buzzsaw whirled and shrieked its way back into his consciousness. What good were his hands if he couldn't make a living from them? He'd be better off without them.

A vision came to him of blood spurting from his fingers like water from a hose. His blood would soak sawdust and snow as the seconds flew by and the shock wore off, enabling the waiting pain to lacerate his mind and topple his body.

It won't be a stump. I'll have a few fingers left. Plenty of people don't have all of their fingers. I could collect compensation for the rest of my life. People cut off fingers and put holes in eardrums just to keep out of the war. It's not so terrible. It takes guts.

Sawdust showered his hat and flew at his face, where the specks of wood stuck around the eyes to freezing tears. Now facing the operator whose head bent low in engrossment, he stretched a hand out toward the saw, as cautiously and curiously as a toddler reaching for a new toy.

His boot sank into a pile of sawdust. Looking down, he recalled his own sawdust piles. In his mind his knee lifted to press against a plank on a sawhorse, and he drew back and forth as he had done ten thousand times, waiting for the piece of wood to drop as its particles had fallen before it.

The sawdust in his life could have made a huge, yellowish mountain into which he could sink and disappear, like quicksand. What had he gained, he wondered, in making sawdust for somebody else?

Crazy bastard. I'm crazy to think about hurting myself. I should hurt the people who crapped on me.

Once again, he picked up the toolcase, this time shouldering it with the disgust a cripple might have toward crutches which he loathed but nevertheless needed.

Keep up the rough abuse and you might get deformed, the doctor had said, twisting his fingers into grotesque hooks by way of illustration. You wouldn't be able to tie a shoelace. Your joints will fuse and your muscles will wither . . .

Farber swore. No more would he be a carpenter, no matter what.

"It's ass-warming time," the laborer shouted as he shifted his body and jerked his head like a prizefighter to avoid the smoke, rising like a black jinn from the barrel.

Farber, nodding his thanks, joined the man and felt the warm blasts of heat. Squinting his eyes against the smoke, he held his hands to the flame and turned them rapidly from side to side, as if cooking them on a spit.

Morris. I'll be like Morris. What's stopping me from going into business?

Although the throbbing pain in his fingers and elbows failed to respond to the aspirin and heat of the fire, a feeling of importance, of achievement, suffused his body.

"You ain't miserable until you're cold," the laborer said, tossing wood into the fire and looking at Farber for an expected nod of agreement.

Farber shook his head as he hoisted the case. "It's worse being out of a job." He walked a few steps and, without turning, shouted, "It's even more worse slaving for somebody else your whole life."

Faint wisps of barrel smoke still loitering in his nostrils and with toolcase riding an inflamed shoulder, Simon Farber performed the ritual he had followed for most of his life. He bought a paper at the newsstand before entering the subway. On the train, however, he did not automatically turn to the classified advertisements and then to *Help Wanted, Male,* where his eyes usually dropped down the column marked *Carpenter.*

Stiff, once nimble fingers found their way to a section his eyes had often glanced over and involuntarily photographed, to be summoned now before his mind. He found it, *Business Opport.* His eyes roved slowly over the boxes of print, announcing capital wanted, capital to invest, and the sale of bars and garages, car washes and laundries.

Next came the grocery store section, heightening his interest. The idea of owning a grocery, having and eating all the food you needed in spite of recessions or depressions, appealed to him. A recollection of the great depression, his father's own inability to find work, came to him. He saw the one-room flat, a gloomy cubbyhole with naked mildewed walls. Winter found rags stuffed in broken windows and black bread soaked in watery soup. The grocer's kid, fat and rosy-cheeked, always had something to eat.

Farber lipread the advertisements under the roar of the train.

[15]

Grocery, Gold Mine
top location, reas.
owner ill, must sell

Groc. Terrific oppty
owner must retire
will sacrifice

Groc. Good corner
Must sell, illness
$8,000 or reas. offer

Broad Ave. Groc.
Conv. loc. new dec.
Liv. quar. upstairs

All the advertisements ended with a phone number
and a request to call within certain hours. One long box,
listing groceries, carryouts, luncheonettes, and bakeries,
completed the column.

List Your Biz With Top Broker in Area
See Us for Buying and Selling
Small Loans Arranged, Low Interest
Timothy Quinn & Co.

Farber carefully ripped the last advertisement from
the paper. He cradled the clipping in his hands, read it over
several times, and then put it into his wallet.

Ideas swirled in his mind of earning enough money to
start his own chain of grocery stores, like Benny and *Benny's Clothes. Farber's Foods,* he'd call the stores, each of
which would send him the weekly gross for his accountants

to play with. Maybe there'll be franchises in other cities. *Farber's Fine Foods.*

Sarah. She's not going to buy this. What can I say to convince her that a grocery store is the only answer?

He'd tell her about Florida, of retiring there in a few years and buying a sailboat. They'd use it all of the time, for fishing, or for taking visiting relatives for pleasure trips. He'd even take Benny sailing. Benny, too busy with his own friends and money, probably wouldn't come, but there was no harm in asking. Sarah would sit on the edge of the boat and dip her feet in the warm, blue water.

Sarah. What else can I tell you? Only two, maybe three years in a store. Okay, forget about the chain of stores. Let's talk about things at hand. Four years of standing in one store, and then we'd have enough to go to Florida and open another business. Life would begin again.

Timothy Quinn and Company.

The wallet in Farber's back pocket felt warm and heavy.

Allan Farber came directly home from school and knew before entering the apartment that he wouldn't enjoy the Christmas and New Year's vacation. A pair of mud-caked boots lay on the doormat. It was too early for his father to be home, which meant no job was found. Suddenly, the sound of his mother's raised voice filled the hallway, removing any lingering joy in him over being out of school for almost two weeks.

"You didn't sign anything, did you?"

"Sarah, I tell you, all we did was have a chat. Nothing's settled."

"I hope not!"

Allan opened the door and entered, exulting in the strong antiseptic solution his mother used to clean the linoleum kitchen floor once a week, on Fridays. When he was much smaller, he used to play on the same fresh-smelling floor, oblivious to its wet hardness, minutes after she was through.

Like reluctant combatants, his parents faced each other. Farber, only a fraction taller than Sarah, still wore his overalls and a thick sweatshirt. His stockiness and open Slavic face contrasted unfavorably against her tall, graceful appearance and thin, long face which gave the impression of forward movement. Only full lips below an aquiline nose and above a strong jaw broke that motion.

They stopped speaking as soon as they saw him. Greeting him with impatient preoccupation, they waited until he went into his room before continuing with whispers. Soon, the argument resumed its previous level.

"First of all, get it in your head I'm disabled. I can't work as a carpenter anymore."

"If you're disabled how could you work in a grocery?"

"First of all, there's a big difference. Pushing a loaf of bread and a few cans across the counter is a little different than to measure and cut quarter-inch trim. If you don't know that, there's no use in telling you anything else."

[18]

She shrugged her shoulders. "The attacks come and go. It's not as if you're a handicapped worker."

His father laughed, not good-naturedly. "So far it's been doing more coming and less going. You know what the doctor said. You want to push me around in a wheelchair?"

Allan thought of the reddened and swollen knuckles which his father held under the hot-water tap on cold and damp days. He listened to a long silence. A good sign, he thought, hearing next the shuffling of chairs around the kitchen table and then, in a low voice, his father.

"It was bad enough before I got sick. Running from job to job, worrying about being laid off. You work for someone else your whole life and get nothing to show for it."

Now his voice was completely calm in its explanation. Allan, sensing safety of passage in the change and feeling thirsty, gathered courage and opened the door.

His father turned quickly toward him. "Stay in your room a little longer. I've got something to talk with your mother about."

"He might as well hear about it now, Simon."

Narrowed, suspicious eyes gave way to a nod. "Okay. Allan, I want to tell you something very important. I'm going into business."

"Your father got fired because of his sickness. He went to see a man about borrowing money. Your father wants to go into business, his own business."

His father grunted impatiently. "Let me do the talking." He paused, looking up at the ceiling intently, as if he

[19]

were searching for a script from which he could read his words. "Allan, you know that the doctor said for me to take it easy. I can't take it easy and make a living at the same time. We need money. Now and for when you go to college. There's a way to make money these days. The grocery business." With that, he leaned back in his chair and simultaneously seemed to dare and forbid anyone to contradict his statement.

Allan smiled. He had sudden visions of being part of a very wealthy family. Automobiles, mansions, swimming pools, and servants. He'd own a Jaguar by the time he was sixteen.

"I went to see a man who specializes in finding stores and putting up money to back people who want to go into business."

"What's the man's name again?" Allan's mother asked.

"Quinn. I told you that already a dozen times."

"Jewish?"

"No, but he's okay. Sincere." Farber's look shifted to Allan, who couldn't help feeling that anything else said would be repeated for his mother's ears. "The store's in Washington, D.C. We sign our name, it's a signature loan, and buy the store and pay him something on account each week."

"Month," his mother corrected. "But why can't he let us sign our name for a store in New York? Why can't we stay here?"

"Because that store is the best one around. Besides, Washington is where the government is. Government

[20]

workers always work, regardless of a depression. It's the facts of life."

"I'm afraid of going to a strange city." She glanced at Allan, who knew that she'd hold fast to her beliefs. She may lose an argument, but she'd bring it up weeks later to turn his father's stale victory into fresh defeat.

His father raised his voice. "What strange city? The capital of the country? It's only four hours by train. Listen, Sarah. Mr. Quinn says Washington may not be a boom town, but nobody goes hungry there. The store's right in the heart of the *shvartzer* area. Negro trade only."

"Suppose there's a race riot? What do we do then?"

"For twenty years I danced like a monkey on the scaffolds. A beam once slipped and killed a guy standing right next to me. So what? That's life. So there's a little trouble with the *shvartzers* now. You ride it out. You treat them right, they leave you alone. Plenty of white shopkeepers in Harlem will tell you that."

His mother, toying with an empty matchbox on the table, was unrelenting. "What do you know about grocery stores?"

"First of all, I know a little about groceries. I buy them, don't I? Look, even Mr. Quinn says he's sorry he didn't go into groceries. That's where the quick money is."

"Quick money," she repeated mockingly. "What's stopping Mr. Quinn from making some quick money in a grocery now?"

"Look, let's stop talking so much!" he shouted. "Do you or don't you want to go into business?"

They looked at each other for a few moments. His

[21]

mother nodded her head slowly. His father, beaming, pressed the advantage.

"Just give me a year, Sarah. That's all I ask. I know I could get a good start in a year. Then I'd hire a man to work for me and you wouldn't have to help. Then we'll have enough to move to Florida and open up another business there. The rest of our lives will be a vacation. You'll see."

Allan, happy because his parents stopped arguing, went to the refrigerator.

Sarah didn't know why she awoke suddenly. She was fully conscious bare seconds after opening her eyes, but she couldn't recall having any sort of a dream, nor did she feel any desire strong enough to have disturbed her sleep.

The only sounds were the low, steady vibration from the kitchen refrigerator and the drone of distant automobile wheels and engines. She closed her eyes and turned over to face the separate bed where her husband slept.

A grocery store. If that's what it was going to be, fine. She wasn't certain if that was what she wanted. She felt secure, though, in knowing that he had the will and drive to succeed. He's no spring chicken anymore, she thought. Her husband, who had never read a book since quitting high school, suddenly had to run to the library. And then, instead of watching television or reading the newspaper, he buried himself with *Retail Sales and Salesmanship* and *How to Run a Business.*

The same things she admired in him, his motivation and energy, also worried her. She felt she was being

[22]

ignored in the household decision-making, especially about moving to another city. Her sacrifices, loss of friends, neighbors and a part-time job, would be hard to overcome.

Of a sudden, a feeling of guilt and selfishness swept her. You got to live, she thought. If a grocery's the only job you can do, you'll do it.

A business was a hard life, that she knew, recalling how Morris' wife Judith had aged during the past few years in spite of their big business success. Judith and she were both forty years old, yet she looked mid-thirtyish while Judith appeared close to fifty. Maybe Judith looked older because she helped Morris in the store and worried along with him about the business. They were having a good Florida vacation now, but was it worth it?

Of course, not only hard work aged you. Having a lot of children to care for and worry about also made you old before your time. Allan was born before she had developed trouble with her uterus. She and her husband never had to face a decision about having more children. Financially, it made things easier, but still Allan cost a lot, with his braces and with college in a few years.

She heard her husband's snoring interrupted by a gasp which sounded like radio static. He cleared his throat. Now it seemed as if she could hear him shouting again. "I'm through with carpenter work. I'm not going back. Lots of people change jobs. I'm going to make it in the store. That's final."

A recorder in her mind next played back his announcement to Allan, "I'm going into business." It would have been better to say, "Your mother and I have decided to go into business."

More disturbing to her now was his decision to go to Washington with Allan and look over the store. Although she really didn't want to go, she was hurt when he suggested that she stay home. "It'll cost more money," the recorder sounded. "Besides, there's no sense in sitting around the store when you could be making a week's salary in the dress shop."

Then he had added that they'd have to tighten belts for a while if they bought the store. They probably could rent an apartment in a white neighborhood, he said, but it would just about break them before they got a foothold in the new business, what with all sorts of notes and bills to pay. Quinn had informed him that the store had good living quarters upstairs.

Living among Negroes frightened her. Not that she believed all of them were bad, there were plenty of good people in all races and religions, she always said, but sometimes when she saw them in the subways or shopping areas she felt that their blackness was an uncoverable sign of their evil.

She pulled a heavy blanket up to her chin and turned away from her husband. Business would be good and they'd be able to move to a white neighborhood, a Jewish one, within a few weeks. Sure of that, she turned again to thoughts of growing old. She wondered how the hard work, much harder than being a saleswoman in a clothing store, would affect her relatively unwrinkled skin and grayless black hair.

Don't stop him. Having a successful businessman as a husband was better than having a crippled ex-carpenter to care for.

She squeezed her shut eyes tighter in an attempt to stifle her thoughts. It was no use. She was excited and afraid.

Wet snow pressed determinedly on the ground under an overcast sky as Farber and Allan left Union Station. Farber had been to Washington before, during the Second World War, when he was stationed temporarily at one of the nearby army camps before shipment to the South Pacific. The sight of the commonplace water fountain and beyond, the Capitol building, and the boxes of hotels to his right, he had seen many times.

Today everything looked dirty and felt grimy, even the little baggage cart provided by the train station. The walls of the station were dark with filth, and the floors were caked with dirt and sputum from hundreds of thousands of train travelers.

For a moment he watched Allan's gawking at the Capitol, and then returned to his own thoughts, wondering whether or not to check the baggage first and see the store, or go to a hotel before doing anything. What about a taxicab? Should they take a taxicab or a bus? A station porter had informed them that the address was a half dozen or so blocks away.

Farber decided. "Come on, Allan. We'll walk to the store. No sense in paying a taxi good money." He handed the boy the smallest of three suitcases. "You carry that until you're tired. If we're going to make money in Washington we ought to start by trying to save it."

Every dollar counts. Every day counts. They should save something even during the trial period of a week. That was the usual length of time, Quinn had told him. After talking with Sarah he had gone back to see the sad-faced Irishman with the long, vibrating dewlaps and the dark-filled bags under the eyes.

"The process is simple enough," Quinn had explained. "You're guaranteed a certain gross weekly. You make a five-hundred-dollar deposit and stay in the store for a week. If the gross ain't seen, you get your deposit back and it's good-bye, Charlie. If the gross is met but you should happen to change your mind, which I hope you don't do for your own sake, you don't want to go back to that rough work, do you? Well then, you lose your deposit, as in all such deposit cases. Now, how much of a down payment can you put down?"

"Not very much," Farber had said. "I've got about five hundred in savings."

"That's not too good. We need two thousand. The money department is hurting, but it ain't hurting too bad. I could place a loan for you with some private investors but their interest rate is a little higher than what you can get at the bank. Okay, you can get a thousand loan from my acquaintances. You pay back one fifteen per month, for twelve months. Okay?"

Farber screwed up his face and nodded as if to agree reluctantly to a stiff bargain. Then he realized he should have shaken his head no, and he switched the movement, but it was too late. Quinn wasn't watching. Just as well,

Farber thought, changing his mind again. "Will I have enough for a down payment?"

"That's all I can let you have. You'll have to borrow another five hundred dollars. Maybe from your bank."

"I have a loan application in for the store for what you told me, about four thousand."

"Okay, good. If that don't work out we'll work out something with Gittelson. He's the guy who owns the store I was telling you about. I already told you it's in a good *shvartzer* neighborhood. Guaranteed gross income of about fifteen hundred per week. Figuring a profit margin of eighteen to twenty percent, that's a lot of good coin."

"*Shvartzer?* What's an Irishman doing with a Yiddish word?"

Quinn returned Farber's grin. "Just borrowing it, Mr. Farber. It's part of the business vocabulary, Jew or gentile."

"Well, Mr. Quinn, how much will that profit amount to? I mean, take-home pay?"

Quinn reared back on his chair, balancing on its hind legs. He suddenly let the chair's forelegs bang on the floor, stood up, and walked around the room. He was a short man but he had a tall man's stance, legs spread wide apart, and with torso swinging from side to side, as if it were a loose, unmanageable weight.

"Mr. Farber, forget the take-home crap. Erase it from your vocabulary. You're going to be a capitalist with a capital C. Forget about the clock. The harder you work for yourself, the more you'll have."

Farber's curious gaze shifted to one of intense approval.

[27]

"You figure twenty percent profit. That's about three hundred a week, and that's only a start. That's pretty good, hey?"

Farber took Quinn's rising from the chair as a sign that the Irishman was bored, that enough had been said, and that the interview, the profitable part, was over.

A wrong turn took them several blocks out of their way as streets darkened in the early evening. Although the suitcases became heavier with each step, Farber exhorted his son to move faster. They passed into a neighborhood of narrow streets, fewer cars, and small apartment buildings, from which only Negroes entered and left.

"Why can't we go to a hotel now?" Allan asked with a hint of a whine to his voice.

Impatient with the boy's inability to keep up with him, and anxious about the black eyes which watched as he struggled with his suitcases, he snapped back, "Because we're not, that's why!"

What's Allan to blame? he thought a few moments later, feeling ashamed. "Only a couple more blocks, we'll be there." He glanced at his son's face. "Look, Allan, we got to let Mr. Gittelson know we're here. Maybe he could even tell us where we could stay."

I hope in a safe place around here, Farber thought. That's all we need, to get lost in the dark.

Every time a passerby caught his eye, Farber saw either a look of anxious curiosity or one of outright hostility. Might as well get used to them now, he told himself, wishing to say the same thing to Allan but afraid of being

[28]

overheard. He even thought twice about joking how he and Allan resembled Spencer Tracy in the movie about Stanley and Livingstone.

They passed a light-skinned woman who held herself up drunkenly in a doorway by hanging Christlike with head down and arms spread on the jambs. She wore an old, heavy army coat with no buttons, and her puffy, eyelid-swollen face shone copper from the light and cold. Her hair, twisted and plaited tightly, made her look like a Medusa with black coils for snakes.

"What you looking at, whitey?" she shouted angrily at Farber, spouting the words in almost one convulsive gasp.

Farber quickly turned his gaze away and hoped Allan had the sense not to look back at the woman. Soon they came to a small street strewn with garbage and covered with broken glass. Although a fresh wind bit and howled, the block danced alive with children, all with runny noses, open cuts, and sores on the exposed parts of their bodies. Several played catch with old beer cans, while others seemed to take delight in bouncing the cans off one another's back and buttocks. One boy whirled the carcass of a dead cat by its tail around his head, and then laughed as he chased other children, threatening to hit them with it.

"Carry you bags for you, mistah?" a boy of about ten asked. He wore a torn Eisenhower jacket with a ragged regimental patch still clinging to the upper sleeve. Knees chalky with cold showed through holes in his trousers. He was accompanied by a girl of about his age, who had pink curlers around which her black hair was tightly spun.

"No, go away," Farber said, pushing Allan by the shoulder to make him move forward and to protect him from whatever menace the children posed. Immediately, he was sorry he gave the impression of being brusque or angry, or even afraid. He had heard that you couldn't show apprehension before these people, just like you weren't supposed to be afraid in front of dogs. They sense it.

"Only a dime, mistah."

Farber now smiled ingratiatingly, lowering and smoothing his voice. "No, sonny. Thank you."

"Only a nickel," the girl said.

"We can do it ourselves, thank you."

"You think we gonna steal them?" the boy asked. "That what you think?"

"No. Please don't bother us."

The girl, walking slightly in front of them, stopped short and stuck out her tongue, carmine over red, pursed lips. She held out a hand with painted red nails and erected her middle finger. "Fuck you, white man."

Although a promontory of windowframe and glass, the store, sitting on the corner of the block, was distinguished from the drab row houses mainly by gaudy, red-lettered paper signs announcing sales. A wooden sign, JG'S MARKET, hung above the double door leading into the store.

Farber, placing the suitcases down to rest his aching

[30]

fingers, guessed that the JG stood for Joseph Gittelson, the owner whom Quinn had mentioned. Later, Farber learned that the customers referred to the initials as the Jew Gyp store.

A large, factorylike building, with broken windows like missing teeth through which showed the darkness within, stood across the street from the store, sharing the intersection with another store, this one with a faded oblong of cardboard in the window bearing BLACK LIBERATION MOVEMENT. A three-story brick apartment house with a chain link fence guarding a few patches of brown grass occupied the fourth corner.

Closer now, Farber saw that the factory building was a school, for carved in stone above its entrance was HOMER P. BRADSHAW VOCATIONAL SCHOOL. For several yards on either side of the entrance a twisted and broken low wire fence surrounded dirt plots covered with broken glass and litter.

He and Allan approached a new group of children and, fearing another encounter, moved quickly. One of them was a toddler who was barely in the walking stage and whose outer garment, despite the cold, was only a threadbare pullover sweater. A little girl, with two tightly coiled pigtails in front of her forehead and three long ones hanging down behind her, shook her head as she ran, making the pigtails twirl like ribbons around a maypole.

Farber's eyes were on the store, a reconverted first floor of a two-story row house which leaned heavily upon the adjoining house for support, as if waiting to collapse. He could see the windows of the rooms above the store where his family's home would be for the next few months. Closer, he read a paper sign pasted on one store window.

CHUCK ROAST
U.S. CHOICE
49¢ LB.

The door window, protected by rusted bars, greeted him with

QUALITY MEATS & PRODUCE
DRINK COCA-COLA

and atop the door itself, a bell rang, signaling his entrance.

A linoleum, parts of which were worn black, or down to brown where the wooden floor showed through, led from the door to the main counter, on which lay pastries, pies, and the cash register. Loaves of bread and more cakes were on shelves built into the counter. Next to the counter facing him was a small candy showcase with the nickel and dime candy on the upper shelves, and lollypops, bubble gum, and other cheap, overly sweetened penny candy on the lower shelves.

To his left and rear, a dimly lit showcase held meat, poultry, lunchmeat, eggs, and butter. Bushels of produce and fruit were tilted in front of the meat showcase and also against the wooden bottom of the larger of the store's two plate glass windows. A huge, walk-in refrigerator loomed beyond the showcase while nearby on the wall was an electric clock advertising a beer company. And above, like a statue of an omnipotent, multi-armed Eastern god, a ceiling fan pointed its still limbs to all sides and corners of the store, packed with shelves of cans and boxes.

The only customer was a boy about three years old who wore a stocking cap on his head to prevent ringworm from spreading. He stood with blank indifference watching Joseph Gittelson scrubbing the butcher block with a wire brush.

Gittelson, with a dirty white apron covering part of his chubby frame, greeted Farber and son warmly. "Mr. Farber, Mr. Farber," he said, patting his bald head nervously with one hand and shaking Farber's hand with the other. "Who else could it be with a white face and a suitcase? Hey, that rhymes! What do you know, I'm a regular poet."

Mrs. Gittelson stuck her head out of a doorway next to the walk-in refrigerator which led to a rear room. "Glad to meet you likewise, Mr. Farber, and you, too, sonny. Hello, hello. You'll excuse me for a few minutes. I'm making dinner. Could I get you a cup of hot coffee?"

"No, thanks, Mrs. Gittelson. We're just passing through. Actually, we're on our way to a hotel."

"Mistah G," the little customer's voice piped.

"Wait a minute, boy!" Gittelson shouted. "Can't you see some important folks right chere? Ah don' care if you was first."

Mrs. Gittelson came out of the doorway, briskly moving her chunky body. She appeared to be made of cubes;

there was not a curve in her whole body. Her hips and shoulders were the sides of boxes. She had no ankles, only straight beams.

"Now, Joe, that don't make sense for Mr. Farber and the boy to stay at a hotel for a week and come here every day early in the morning till late at night. They can stay in the back or upstairs." She looked at Farber. "We got two beds upstairs and even two cots in the back. You can stay here for the week, if you want."

"But where will you stay?"

"Do you think we live here?" she blurted out. "In this neighborhood?" She laughed as Farber blushed. He realized that she didn't know that he, Sarah, and Allan would live on the premises if they bought the store.

"Oh, we don't sleep here," she continued. "We have a house in the suburbs. The cots we use to rest on during the day."

Gittelson held a finger to his lips. "Sh, don't tell him that. He'll think we're not busy in the store during the day." They all laughed. "Actually, Mr. Farber, we're quite busy. Grocery stores in this neighborhood, well, let me tell you, it's so busy that every grocer and his wife needs just one fork and one spoon. They never eat together."

"Well, we've got more silverware than that here. That's just a saying," said Mrs. Gittelson. "And speaking of eating, you could even eat here, Mr. Farber. There's no restaurants in the area. We'll just figure on a few dollars a day for room and board for you and your son."

It was a bargain, Farber thought, nodding his approval, even though it bothered him that she was so quick

[34]

and matter-of-fact about it. She must have talked it over with her husband before. Anything to make a few dollars.

Why am I thinking like that? With me everything is brought down to money. Here are two, good, hardworking people and I'm saying that they're letting me into their house because of a few lousy dollars.

Before entering the kitchen they passed through a large, windowless room piled high with cardboard boxes, some empty with flaps like limbs, and some filled, heavy with canned goods. The kitchen was old; its walls of dark green had not been painted for many years. Stains of rust caused by broken water pipes showed through the paint on one corner of the wall. The floor was covered with cracked linoleum. Another door led to a back yard.

Farber heard the loud voice of Gittelson finally acknowledge the little boy.

"What you want, boy? You got any money? Huh? If you ain't got no money you better go home and get you some from you mama. Ain't no good you just standin' there. Now, what you want?"

"My mama said buy a bread in the white Jew store."

"Okay, where you money?" Gittelson replied promptly.

Farber and Allan ate a meal of cold cuts and potatoes which Mrs. Gittelson prepared. In the evening, for a short time before the store closed, Farber stood watching a few of the customers.

They came in, indigenous foreigners in the land, with

[35]

their dark faces and hands, heavy eyelids over unmerciful eyes, and pouting, everting, impatient lips under cavernous nostrils. Even the whites of their eyes were dark and gray.

"Gi' me loaf a brea'," they said in a soft and lazy tongue, ignoring time-consuming consonants and often clusters of syllables. The *r* was dropped in door, making it sound like dough; yet the dough used in bread was slightly more relaxed and drawn out when pronounced by the educated. The customers' *dough* for *door* was quicker, usually spat out in a petulant burst which, like a report from a revolver, made a speaker's head jump perceptibly backward a half inch or so.

Negroes weren't new to Farber. One, a shoe salesman, lived on the street, and got along nicely on the predominantly Jewish block. The Negro laborers on the job, except for their drawling speech, were no different from the other men. Nobody paid any attention to color.

"You all new here, ain't you," a fat woman addressed him.

"This here's Mistah Farber," Gittelson replied before Farber could answer. "Maybe you treat him right he stay on here and buy this here store."

The woman nodded her head with its hair rolled up in stiff braids to form a prickly crown. "You sellin' out, Mistah G?"

"Maybe. Gonna take my Missus and go to Florida and live it up for a while." He laughed.

The woman, sour and unsmiling, finally grinned. "You got all that money you got off us, Mistah G. That ought to get you *somewheres.*"

[36]

Now Gittelson forced a grin. "Miz Thompson. You stop it, now. Hear?"

She shook her head and switched her blue-black eyes to look at the shelves behind Gittelson. "Gimme one them cans sardines." She also ordered potatoes and a cut of fatback before handing Gittelson a notebook into which he scribbled the bill and then the same figure into his own notebook, kept under the register. When she left, he turned to Farber.

"Goddamn black bastard. What *chutzpah!* I sweat my tail to the bone to rub a few pennies together and she gives me lip. They send her a relief check every month so she could have a *momser,* a bastard baby, once a year, every year."

Mrs. Gittelson heard him shouting and stuck her head outside of the storeroom. "What's the matter?"

"Goddamn Thompson woman. She's shooting her mouth off how much money we got off them. Boy!"

His wife turned toward Farber. "Mr. Farber, your son and me fixed the beds upstairs. Now, don't worry about the heat. Joe will put enough coal for most of the night and he'll fire the furnace first thing in the morning." She looked back at her husband. "Joe, it's almost ten o'clock. How about closing the store? Tomorrow starts the new week and the new life for Mr. Farber." She threw a smile at Farber and returned to the kitchen.

Gittelson rubbed his cheek and stared at Farber. "Ah, Mr. Farber, there's a delicate matter I have to discuss with you. Now, you don't know me and I don't know you. I could be honest or a crook. The same with you. So why worry about it? What I have in mind is the store when I'm not around or when you're not around."

"What do you mean?"

"Well, to prevent either you or me from stealing from the store while it changes hands, I have keys both to the front door and to this door." He pointed to the door to the storeroom, kitchen, and living quarters. "When me and the wife leave at night, we'll lock this door and the front door. Now it's not that I think you're dishonest, but I think it's best, for both of us."

"I never took what wasn't mine in my whole life, Mr. Gittelson." Farber was incensed, but he was also tired from the journey and the excitement of the day. He didn't want to argue and wished that Gittelson had just locked the door without making a fuss over it.

"No, no, no. Don't get me wrong, Mr. Farber. When the store changes into your hands and I'll stay with you a couple of days or drop in a couple a times a week to give you a hand until you're broken in, you'd keep the keys to the front door. They're yours. I wouldn't want them."

Farber shrugged his shoulders. That was business, he thought. Good business wasn't a matter of politeness. He'd have to learn that.

Allan, awakened by a sound of pebbles rolling down a sandy, rocky hill and by the screeching of the wind, listened intently. Darkness filled the room; not a speck of light beamed through the bedroom windows painted black by Gittelson to save money on shades.

Rainfall began to splatter on the roof. He shivered in the dark, cold unfamiliarity of the room and the hardness

[38]

of the bed, as he strained to listen to the irregular down-pour, but his father's snores now smothered the sounds.

He pulled his overcoat used as a blanket up to his neck and curled his legs up to keep them warm. It was probably early in the morning, he guessed, since it was so cold and Mrs. Gittelson had said it would be when the fire in the coal furnace went out sometime late at night or early the next day.

The noise came between the snores. No, it wasn't rain, he decided. It was a dry, scrambling sound. In his fully awakened state, the wind was not the wind, but the squealing and slithering of unknown things alive.

He woke his father, who groaned from being made suddenly aware of the cold. They both listened for a few moments to the scampering and screeching which resembled the sound of a quickly turning rusted wheel.

"Rats," his father said. "We'll soon get rid of them. They're in the walls. On the beams and plaster. Go back to sleep."

Allan listened to the sounds of sleep, the snoring and heavy breathing through the mouth, returning to his father as the rats bounded and scurried. He listened to them for a long time, thinking of how he hated them, and began to associate them with the store and then the Negroes he had seen today. He wanted to cry, and tried to think of the good things that the store would bring.

He thought of how he'd miss his friends if his parents would buy the store, and how he'd probably be the only white person in a colored school. He became angry with his parents for not thinking about him and decided that he

[39]

didn't want them to get rich from the store.

The money was not important. Nor was a sports car or a swimming pool. He wanted to go home. He hoped that something would go wrong with the store and that they would have to go back.

In the morning Farber awoke and found his son still sleeping. It was six fifteen. Farber lay still for a few minutes, feeling the aching of his joints and listening to the wind as it worked its way among the crevices and cracks of the window. He wouldn't be out there in the wind anymore, he said to himself. No more hammering frozen wood. This was a new life. Even Mrs. Gittelson said so.

What bothered him though was what the little boy had said about the white Jew store. It amused him to be called whitey by them, for it placed him among the great American gentile Caucasians, but he could not stand anti-Semitism.

Before Gittelson had left last night Farber questioned him about not telling the boy off.

"Jew hating is a tradition here," Gittelson had said. "That *momser* and all the rest of the kids think all Jews are white and all whites are Jews. It don't mean nothing. Don't even think about it."

"Hell," Farber now said out loud as he shaved. He wasn't going to put up with anti-Semitism, tradition or not. He worried how Sarah and Allan would be able to cope with it.

He finished dressing in time to hear the arrival downstairs of the Gittelsons, speaking in low voices. In a few minutes, there was the sound of furnace grates grinding ashes into a receptacle, and he knew that Gittelson was preparing a new fire. He descended into the kitchen and felt the warmth of the rising heat from the furnace and from the gas burners where Mrs. Gittelson boiled water for coffee.

"Good morning, Mr. Farber," Gittelson said. "Ready to begin a new life?"

"First let him have his coffee," his wife said. "Is the boy still sleeping?"

Farber nodded. "Yesterday was a big day for him. What time do you open the store?"

"Seven. Early enough to get the workers. They buy lunchmeat, fruit for lunch. Then we could close for a half hour but we don't. Nobody comes in. Eight o'clock begins the schoolchildren buying stuff for their lunch. But you won't have that now, because it's Christmas vacation."

"That's a good reminder for me to tell you something," said Mrs. Gittelson. "Right, Joe?" Her husband nodded, already knowing what she had in mind. It was a well-rehearsed nod. "About the guarantee, we won't exactly meet it."

"That's right," her husband said quickly on cue. "The kids are out of school this week. They don't come in for breakfast in the morning and they don't come in from the school across the street for lunch." He looked at Farber's bewildered expression and pretended that it came not from the guarantee business but from not knowing about the existence of the school. "That's the high school across the street. It's a trade school. And they come in here, forty, fifty at a time. They look like seventeen-year locusts. You'll see."

Farber stuck to the issue. "Mr. Quinn said the guarantee was a thousand dollars a week."

Gittelson chuckled. His shoulders moved up and down, forcing him to place the coffee on the table. "No problem. We'll break that thousand dollars this week, easy. But in case we're short about a couple of hundred, you'll know it's because of vacation. You just make sure your signing arm is okay for the contract come next week."

"It'll be okay," Farber said, wishing to drop the subject. He wanted to believe them.

They finished their coffee and entered the store after passing through the storeroom. The store was cold, yet the odor within was friendly, despite its staleness and unfamiliarity. During the evening the closed store had become almost vacuum packed with itself, blending with all the odors of hundreds of products to produce its peculiar smell, a mixture of smells from vegetables and fruit, fresh or rotting, bushels of onions, potatoes, cabbages, lettuce, collards, and turnip greens, wrapped and unwrapped candy, packaged cereal and a hundred other packaged goods, mop-washed linoleum floor, grease-stained sawdust behind the meat counter and under the butcher block, the uncovered jar of pickled pigs' feet on the counter, old flypaper still hanging since last summer, bags of soft coal, a tank of kerosine, the stagnant ice water in the soft-drink case, and the electric motors of the meat showcase and walk-in refrigerator.

Farber shivered with anticipation. It was soon going to

belong to him, the store and the smell which will bring a good life. He breathed deeply, savoring the smell as if it were perfume.

"First thing today," Gittelson said, "we got to put up the Christmas crap. We're already late with it."

He said *we,* Farber thought. The store almost belongs to me.

He helped Gittelson decorate with Christmas trimmings, which, although old with a storage-box look, nevertheless sparkled against the surrounding dirt and grayness of the ceiling and walls and held their own against the reds and oranges which colored the shelved packaged goods.

During the day, and the days of the week that followed, throngs of women buying foodstuffs for the holiday kept the store busy. Children stormed inside clutching pennies and nickels begged from their fathers and men around the house, or grasping soda pop bottles whose deposit worth was two cents. Often bunches of them followed the leader, the child holding the coins or bottles, from whom they would beg a piece of the candy prize.

The door opened and shut incessantly, and its wood banged against the bell fastened on the top frame, making antiphonal sounds of a strange, untiring inanimate chorus. The door remained shut only long enough to be opened again, as customer after customer in an almost trancelike state asked for and received goods in words that became a litany throughout the day, as if both buyer and seller had memorized their complete conversation, including small talk.

[43]

Farber was both delighted and apprehensive. From the nightly tallies with the Gittelsons over the cash register receipts and the credit books, it looked certain that the weekly guarantee would be not only reached, but surpassed. The thought of his buying and owning the store, finally, made him nervous with fear that he would not be able to make a go of it. He worked hard during the week, trying to learn and pack in as much as possible about the grocery business so that he would avoid making the mistakes of the inexperienced.

Foods that were completely unknown to him became as familiar as salami and rye bread had been; the unrelieved pasty whiteness of fatback, twenty-nine cents a pound, streak of lean, which, he discovered, was an apt name, at sixty-nine a pound. The oddly shaped hog jaw also sold for sixty-nine.

He hated to handle the brown, sweaty pigs' knuckles. Even at the relatively high price of forty-nine a pound, he thought that they were fit only for the lowest of infidels. Not only was it nonkosher, he believed, but it embodied everything that was antikosher.

New physical movements and different muscle use made his body ache, but it was a soreness of satisfaction and not arthritis. He learned how to cut open a chicken, draw out the giblets, and snip away the inedible parts, the dark green bile from the liver, and the intestines. His carpentry skill made it easy for him to measure by eye portions of pork chops before cleaving away. The art of displaying meat in the showcase, slicing veils of staleness from the lunchmeat, moving fresh or better-looking meat to the

[44]

front, and taking advantage of the lights, was taught to him. Nothing was wasted. Old slices and bones were to be presented with much fanfare to the customers for their pets. He even learned not to spill any kerosine from the tank from which he pumped the liquid fuel into customers' jars and cans.

Gittelson proved to be a good teacher. "Always push, always remind. Ask them if they need anything else. They forget. Tell them today you got nice spareribs, chickens. Don't volunteer the price until after you cut so they'd be obligated. They're going to whistle at the price, any price. Don't pay attention. Even if you give something for nothing, they think it's too high."

Farber enjoyed hearing customers call him "Mistah Simon," which made him feel like a plantation boss in the old South. Before long he began to understand more clearly their speech, with the whining, rising and falling inflection.

Gittelson told him a lot of them were recent arrivals from the South who moved in and chased away to better neighborhoods the older, more established Negroes. Farber found some of the Southerners cute and appealing, almost like children.

The children themselves seemed to lack identity. Seldom did Farber hear them call each other by name. Even the parents, possibly because they had so many children, called their offspring "boy" and "girl" or "sister" and "brother."

Gittelson's own speech fascinated Farber more than that of the Negroes. The storeowner, much like a comedian doing vocal impressions or imitations, changed accent and inflection when speaking with his customers.

"Wha-cha say there, man?" Gittelson asked one youth. "Where you been las' few days? Ain't seen you, no-how."

"Been aroun', Mistah G."

"What can ah do for you?"

"Pack a cigarettes. Luckies."

"Now, wait you one minute, James. You know you too young to smoke an' ah too smart to sell 'em to you. You want me to get lock up?"

"They for my brother."

"He come in an' get 'em, then."

"He sick, Mistah G."

"Sheet, James. You talk trash. You 'speck me to believe that?"

At that point Farber glanced over at Mrs. Gittelson, who was laying out eggs on display in the showcase, apparently unmindful or unconcerned about the drawing out of the word *shit* by her husband. For a moment she reminded Farber of a mother hen, gazing blankly in front of herself, coldly indifferent to the warmth her feathered behind was providing for her eggs.

"Bring me a note from you brother, James. Then ah see what ah can do."

Farber, watching the youth shrug his shoulders and leave the store, smiled to himself. If he'd close his eyes, he wouldn't be able to tell the difference between Gittelson and the customers. Actually, Farber told himself, the Gittelson feat was not surprising or unusual. He remembered

[46]

hearing stories of Jewish shopkeepers in New York City learning and speaking enough Spanish to deal with their new Puerto Rican clientele.

On the following Saturday night, the end of the week, Gittelson closed the store with a terse, "This is it." He carried the credit book and the tally from the cash register to the kitchen, where they added the week's gross income. It came to eleven hundred fifty-three dollars and thirty-nine cents.

"Well, Mr. Farber," said Gittelson, "that's that. I say we take inventory, dollar for dollar, on Monday. Plus three thousand dollars goodwill and fixtures. That's what Mr. Quinn said. Right? We could sign the papers Tuesday with the lawyers. Can your wife come down?"

Farber nodded, his mouth dry from breathing through it during the computation. Later, when the Gittelsons left, he called long distance.

"Sarah," he began, "you've got to come to Washington. Right away."

Toward the end of Monday morning, her first day in the store, Sarah found that her fears of hard work were greatly exaggerated. It was almost like selling dresses, though she realized that four people were doing the work of two in the grocery. The Gittelsons were eager workers, and even though the store was as good as sold, they still insisted on doing the difficult chores, such as putting the new stock away and cleaning the refrigerator and showcases.

It was just as well that the Gittelsons did the work

today, she thought. She was still tired from the train ride yesterday and from staying up half the night listening to the rats. A complaint to her husband brought the promise of getting an exterminator as soon as they moved in.

Her thoughts were interrupted by shouts of curses as a large, bulky man in a gray uniform bustled into the store, carrying by a handle tucked in the crook of his arm an unwieldy basket of bread. He looked around the store, now empty of customers, and fixed his eyes on her, and then her husband. Gittelson was in the kitchen lunching with his wife.

"Those black bastards," he said, breathing heavily and dropping the basket near the bread counter. "Excuse the language, lady. You must be the new people Gittelson was telling me about." He paused, turning to the street. "Well, those black bastards didn't even wait for the truck to stop rolling and me to put up the hand brake. I pulled up in front here and two of them jimmied the back lock while I was still rolling."

"They opened it from the outside?" Sarah asked, unable to take her eyes away from his puffy, perspiring face.

"Sure, how else? I don't carry niggers inside with the bread."

Sarah shook her head. "They broke in just to steal bread?"

"Not bread. Pies and cakes. Sometimes they break in just because there's a lock. Like those guys who have to climb a mountain because it's there."

Farber now spoke. "Why didn't you run after them?"

"What'll I do when I catch them?" The breadman

[48]

motioned toward his trouser pocket. "Look, when one of them puts his hand in his back pocket, you don't know what the hell's going to come out. Excuse the language, lady."

"That's okay, mister," Farber said, hoping his words conveyed a tone of understanding and forgiveness. "I'm Simon Farber and this is my wife, Sarah. This is her first day in the store. We're thinking of buying it."

"I'm Jimmy the breadman. Superstar bread. I've been out for the holidays but Gittelson told me about you the other week."

Jimmy placed the huge, wide plastic basket on the floor and unloaded bread into the shelving which formed the front half of the counter. He worked fast, placing the fresh cellophane-wrapped loaves behind yesterday's bread, which he squeezed and pressed upon to impart to the next customer who squeezed them a feeling of soft freshness.

"I'll tell you one thing, Mr. and Mrs. Farber. I'm getting out while I'm still in one piece. I don't care what they do to my truck. The hood's bent in where they jump on it. Dirty words scratched all over in the paint. I don't know how many flats I changed from ice pick jobs. That's just mischief. Okay, but where it hurts is when they get at *you*. I don't care if they tear up the lock and get in. We put in a double lock, that means double keys and that slows me down every day. Stopping, unlocking, locking. But you know something? They break in faster than I can open with my two keys."

"They're boys," said Farber, wishing to change the subject lest Sarah became worried. "How much bread to-day?"

[49]

"They're regular Houdinis," Sarah added.

"After age fourteen they're no more boys, Mr. Farber. I caught one breaking in, he was about thirty. I said, 'What you think you're doing?' He looked at me as if I just only stopped him tying his shoelace on my doorstep. He shrugged his shoulders and walked away. Like nothing happened. Like I asked him the time and he didn't know it."

"Call the police," Sarah said.

"They don't come, missus. You never see one around here. What are they going to come for—a stolen cake, a broken door? They got murders to take care of around here. Don't tell me about Alabama and Mississippi. I'm not interested."

Gittelson, who had stood unnoticed by the storeroom door, clucked his tongue. "Look, Jimmy. Just put the bread and go. We don't need politics here." The grocer turned toward Farber. "Deliverymen, they're just like barbers. Always shooting with the mouth."

Jimmy ignored Gittelson. "And when there's trouble, the cops come later because they don't want to incite the niggers. You got to move among them like they were bees. So the crime goes on because they know nobody can stop them."

"Okay, that's enough craptalk now," the grocer said angrily as he stepped into the store. "What do we owe you?"

The breadman pulled a pad and pencil from his jacket to tally the bill. "Four ninety-two," he said to Farber, who looked helplessly at Gittelson.

"Pay the man, Mr. Farber. Go ahead, just take it out of the register."

"I didn't know whether I should, Mr. Gittelson. It's still your money."

"That's all right. First check his figures. And did you count the bread?"

Farber, embarrassed, shook his head.

Jimmy placed the bill on the counter. "The number of bread's on the paper." He did not appear concerned about Gittelson's effrontery, as if he expected it from all the shop-keepers on his delivery route.

"Never mind what they say about philosophy and the weather," Gittelson continued. "Always count what they put in. Sometimes you can't tell what they put in. Some-times you can't tell yesterday's bread from today's."

"Yeah," Jimmy laughed, "I can tell the store ain't been sold yet." He looked at Farber. "If you owned it now, he wouldn't be so worried about being cheated."

Farber rang the no-sale key and scooped up money for the breadman. "Yeah," the latter said as a friendly, parting gesture in appreciation for the money and recognition of Farber's newness, "the cops around here, their hands are tied by the Supreme Court. So why should they bother? See you tomorrow."

"Big fat mouth," Gittelson said. He returned to the kitchen, content in sitting and drinking coffee while the Farbers waited on customers. They listened to him tell Mrs. Gittelson what had happened and then smiled to each other.

"Scary," Sarah said.

[51]

"We'll get used to it."

"I'd like to take a walk. My feet are killing me, standing up all day. Maybe the circulation needs some exercise."

"Be careful," he said. "Don't go far. And put on your coat. It's cold outside."

Icy dirt caked the sidewalk, spilled into the gutter, and then edged cautiously onto the street where the heat of traffic kept it in abeyance close to the curb. The sky was gray, and the wind came in strong cold gusts which rattled coverless and empty trash cans and sent torn newspapers flying and hugging trees and lampposts.

If there would be precipitation, Sarah thought, it probably would be snow. She hoped for a day of warm rain to wash away dirt on the streets and buildings.

She looked at the people—her new friends, neighbors, and customers. She had often seen colored people on the subways, and once or twice had driven through Harlem, but not since a few years ago when the civil rights battle began. There was a colored family who lived on the street, the old street, she corrected herself. And one of the girls who had worked with her as a salesclerk was colored. Edna Mae Washburn. They all had such funny names.

The faces on the men, women, and children weren't all dark. One boy, she noticed, who swept the length of his sleeve, from the shoulder to the cuff, under a running nose, was as white as anybody could be. His hair was straight and shiny, and he had a certain darkness under his eyes, like someone who suffers chronic loss of sleep. Other faces were soft brown rather than black. She wondered where color began and where it ended.

[52]

Soon she passed a young man with a cap and noted that she had seldom seen a colored youth without those brimless little head covers with visors. They even wore them in New York on the hottest days. It was like a uniform for them. Maybe they were ashamed of their hair, she thought.

Of a sudden, she felt someone behind her, dogging her steps. She turned to see the young man with the cap, who winked at her and began to speak in a singsong fashion.

"Where you going, baby? Huh? Where you going? How about you come with me, huh?"

"Leave me alone," she whispered in a voice dull and dry. Loudly now, she repeated what she had said, but he only grinned.

"Come here, white baby. Come here." He marched closer to her and made sounds similar to short bursts of escaping steam, or to someone calling a pet cat.

She looked around, seized with fear that the street suddenly had become deserted. Not a person, not a passing automobile, were to be seen.

"Hey, white pussy. Not so fast. I got something big and mean for you."

Certain that she was going to be raped, her mind churned dizzily. Should she scream? Who would hear her? All doors and windows on the block were closed tightly. The street was a ghost town. He was going to pull her into an alley or someplace, of that she was convinced. Who would help her?

She began to run on legs that barely obeyed her to the corner, but he kept up with her merely by lengthening his

[53]

stride. Turning the corner, she cried with relief when she saw several young men standing around and stamping their feet to keep warm.

At last, she thought, turning to her pursuer to watch him slink away, frightened by the youths. He seemed, however, to gain new courage when he saw them.

"That's my gal," he shouted.

"Where you get that white meat, Ernie?" someone asked him.

Her fear turned to absolute panic. What began as instructions from her mind for a scream came out instead a low, bubbly moan. Her legs now failed her completely, and the youths interpreted her confused halt as a sign that she was interested in them. They surrounded her, and one of them reached out for her.

"A white mothah hooker," he said, grabbing for her shoulder. His arm was brushed away by Ernie.

"You ass off that, mothah!"

"Oh, please, please, please!" The tears had finally come, and she was grateful, for now she had an ally to convince them that her show of fear was not pretended. "Please let me go. I want to go home."

"She want to go home," another youth mocked. "This is you home, mothah."

She shook hysterically now and could only murmur, "No, no, no," in a voice that was barely audible, yet she was able to notice a taller, older man standing away from the circle who smiled at her. Was it a concerned smile or was he merely enjoying the spectacle? she wondered, trying to plead with her eyes.

[54]

Another youth reached for her breasts, well-covered and protected by a thick coat and sweater.

Ernie shouted again, "You ass off that," as he lashed out to slap the youth hard. The two then traded rapidly thrown punches for a few seconds until they were separated by the tall man.

"He better get his ass off that," Ernie protested to the man, who wore a stiff pompadour of black, oily caves and crevices, and shiny black pants with a white leather jacket.

"You all's ass better get off that or the police be down here," the man warned. "She ain't no hooker. She lost." He smiled at her and then quickly snarled, waving a hitchhiker's thumb, "Get you ass out a here!"

As she turned toward the direction of the store, the hand of Ernie came under her coat, under her skirt, and encompassed a warm buttock. The hand, hard and icy, squeezed tightly, transmitting an electriclike shock which jarred her from her paralyzed state and sent her off with a leap and a gallop to their laughter.

She tried to hide what had happened, but her tears broke down her defenses. Farber went for the cleaver at the meat block but she and the Gittelsons restrained him. They argued about calling the police.

"It's all over now, why call the police?" Gittelson said. "No use to get excited," he continued, more worried about what effect the incident might have on the sale of the store than about the incident itself. "Such things happen. Nobody was *really* hurt."

"It was broad daylight," Farber cried, almost with tears to match his wife's.

[55]

"Daylight to them is to better see broads," Gittelson joked weakly.

"Broad daylight, smoard daylight," Mrs. Gittelson said. "Listen, honey. Take my advice. You don't go walking around here alone nighttime, daytime, anytime, if you're a white woman. You just don't do it, that's all."

"I can't stay here," Sarah cried. "I don't want to live here."

Mrs. Gittelson took her by the elbow. "Look, honey, I'm telling you. Everything's all right. You'll forget about it."

"Don't buy the store, Simon. I don't want to live here."

Mrs. Gittelson became impatient. "Look, Mrs. Farber, take it easy. You're excited. Overwrought. Maybe you ought to go upstairs and lay down for a while."

"And listen to the rats?" Sarah shot back, looking only at her husband. "It's bad enough they keep me up all night."

"Rats, smats," said Gittelson, more nervous than before. "Look, do me a favor. The man from inventory is going to be here in a few minutes. Don't make a mountain out of a molehill. So a *shvartzer* patted you on the *tokus*. So what? Some ladies should be happy that they still could get a man to look at them." He began to laugh, but stopped when he saw Farber's face.

"Don't talk to my wife like that. You take your damn store and you know what you can do with it."

[56]

"Now, now, Mr. Farber," Mrs. Gittelson said. "You got every right to be overwrought." She turned to her husband. "Shut up, Joe. Can't you see it's a traumatic experience?"

But now Mr. Gittelson raised his voice. "You shut up, yourself. *Dramatic* experience. Big deal! And you, Mr. Farber, don't do me no favors. You want the store, okay. You don't, I'll just take your five hundred deposit and wait for the next buyer to come along. And believe me, that won't be long."

The five-hundred-dollar deposit, Farber thought. He had worked hard to raise that money. From Quinn he had borrowed one thousand. The bank gave him four thousand, five hundred of which went to complete the two thousand down payment. There had not been a penny remaining for the deposit. He had a choice of selling the car and some furniture or asking Benny for a loan. He did not ask his brother.

Farber could not back out now. It was too late, too confusing, and he had a bad headache. "Okay, relax," he said. "Come on, Sarah. Maybe you better lay down for a while."

The man placed his portable adding machine on the counter and nodded a hello to the Gittelsons and Farber. He worked for a few minutes with the machine, adjusting its paper and trying it out before he spoke. "All set? This is going to take at least four hours, maybe more. We'll start with the cans."

[57]

He was a tall, heavy man, but with narrow shoulders, and he wore an old suit with a red and blue sport shirt under it. He continually pulled on his nose, using either hand, and Farber wondered how the man's small nose was able to keep its size. Without further introduction or instruction, he nodded again, this time to Gittelson. "Ready when you are, C.B."

The grocer walked briskly to a corner shelf, kneeled, and began. "Six cans of salmon at fifty-nine each," he shouted as the man began to punch keys on the machine. "I've got nine here of sardines at nineteen." Both he and the man worked quickly, and each time a shelf was completed, the man tore off a snatch of paper and lanced it on a spike file.

Farber wondered what he was supposed to do while the two of them counted. He marveled at how well Gittelson knew his job, as if the grocer had rehearsed or performed the role many times. Maybe Gittelson had, he thought, wondering whether it was possible that the grocer made a racket of collecting deposit forfeitures after scaring prospective buyers away. Nonsense, he reassured himself. Word gets around. Quinn would have told him. It was more likely that the business had been up for sale many times but each time the buyer had backed out at the last minute after discovering the store to be a lemon.

Farber now suspected some unholy plot between grocer and stock taker, even though he was told that inventory men were part of honest firms established to set a store's worth. Yet, he decided to watch the grocer closely in the counting, as if that would help offset or prevent still more outrageous collusion and possible subsequent disaster. At least, he would appear busy and in tune with the meticulous and serious business of inventory.

The papers were signed the next day.

The lawyer for the Gittelsons showed up in a loose-fitting suit. His thinness emphasized the misfit, while his shirt, several sizes too large, made his badly shaven, colorless neck look like that of a plucked chicken. The shirt also allowed some chest hair to ride obscenely over the top of his tie knot.

They sat around the kitchen table, Farber, Sarah, and the Gittelsons with their lawyer. Sarah had hastily cleaned the table of the roll of salami, bread, and a large bottle of soda when the lawyer arrived, but Farber could see crumbs of bread which attracted a roach, unmindful of the daylight and human activity. Both roach and crumbs were brushed to the floor, the insect owing his life to Farber's unwillingness to crush in front of company.

But the lawyer missed nothing. "That's right, Mr. Farber. Leave it to the sweeper."

"I'm the sweeper," Sarah said, blushing in her wish for something to say so as not to appear dumbstruck by the professional man.

Farber watched as the lawyer's long, skinny fingers unsnapped the briefcase and took out papers and notebooks. The papers looked legal as lawyers' papers should, Farber thought, not failing to notice the first word,

WHEREAS, printed large at the beginning of one page.

"What time's your attorney going to show?" the lawyer asked him.

"I don't have one."

Shrugging his shoulders, the lawyer slid his hands gracefully over the papers, putting one to his left, several in front of him, and a few to his right. He licked his lips and read one of the papers while his audience watched reverently. "Well, everything looks okay from where I stand," he said as he began to write something.

The rustling of the important papers and the scratching of the pen made Farber respect the man for his education and knowledge. The lawyer's hands were manicured, hairless, and unveined.

Farber looked at his own hands, not yet gnarled by arthritis, but still chapped with creases and cuts packed with black grime. Veins bulged like a surface pipeline.

The hands of a man who worked with his hands, he thought. A carpenter. What was that lousy lawyer but a lousy shyster lawyer? A doctor you need, but who needs a lawyer? Even work as a carpenter, building houses, shelters for people, was more important than being a lawyer, a man who made up big words with his fellow lawyers and then charged you money for explaining what they meant.

He wished he could buy the store like he bought a pair of shoes, for he now felt that by not having a lawyer to represent him or to counteract whatever tricks the Gittelson lawyer might have he had made a bad mistake.

Yesterday, when alone with Jimmy, the breadman had whispered that the Gittelsons were also supposed to put up a five-hundred-dollar deposit. If they'd back out, Jimmy said, you'd get it.

Why didn't Quinn tell me that? But Quinn's not a lawyer. Why should he have mentioned it?

Jimmy had said that not having a smart lawyer was bad. And then, seeing how worried Farber had become, tried to make him feel better by saying that in case of default on either side, the lawyers would get most of the deposit anyway, so don't worry.

Farber now thought that he might ask the Gittelson lawyer to act for him, too. No. How could a lawyer cheat himself? It would be all over soon, as soon as he signed his name. He wouldn't be a carpenter anymore. He'd be a storeowner.

Nevertheless, Farber leaned back, feeling completely out of his depth. He waited for deceit as a small boy waits for an inoculation.

The lawyer cleared his throat. "Now, my clients are acting both as the seller and the lessor. The sale of the store, the name, the goodwill, et cetera, is clear cut. Three thousand. Plus four for inventoried stock and fixtures. Which leaves a grand total of seven thousand, from which I deduct the down payment of two thousand dollars. You say you have a bank loan for thirty-five hundred. Add your deposit of five hundred. That leaves a stipulated promissory note of one thousand to be paid off to the tune of one hundred dollars a month, plus interest."

What was a lessor? Farber wondered. He glanced over to Sarah, hoping that she'd understand what the lawyer was saying, but she looked at him as if to beg him silently to pay attention and try to understand. She knew him.

"Well, as a matter of fact," the lawyer continued, "the situation with the lease is pretty much cut and dried. I'm sure you'll agree with that, Mr. Farber."

The Gittelsons nodded. They sat closely together, side by side, chair to chair, both with hands clasped over their corpulent midsections, twiddling their thumbs. Their heads were bent at an angle, his to the left, hers to the right, giving an impression of a well-fed, satisfied, two-headed monster.

"Now, you as the lessee, Mr. Farber, well, I'm sure you've read the terms of the lease. It's a cut-and-dried contract in black and white. We've got the rental figure for the property owned by my clients. One sixty monthly. Three-year lease. Repairs made by the lessee. My client will repair major defects."

"Just a moment," Sarah said. "If we're buying the store, why do we have to pay rent also?"

The lawyer smiled patronizingly. He pulled off his glasses, leaving a deep-cut mark in the nose flesh. "You're buying the business, per se, not the land, the property, the upstairs, and the house itself."

Sarah felt foolish.

"Now, let's see. The usual stuff here. Nothing out of the ordinary. One thing, Mr. Farber," he said, scanning his papers. "You've got to provide some security here to Mr. Gittelson to assure the return of the premises in good condition."

Sarah saw a chance to strike back. "What do you

mean? You mean we have to give you more money?"

"Not *me!*" the lawyer protested, laughing. "Well, let's see. It's a small sum. About five hundred dollars."

"What for?" Farber demanded, convinced now that he was being cheated, and determined to stop, hold, and fight at this point.

"To assure return of the premises in good condition."

"Nothing's the same after you use it," Farber said. "It's going to get a little older."

"Consider it a savings fund, Mr. Farber. And it protects both you and Mr. Gittelson."

"How does it protect me?"

"Well, Mr. Farber, in case Mr. Gittelson goes broke, God forbid, and can't make repairs, you get the money back."

"But it's our money to begin with," said Sarah.

Seeing the spouse of Mr. Farber take part in the proceedings, Mrs. Gittelson was moved to do likewise. "It's to protect you."

Farber was elated. He felt he had caught them conniving and had shown himself to be a shrewd businessman who did not need a lawyer's services. "In other words, in case the property isn't the same, you get to keep the five hundred. I'm sorry, that's not in the deal."

"Now look here, Mr. Farber." The lawyer removed his glasses again for emphasis. "This means only if there are big changes. Damages. Like a hole in the wall where the hatchet hit after your wife missed you."

[63]

The Gittelsons joined his laughter, cut short by Farber's steely voice.

"My wife doesn't do that, Mr. Lawyer."

"All right," the lawyer said, "this protects you if the lessor goes bankrupt."

"Speak plain," Farber said, believing that now he was in control. "What's a lessor?"

"The landlord. The owner. Wasn't that clear to you?"

"It is now."

The lawyer smirked and mocked, "It is now." He paused to shake his head, as if to show his patience was wearing thin.

"I don't have the money anyway," Farber confessed.

The lawyer glanced at the Gittelsons, and the two-headed creature nodded in unison. "No problem," he said. "We could arrange to have you send me fifty a month, until you reach five hundred. Let me state here and now that this money is your private, personal account. In no way is it to go to myself or my clients, unless of course there are damages."

"Okay," Farber said without looking at his wife. He picked up the contract, ready to sign, but realized that they'd think him inexperienced if he signed too quickly. He forced himself to read at least some of the words.

Sarah signed in a moment, as if she was unwilling to prolong whatever she suspected was unpleasant or painful in the contract.

A strange sorry-glad feeling came over Farber. He told himself that he did the right thing and tried not to think of the numbers that came to his mind. One fifteen to Quinn.

[64]

About one fifty to the bank. One hundred to Gittelson. One sixty for rent. Fifty for the lawyer. What did that come to?

He shuddered, and heard the droning of the lawyer which seemed so far away.

The jarring of the bell atop the doorframe signaled entry of a man shaped almost like a huge ball with limbs. His kinky hair, mixed black, gray, and white, was grown out naturally, overlapping his ears, and making it look like a poor imitation of the wig English judges wear.

In spite of the cold, he wore an army khaki shirt and trousers. As he moved, the end of the shirt and the top of the trousers failed to meet, revealing white lint sheltered in a black navel.

"This must be my new, neighborhood friendly corner store," the man said. "I guess my friends the Gittelsons must be gone by now."

"Moved out last week," Farber said. "What can I do for you?"

"That's right," the man replied. "What can you do for me. It's your world. I'm just merely passing through."

"What did you say?"

"Surprised, eh? By my accent? I don't speak 'cul-lud'? Well, I'm a bit different from the niggers you see around here."

Wary, Farber said, "That's very interesting."

The bell sounded again. Mother Matthews, a light-complexioned woman who lived by herself, entered. Although she was plump, Farber thought that she bought too

[65]

much food for one person. He suspected that she had many male friends, notwithstanding her claim that her business was psychological counseling.

The man bowed and smiled. "Why, hello there, Mother Matthews. How are you?"

"Fine," she said brusquely, turning to greet Farber.

Farber smiled hello at her, and looked impatiently at the man. "What can I do for you?"

"Don't like small talk with the colored trade, eh, Mr. Farber?" The man looked at Mother Matthews for approval, but she glared in return. "Tell you what. Why don't you wait on this here lady first. I'm in no hurry."

The man turned an empty soda crate sideways and sat on it. For a moment Farber felt concern, afraid the man was a holdup artist, waiting for the customer to leave. But Mother Matthews saw and knew him, and could identify him for the police. The man wanted something, but what? Farber smiled to himself. Maybe he just wants groceries.

"Well, ah think ah'll just take a bread, couple strips bacon for a little late breakfast," Mother Matthews said. "And put it on the book, Mistah Simon."

"I haven't seen you for a while, Mother Matthews." The fat man wheezed his words out, lowering his eyelids to appear rugged and mysterious.

"Been keeping myself occupied." She picked her credit book up, nodded her appreciation to Farber and walked out without saying anything else to the man.

He looked after her, puckering his lips as he watched her buttocks sway away from him. He kissed the flat of his hand and blew the kiss across to her just as the door slammed.

[66]

"Boy, I'd like to get a piece of that fancy stuff." He shook his head. "Ha. She didn't even want to chat with me. That goddamn whore."

"She's not," Farber said. "She's a psychological counselor."

The stranger laughed uproariously and almost tipped over his soda crate. "Man, let me tell you something. You can work at any job in the world, but if you're a whore in your spare time, you're still a whore. Yeah, I can tell her kind a mile away. Low nigger type."

"I don't like to hear that kind of stuff, mister."

"Low nigger, for your information, is not a derogatory term. It's a descriptive term, meaning a black who doesn't have much black blood. Look at her light skin. She's the leavings of some son of a bitch white man."

"Mister, I said I didn't like that talk."

"Oh, well, she can't help having that poisoned white blood. They beat our men with chains and bred our women as animals."

Farber nodded with acknowledgment.

"I know you, Mr. Simon Farber, but you don't know me. Call me Tammu. Funny name, isn't it? Well, it's my own, or rather a name which denotes my African heritage. I used to have a plantation name like Jones, given to my forebears by yours."

He walked over to the soft-drink case, opened it, and pulled out a Pepsi Cola. With his head tilted back and soda bottle raised high, he drained the contents in one gulp. Soon a low, heavy noise, like the faraway sound of a volcano, came rumbling from his midsection. An eruction rolled above his lower lip and dropped to wet his shirt. His thick, moistened lips opened to receive his tongue which whipped around the periphery, soaking up the remains of the bubbly, lavalike liquid.

"Me, oh, my," he said. "Excuse me."

Farber calmly clenched his fists. He knew he could easily throw Tammu out of the store. "Look, I'm very busy, Mr. Tammu."

"All right, sir. Permit me to introduce myself more fully. I am General Tammu, founder and leader of an organization that now solicits your support. We need donations from community business leaders such as yourself to help us achieve our goal. Which is liberation for the black man."

"I'm sorry. I can't afford to help you."

"You can't afford not to help us, Mr. Farber. You see, if you contribute, my supporters will trade here. If you don't, they won't. Some may even do rash things."

"Like what?"

"I hesitate to venture a prediction at this juncture."

"Get out, or I'll call the cops."

"As you wish, Mr. Farber." He walked to the door and, without turning around, said, "Think it over."

For a long time Farber sat on a stool, grateful that no customers came in and that Sarah was busy cleaning and cooking. Several times he thought of calling the police.

They wouldn't do anything until Tammu breaks a window or something. There's nothing illegal about a boycott. If the *shvartzer* did make a threat, how could I prove it? It's the old protection racket. I can't tell Sarah anything. Things are bad enough as it is with her.

[68]

Farber made up his mind to do what he could alone. His first step would be to grab Tammu and remind him that he walked out without paying for the soda.

They spied each other at the same time and both stopped what they were doing.

Allan, with his hand still holding the kitchen door-knob, and the rat, lying on its back on top of the refrigerator, holding and cradling on its abdomen an egg, which it sucked through an opening at one end, much like an infant with a bottle. The rat sniffed and blinked at Allan. In a moment, it continued undauntedly to suck on the pole of the egg. Next to the animal was a cardboard egg holder with the cover ripped off, as if by human hands.

Gray, with a squirrelly, coarse-furred coat which stuck in oil-greased patches, the rat kept an eye on Allan as it unhurriedly drained the egg. Suddenly, it permitted the egg to roll off its stomach, and Allan heard the empty faintness of the shell's breaking as it hit the refrigerator top and rolled off to smash on the kitchen floor.

The rat righted itself, stood on its hindlegs, and rested a foreleg on the egg box while it licked spilt egg from its chest. It resembled a drunken man leaning against a corner pole and nodding his head.

Transfixed by the audacity of the rat, Allan was curiously amused yet wary of the creature which virtually ignored his presence. Almost at the same time, he called his father and screamed, "Scat!"

The rat looked up, paused, and strolled to the edge of the refrigerator where it jumped noiselessly to the floor without breaking stride. It scurried along the sides of the kitchen to the door, passed within inches of Allan's feet, and then disappeared among some boxes in a dark corner of the storeroom.

Allan felt as if the large and ugly animal had contaminated him forever.

"What's the matter?" his father asked.

"A big rat was on the refrigerator. It's in those boxes."

His father picked up a broom and advanced to the boxes. He pushed them aside and found a hole in the wall no larger than the circumference of an eyeglass lens.

"I don't know how he got through that hole," Allan said. "He's five times bigger."

"They could squeeze through anything," his father said, grunting. "All right, go to the five and ten and get a couple of rat traps. The best they got."

An excitement filled Allan, the adventure of the hunting and killing of an animal. In an attempt to prevent any possible future flagging of his father's enthusiasm, he said, "It was like Dracula sucking on blood. It was big, like a cat. I don't know how many eggs it ate."

He followed his father into the kitchen. Aside from the shattered egg on the floor, they found only one other destroyed, its shell lying among the insult of the rat's droppings; a white oval emblem of health in the midst of elliptical, black reminders of filth and disease.

"Eccch!" Allan said.

He swore vengeance on Dracula, not for eating the egg or leaving droppings, but for not being afraid of him.

For some reason, the banquet was strangely silent. The

waiter made no sound as he held the tray low to offer Farber a cocktail glass.

For a moment, Farber held the delicate glass in his thick, red hand, but then the coldness of the glass made him loosen his grip and it fell to the ballroom floor. From far away, the shattering sound came to him.

"Simon, wake up."

He heard his wife and then felt her fingers sticking hard into his shoulder.

"I heard a noise."

He sat up for a moment and then got out of bed, shuffling with his feet as he searched for his slippers.

"Be careful."

Head heavy with sleep, he went down the stairs and into the store. He saw a hole in the window, with large cracks running like lightning. In the center of the floor, like a stage performer in a spotlight, a brick lay in a rugged circle of light projected through the hole from a streetlamp.

Just a brick, he thought. He had seen so many of them, but on construction jobs. What was this brick doing on the floor of his store?

He examined the brick, faded and chipped. It must have been taken from a demolished house, he thought, or pulled from one of the sidewalks made of bricks worn smooth by tens of thousands of shoes.

Who would want to throw it through a window? And for what? Exercise? Only more profit for the glass manufacturers. He had a vision of a fat manufacturer of plate glass sitting at a desk, smoking a cigar and smiling at the thought of another broken window.

He shook the sleep from his head. Bastard, he thought.

"What is it, Simon?" Sarah stood at the door in her nightgown, arms folded in front of her, shivering in the cold as she spoke.

"Go back to bed. Nothing." He saw Allan standing behind her. "Allan, go get the broom and dustpan. Somebody threw a brick."

"Who?" she asked.

"A *shvartzer,* who else? Maybe he was drunk or maybe he tried to break in. I have to get a piece of lumber and cover the window or else somebody else might try to get in."

"Call the police first."

Without answering, Farber walked over to the cash register, which he kept open nights on the advice of Gittelson. Leaving the drawer out, Farber was told, prevented a burglar from smashing the register to break into it. And always leave some money in it, the advice had sounded, or else the burglar might search around until he did find some.

He lifted out a coin and walked over to the telephone booth. "I want to report a broken window." He reported what had happened.

"All right, Mr. Farber," a police officer said, "it's on the book. We'll send someone around in the morning."

"You're not coming down now?"

"We see them all the time. We're pretty busy tonight. Like one gentleman of color got his throat slashed from ear to ear with a broken whiskey bottle swung by his wife while he was drunk to the world." The officer paused and blew air through his lips. "If you have insurance call

[72]

and tell them the police have a record."

"I think I know who did it," Farber said, his throat tightening."

"Who?"

"A man called General Tammu."

"We know him, Mr. Farber. We'll talk to him in the morning, too. Best you get some sleep now. Okay?"

"Mr. Gittelson, hello. Good morning. This is Simon Farber." He closed the door of the telephone booth and at once smelled the stink of cigarettes smoked and drops of liquor spilled and urine surreptitiously discharged.

"How're ya doin' there, Farber? Raking in the *gelt?*"

"We had a slight accident last night, Mr. Gittelson. Someone smashed my window."

"It happens, it happens. What you have to do is get a new window."

Idiot, Farber thought. "That's what I called about. The insurance." He laughed nervously. "What's the name of my insurance company?"

"Farber, I got news for you. You don't got insurance for plate glass. No company wanting to stay in the black, if you get the joke, will stay in the black, if you get what I mean. Not even Lloyd's of London would write you a policy on glass there. You make up for it by raising the price on a few items."

"I can't do that."

"Look, I lived and worked there for years. The *shvartzers* stole from me, broke my windows, and took swings at me a couple of times."

"Why didn't you tell me that before I bought the store?"

"Look, it's a good living and we all face danger one way or another. Every time I get out of a slippery bathtub or cross the street . . ."

Farber gently replaced the telephone receiver.

Approaching the room, he stopped, afraid to go in. He braced himself against the door, hoping to learn what was in store for him before he entered, but the teacher's voice could barely be heard over the chattering, the shuffling of chairs, and rattling of desk tops.

Earlier, when he and his mother had arrived at the school to have him admitted, he had felt that his outlandishly pale skin wasn't only the wrong color, but didn't quite fit, squeezing and tugging him like a suit several sizes too small. The stares, indifferent, curious, and even hostile, seemed to contribute to the hot pastiness which coated his mouth and throat. Breathing was difficult; speech almost impossible.

He was glad his mother left after he had been assigned to a class. He didn't want her to suffer from any thoughts about his being in not only a colored school, but a Christian one, for the signs of the past Christmas holiday were still around. In his predominantly Jewish school in New York, Christmas was observed by the singing of "Jingle Bells" and a week's vacation.

Allan clutched a paper his new homeroom teacher had given him, along with instructions where to find his class, which was taking history with Mr. Johnson. He now pressed his ear against the door, but a sharp rap of stick against wood from within the room made him jerk his head away. He heard a shout from the teacher for silence, and in the ensuing quiet, the enunciation of each word in a way customers in the store never spoke.

"It's just not right for us to wait for the white man to do our job. We must all take part. When we reach our goal, we'll be able to say that American Negroes, one for all and all for one, worked together to win our rights."

Allan saw his homeroom teacher watching him from down the hall. He gasped, pushed the door open, and encountered more shouting from Mr. Johnson.

"Robert, I told you to quit playing with those cards! You hear me? Put them away!"

Mr. Johnson's eyes widened when he saw Allan. Then he smiled broadly and motioned the new student forward, taking the paper and writing something in a notebook.

The classroom was packed with boys and girls, all of them Negro. All the seats, as far as Allan could see, were taken. Crumbled papers, pieces of fallen plaster from the ceiling, discarded workbooks, comic books, and other debris lined the aisles. Several broken window-panes permitted wafts of cold air to enter the already chilly room.

Allan did not dare look directly at his new classmates, but from the corner of his eye he saw a few point at him, snicker, and whisper among themselves. His eyes found refuge in the teacher's face, covered with light skin broken by Caucasian features. Mr. Johnson's heavily pomaded hair, wavy and tightly curled, looked like a pelt of Persian lamb pasted on his head.

The teacher showed pleasure at Allan's appearance by

[75]

gripping the boy's hand and shaking it too high and too low. "Class, I'd like you to welcome Allan Farber. He's joining us and I hope you'll treat him warmly and make friends with him."

Allan walked through a gantlet of eyes that were black olives, emotionless, secretive. He sat on a chair temporarily placed at the rear of the room, next to the cloakroom door. Although isolated, he felt snug in being able to watch the others without being seen.

He thought of his last day of school in New York. All the students had known he was transferring but his homeroom teacher made the news official as soon as the class had recited the pledge of allegiance to the flag.

"Boys and girls, our class president is going to see the nation's president," she had intoned.

The class had returned her smile. Her jest, however, did not affect Allan's pride in knowing he would be going where important people lived and worked.

Both class and teacher had been sadly silent as he then turned his duties over to the vice-president. Gentle applause followed. The vice-president, a slender reed of a girl with worn heels, bade him farewell. The class athlete then began a smart-alecky cry of "speech, speech" which was picked up as a sincere request by the other students.

Attentively, with their elbows propped against desk tops, and with hands clasped in front of their mouths, they had listened to him. He spoke haltingly, merely repeating what he had heard his father say. Washington, D.C., wasn't that far away. One day he'd be back.

The vice-president then presented a gift from the class,

[76]

an inexpensive wallet with his gilt-engraved initials already chipping.

Mr. Johnson rapped on the desk again. He stood like a lone peak in front of a field of bobbing black hair. Shocks of frizzly hair grown out in natural dishevelment had the appearance of used steel wool. Several boys competed with the girls for length. One girl whose hair was longer than any of the others appeared to be balancing a woolly water-pot on her head.

As soon as the teacher turned toward the blackboard, on which he began to write a list of names, some of the students, heretofore content with whispering or reading comic books implanted into textbooks, started a movement of arms and legs. One boy walked around the room while another rose to look out the window.

For no apparent reason, a husky youth with arm muscles road-mapped with thick veins struck a boy sitting in front of him, while a girl removed chewing gum from her mouth and threw it at another girl in whose haystack-stiff hair it landed like a grasshopper. A boy with hair like an embroidered wig who sat immediately in front of Allan leaned over the aisle and cupped the breast of an unprotesting girl. She looked back at Allan, put her hand over her mouth to stifle a giggle, and then brushed the boy's hand away.

Allan, envious and embarrassed, felt his face redden. He shifted his eyes to Mr. Johnson, who still stood with back to the class. He appeared oblivious to the constant shifting and whispering. A bare moment before the end of the chalk sounds, the students, seemingly endowed with an

[77]

extraordinary sense, halted their activities. Bodies slipped back into seats, and hands and arms returned from across aisles. It was almost as though a busy puppeteer manipulating the scene had to end the mischief in order to pull the strings that turned the teacher.

Allan was sure that the teacher knew what went on but could not do anything about it. His sympathy went out to Mr. Johnson, who, apparently responding to the psychic communication, addressed the boy.

"Allan, we're in the midst of Negro history in America. I'm sure you'll be able to catch up quickly."

Again he turned to the board, accompanied by renewed student activity. Now Allan saw the breast-cupping student shoot a hand across the aisle, this time to squeeze the girl's thigh. She continued to comb her hair with one hand and patted his fingers with the other. Suddenly she stood and slipped past Allan into the cloakroom, to be followed by the boy. None of the other students saw them leave. Without bothering to conceal themselves from Allan, whose rear seat enabled him to see around the cloakroom passageway, they kissed and fondled each other to the sound of the teacher's board scratching.

Allan kept the tail of one eye on the teacher. He half hoped that Mr. Johnson would turn and notice the empty seats and hear the illicit sounds coming from the cloakroom. He breathed rapidly through his nose and mouth as he watched the boy lean over the girl and put his hands under her buttocks to lift her to his groin. The boy, panting, gyrated his hips as he pressed against her. She seemed unaffected.

Suddenly, he stopped and loosened his grip. She adjusted her dress, hesitated at the passageway to look at the teacher, and then sneaked back to her seat. He wiped a wetness on his trousers with the sleeve of a gray coat hanging on a peg. In a moment he scurried to his own desk.

Now completely astounded, Allan was able to gain his composure only when the teacher faced the class and called on him again.

"Allan, I've just written several names on the board. Can you tell us which ones you've heard of before?"

Allan stood, not caring now about being exposed in his vantage point. He was too excited by what he had seen. He answered with a tense, shrill voice.

"Booker T. Washington and George Washington Carver."

"Very good, Allan. Be seated." He pointed to the other names, ticking them off. "Frederick Douglass, Crispus Attucks, James Weldon Johnson, and all the rest of them will be quite familiar to you as time passes. This man, for example"—he tapped his finger on the board over another name—"Jean Du Sable, was the first non-Indian to settle Chicago. Now, he wasn't white, but Negro. So you see, the first white man in Chicago was a Negro." He laughed, but none of the students joined him. Moments later, however, the husky youth who had struck his neighbor clapped his hands and neighed like a horse.

"Robert, I fail to see any reason for that ugly sound."

Robert muttered in a low voice and shook his head.

"Speak up, Robert." Mr. Johnson's light face grew gray. "If you have anything to say in your defense, say it."

"You was laughin' you-self."

"All right, Robert. I laughed for good reason, but you were having a good time at my expense. I can't help believing that you're taking advantage of the fact that I'm your homeroom teacher. You seem to forget that you're here because you failed this class last year."

The teacher glanced to the rear of the room where Allan sat. Allan was sure the speech was for his benefit, to clarify the presence of Robert, who was larger and looked older than any of the other students.

Mr. Johnson showed satisfaction in unveiling his authority with the proper belittling remark, proving, it appeared, that he would not let anyone forget he was in control of the class in spite of an occasional friendly joke. He pointed a strict, stiff finger at Robert. "Pick up your book and begin reading at the top of page eleven."

Robert hung his head low and read, mispronouncing words, stumbling over others, and finally lowering his voice to a whisper.

"Speak up!" the teacher commanded.

"Mothahfuck!"

Mr. Johnson again looked in Allan's direction. He strode quickly up to Robert's desk to face the youth, who rose out of his chair to stand a head taller than the teacher.

"Robert, you come from nothing, you are yourself nobody, and your children, and I hope to God you never have any, could expect nothing from you."

"Nobody call me nothin'," Robert said, swinging his fist in a vicious arc to wallop Mr. Johnson on nose and mouth. The teacher fell backward against students and desks, pursued by Robert, who unrelentingly pummeled with both fists, punching through the teacher's upheld non-protective palms to strike him on the face and chest.

None of the other students moved. Allan remained seated, as though paralyzed. Only when blood gushed from Mr. Johnson's nose did Robert stop. He ran from the room, but retraced his steps seconds later to rush to the cloak-room, where he snatched his coat, the same gray one which had been used to wipe the amorous student's trousers.

Shouting by the students through the open door brought other teachers, including a woman who appeared to Allan to be the principal since she was much older and had an authoritative bearing. Two younger male teachers lifted Mr. Johnson to his feet and, with his arms dangling over their shoulders, helped him leave the room.

Before reaching the door, Mr. Johnson turned to face Allan for a moment. A look of embarrassed pain in the teacher's expression made Allan think it was due to the beating and the blood.

The elderly principal shook her head of sparse white hair as she watched the trio leave. She then faced the class and stood for a moment, the light reflecting in her glasses. Her voice was coarse, as though toughened from years of shouting.

"I don't suppose I have to tell you how terrible this all is. The boy will be expelled. I suppose that is what he wanted. Now, I must ask each of you not to go telling everybody what happened here. This is a school matter, but

[81]

you would be surprised how terrible rumors travel. You would see it on the first page of the newspaper how a teacher was slashed by a knife. Or how there was a big razor and chain fight. We know that is exaggerated. And we are not going to issue any press releases each time there is a misunderstanding."

She spoke until the bell rang. In the midst of the bustle to leave, Allan momentarily forgot about the beating as he stared at the rounded breasts of the girl in front of him.

Tammu came into the store, nodded a greeting to Farber, and leaned up against the meat showcase with his arms folded in front of him. He watched Farber wait on another customer. When his turn came, he jerked a thumb toward a man who had come in after him. "Wait on that gentleman, first, if you please."

Farber knew why he had come and was careful not to betray any signs of nervousness. As he packed a bag for the customer, he watched Tammu from the corner of his eye. The Negro was breathing heavily, pitching his chest against the folded arms. Although the store was not warm, perspiration popped out of his forehead, and the black skin glistened under transparent beads.

The customer left and Farber turned to Tammu. He was glad Sarah was napping and Allan was away at school. If there was to be trouble, let there be. He knew he could handle Tammu. The man was fat, slow, and probably out of condition. The only good thing the years as a carpenter had given him, Farber thought as he nodded to Tammu, was a hard, well-muscled body.

"Mr. Tammu. Anything I could help you with?"

"You've helped me enough, Mr. Farber. You've helped me pass an otherwise quiet morning in the company of two police officers. I came to thank you."

"They asked me if I knew of anybody who'd want to break my window."

"Me? Break your window? Why should I want to break your goddamn window?"

"You threatened me."

"What's that supposed to mean?"

"It's pretty bad that I have to pay for that window out of my pocket because no insurance company would insure anything around here."

"Why not? This is a good neighborhood, even though it happens to be black."

"A broken window happens in a good neighborhood?"

Tammu was forced to smile. "Well, I had nothing to do with that incident. I sleep during the night. My campaigns are carried out during the waking hours."

"If you say you didn't do it, fine. I take your word. But do me one favor, leave me alone. All I want to do is make a living. I'm not interested in your campaign or philosophy or anything else you do."

"Nor am I interested in frustrating someone from making a living and establishing his identity."

"Okay, Mr. Tammu." Farber paused. "Do you want anything?"

[83]

"General Tammu, if you don't mind. No, thank you."
He put his hands into his pockets and looked glumly into
Farber's eyes. "So you want a place in society, huh? And
you think you could buy it with money?"

Farber picked up a wet rag and began to wipe the
countertop. "General, I know you're a very important person. You're well educated. But I don't know why you keep
pestering me, a small storekeeper. What do you want? Do
you want me in your organization?"

Tammu, laughing, reached for his cigarettes. His lips
tightly grasped a cigarette and his hands were able to light
a match, but his body shook so from laughter that he had
difficulty in applying fire to the end of the cigarette. After
he did, he spoke.

"Do you know something? You interest me. You're
typical. Jewish, I mean."

Farber bristled. He clenched his fists.

"Now, now, Mistah Simon. Relax." Tammu spread
his palms outward and said in a Yiddish accent, "Enjoy,
enjoy. Let me finish."

"I don't want to hear any anti-Semitic shit. Especially
from you."

"Especially from a *shvartzer,* huh?"

Tammu closed his mouth and blew air until his cheeks
filled like a balloon. He slapped a cheek playfully to force
the air out in bursts. "Sir, oh, sir. Did you ever study a
thesaurus?"

"I don't know what that is," Farber said, strangely
thinking of the word *lessor* and the Gittelson lawyer.

"It's like a dictionary. Has all sorts of definitions. Look

[84]

up Negro, for example. I'll tell you what you see. You see all sorts of terms beginning with the old, all-time favorites on the hit parade—nigger, shine, coon, and sambo. Then you see dingy, spook, jungle bunny, smoky, crow, jig, jigaboo, boogie, buck, and spade. And in parentheses you see dial and derog, U-S. That stands for dialect and derogatory, United States. Meaning that this here country has nothing but nice words for us. There isn't a complimentary expression for us. Now you people come along with a new one. *Shvartzer.* Well, thank you very much for enhancing the English language. We need more synonyms for the black man. We suffer a paucity of them."

An angry and embarrassed flush suffused Farber's face. "There's nothing ugly in that word. It just means black."

When he saw Tammu shake his head in a manner indicating that the explanation was unacceptable, the grocer raised his voice. "I even hear your people say nigger. And what about words that I hear them use all the time? Honky and Mr. Charlie. That's all I hear."

"Put it in the thesaurus under white hypocrite."

"You're a very decent people," Farber said, hoping he sounded sarcastic enough. "I hear five-year-olds use a word I never heard until I saw a colored person."

"I assume you mean *motherfuck.* Let me give you some historical perspective regarding that old expression. It's my guess that it began on the Southern cotton plantations when white Christian slaveowners lay with their black female slaves, making them heavy with child. Soon nobody knew who was their mother. When you don't know your mother, you're in sad shape, especially when it comes to making

[85]

love. So back in those days, motherfuck was coined. It meant taking a chance. Down through the generations, the word changed its meaning to, 'Oh, what the hell's the use? It's whitey's world, anyway.' "

A group of children came in, carrying empty soda bottles. They ran over to the candy showcase, pointing with the bottles at the candy they wanted.

"Watch the glass, watch the glass!" Farber shouted.

"With the little ones it's candy," Tammu said, heading for the door where he met a derelict carrying a large paper sack. "And with the old *shvartzers* on the plantation, it's wine and sex."

"Oh, General," Farber called. "You owe me for the drink the other day. Ten cents."

Tammu shrugged his shoulders, stuck his hand into a pocket, pulled out a dime, and tossed it at Farber, who made a three-fingered catch. The Negro, momentarily stunned by the grocer's performance, stood silently at the door.

"I used to catch nails that way," Farber said.

Shortly after Tammu left, the noon bell clanged at the Homer P. Bradshaw Vocational High School. Farber, who had been warned by Gittelson of the lunch hour rush, hurriedly called his wife as the store became packed with pushing youths who shouted orders for candy, soft drinks, and cakes.

"Give me a Coke," the first demand came.

"That'll be ten cents and two cents deposit on

[86]

the bottle," Farber said, lifting a bottle from the soda case.

"Ah'm gonna drink it here."

"Okay." He handed the bottle to the student in exchange for a dime.

Sarah arrived to make sandwiches and serve hot coffee behind the meat showcase. Each time she passed an item, the student gave her money which she dropped into a cigar box of change. There was no time for her to run to the register.

Farber found it hard to find a pleasant face among them. They ranged in age from about sixteen to nineteen, and all of them had either a harassed or tight, mean look. When they laughed among themselves, they laughed loudly, but when they saw him watching them, they stopped suddenly and scowled. It was as if they objected to not only his attempted entrance into their world, but his very presence.

"Give me a pack a Camels and a orange soda."

"Drink it here or take it out?"

"Drink it here. How much?"

"Twenty-eight and ten. Thirty-eight."

"Man! Since when cigarettes twenty-eight?"

"I don't know. I guess for a while."

"They twenty-seven just a few days ago. Man down the corner sell them for a quarter."

"Okay, sonny," Farber smiled good-naturedly, "for you, I'll make it twenty-seven."

The boy took the cigarettes with cool detachment, as

if he had caught the grocer red-handed, but was too magnanimous to press the point.

Farber heard the smashing of glass from the outside. "Sarah, stand by the register a minute," he said, passing through the students until he could look out the window. Five youths who had bought sodas were rolling and smashing the bottles in bowling alley style.

He rapped on the window with his knuckles and shook his head, much like a disapproving father. The youths looked at one another and laughed.

Farber, outside now, began to gather one or two unbroken empties. "I don't mind you taking the bottles outside when you said you'd drink them inside, but I do mind losing the two cents on each bottle which I pay deposit on. And who's going to clean up this mess?"

"Okay, mister. Here you two cents," one boy said, throwing the pennies at Farber's feet.

Farber kicked at the pennies angrily and made a motion as if to strike the youth, but stopped when he saw him reach into his pocket. A knife, the grocer thought, hearing his wife calling him.

"You wife want you, mister," a boy said.

"Yeah, yeah. Don't let me catch you guys breaking any more bottles," he said, fighting to hold back his temper.

The crowd by now had thickened with the arrival of the girls, who apparently were let out for lunch a few minutes later. The shouting and pushing rose to new levels, as boy welcomed girl with voice and hands. No space in the store was unoccupied.

Each time Farber turned or stooped for an item, merchandise was secreted into pockets and pocketbooks and under and above blouses, sweaters, and skirts. Bags of potato chips, chewing gum, cakes, fruit, even bars of soap, disappeared into the quicksand of flesh and clothes. When the grocer faced front, teams of two or three operated effectively. One boy stood nonchalantly beating a rhythm on a shelf, at the end of which boxed crackers in a row fell one by one to the floor, unnoticed and unheard by Farber. The boy's accomplice easily picked up and concealed the boxes, which he would later sell to his fellow students.

"Ah give you a five-dollar bill!" a voice screamed above the others.

"No," Farber said to the shouter, a massive youth with stringy hair who dwarfed the other students. "You made a mistake. You gave me a one."

The youth, menacing large over Farber, slammed the candy bar he tried to purchase on the counter. "Dabba, dabba, doo! Mr. Grocer Man, ah give you a five. That's all ah had."

Another boy impatiently waiting his turn to buy something laughed. "You never had no five in you life, Fat Nasty."

Fat Nasty, his anger stoked by the traitorous lack of support from a fellow student, murmured a threat to the student without turning to face him. "Ah take care you later."

"Sheet," the heckler replied.

Fat Nasty ignored the boy but stood staring at Farber, who swallowed saliva and said nothing as he saw in the

[89]

corner of his eye a girl walk out with a large bag of un-bought potato chips.

"Ah give you five dollar and you give me change for one. You jew me out of them four other dollar."

"First of all, sonny," Farber said, raging over use of the term jew, "I don't like you to talk to me that way." He walked over to the register, pushed the no-sale button, and caught the drawer as it rang out. He lifted the sliding drawer, with its compartments of paper money and coins, up and out from under the safety latch which attached it to the main machine and placed it on the counter.

"See. I don't even have a five in the register." He shuffled the paper money and showed only ones, and one ten-dollar bill.

"What you say about that, Fat Nasty?" the heckler continued. "The proof don't lie. That mean the liar must lie."

Fat Nasty looked at the student, at Farber, and then back to the cash register drawer. With a lightning sweep of his arm, he sent the drawer flying on the customer side of the counter, where it scattered pennies, nickels, dimes, and other coins. Dozens of hands clutched for the paper money and then grabbed for the coins. The students kicked each other on the shins and stomped each other's shoes to get at the money.

An outcry came from Farber. "That's my money! Give me my money!" He rushed from behind the counter to join them in the mad scramble, knowing that he would never regain that money.

"I'm going to call the police!" Sarah cried. She headed for the telephone booth but her way was blocked, not intentionally, by the excited students.

"Sarah! Come back here." Farber grabbed her by the arm, leading her back to the other side of the counter where they watched helplessly as the floor was picked clean within seconds. Those who pocketed the money quickly left. The others guiltily marched out, leaving the store empty.

"Animals!" spat out Farber.

"I'm going to call the police."

"What good would that do? The money is already in their pockets. By the time the police get here, they'll be back in school. They could say it's their money. All money looks the same."

Farber did not want the police. He was afraid the students might retaliate by boycotting the store, yet he was deeply disturbed at being humiliated by the stealing, and by Fat Nasty, the bottle breakers, and the boy who had argued about the price of cigarettes.

"They were like native boys diving for coins in the South Sea islands," Sarah said as they cleaned up. "How much was in the register?"

"What do you know about the South Seas?" he snapped at her. "A lousy thirty dollars or so. I'll call the insurance company. I'll even get it back from the *shvartzers*. Don't worry."

"How?"

"Prices go up for them. No more twenty-seven-cent cigarettes."

"You're supposed to sell them for twenty-nine. Everybody does."

"The man down the corner sells them for a quarter," Farber said, wishing to show Sarah that twenty-eight was enough.

[91]

"You believe that boy?"

"Prices go up for them." He glanced around the store. "Look at the shelves. Almost empty. We didn't sell that much. Natives, you said. Locusts is more like it. Stealing, destroying."

"We should have never come here," she said, a tear brimming in an eye. "We have no business here."

Farber's pent-up anger exploded. "An accident happens and she's ready to pack up! I didn't come to Washington to go home with my tail between my legs."

"Then let's close the store every day at lunch time."

Farber did not reply. They were quiet for a few minutes until he spoke. "You gave me an idea. Come on, let's clean up."

The next day at noon several dozens of students hurled themselves against the locked doors of the store.

"Open up, open up. What this, a Jew holiday?"

The kitchen window on the side of the building flew up. "Come on over here, boys," Farber said.

They came and formed a line. Back and forth through the window passed goods exchanged for money. Inside, next to Farber, was a table laden with most items the students wanted. Sarah stood next to the cigar box of change, helping where she could, and running to get things not on the table.

Later, he smiled and patted her on the back. "We're learning. We're learning."

Instead of meeting his relaxed and satisfied smile with one of her own, she began to sob. "I'm learning, too. I learned my lesson. I had enough and I'm going home."

[92]

He purposefully waited a few minutes after school until most of the students left before he gathered his books and put on his coat. Outside, he immediately recognized as classmates two boys who sat on the curbstones, oblivious to the cold which penetrated through their corduroy pants.

One of the boys, whose large, black, penetrating eyes gave him a sensitive look, turned to Allan. "Hey, mothah! Where you goin'?"

His companion, a chunky youth with an almost flat nose resembling an inverted V over lips that looked like a rounded, comic valentine heart, compounded his friend's question. "And where you from?"

His stomach turning, Allan knew that the questions were a prelude to a fistfight.

The chunky one stood up close to Allan. "Hey, James. Maybe he got some money."

James, his intelligent eyes surveying Allan, ordered him forward with a curling finger. "You got any money, white boy?"

"A quarter."

"Give it to us and we let you go," the larger one said, his lips loose, as if the muscle fiber supporting them had torn and snapped like an overladen cable. "Else we mash you ass, mothah."

"Leave him be, Ferry. Ah whup his white ass." James stood up. "No white boys allowed around here. How come you white ass here?"

"I live here," Allan said. "A few blocks away. My father owns the grocery store."

"Hey, that right," Ferry said. "My mom buy there. She say new Jew move in."

James, his eyes sparkling with mischief, grinned. "Jew? You crucified the Lord Jesus."

"I didn't crucify anybody," Allan said, preparing himself mentally for a fight. They were both bigger than he, and he knew that he could do no more than defend himself by blocking their blows.

James' grin widened. "We don't care anyway about the Lord. We tease you. Jesus was a white mothah, anyway."

Ferry said, "How about that quarter?"

"Yeah," James added. "Give me that quarter and you can join our gang. You be the new member of the Black Brigade."

Allan gave James the coin, glad of the cheap ransom. "That's for initiation?"

James pocketed the money, eyeing him uncertainly. "Yeah, that's for that. You come with us, and we show you our headquarters."

Allan followed a pace behind them as they led him down the street into the next block, behind a rotting frame house to a yard at the end of which was a garage. A spray-painted white X was on a door through which they entered. White X's were on the walls, ceiling, and even the cement floor of the garage, which was bare except for a few empty soda crates.

James and Ferry walked under the ceiling X and raised their right fists. "Mighty X, mothah of us all. We come to you to receive us," they both intoned.

Allan repeated the first gesture and intonation.

[94]

James smiled. "Like Mr. Johnson say 'fore he was whupped by Robert, you the first white boy to settle in this neighborhood. The first new man in the black gang is a white boy."

All three laughed, Allan the loudest.

Sarah, sitting on a chair in the semidarkness and clutching a broom held across her lap, cried softly so as not to awaken her husband and son, nor to interfere with her listening for the approach of the rats. Her whimpers were soft and the tears small, as they had been on several previous nights when her mind, aching for the past familiar life, refused to permit her fatigued body to sleep.

It had been two weeks since the incident. Even now, whenever she stepped out of doors into the cold, to take the trash out, or hang up the wash, the sensitized portion of her buttock touched by the interloper became chilled before any other part of her. It seemed as if she still felt his nails, the palm of his hand, and the roughness of the callus line. Sometimes at night, going into a cold bed, she felt it.

She cried for the warmth of her apartment in New York. Here in the store or in the adjacent storeroom and kitchen and the rooms upstairs it was always cold. The continual opening of the store door sent cold air rushing throughout the house, too fast for the small furnace to catch and influence, despite the aid of an electric heater on the floor behind the counter. She wore two sweaters, an old pair of her husband's trousers with legs rolled up to her knees beneath a woolen dress.

Her husband used to complain so bitterly about the cold on the job in New York. He was strangely silent about it here, however. Maybe because he was used to severe cold, and this weather was comparatively mild for him. Or maybe he felt guilty about her being in the store all of the time. His arthritis seemed to have disappeared. Maybe it was all a state of mind. No, it couldn't have been. She had seen the swelling and had heard his moaning. But then, even if it was mental, the store was good for him.

She thought back to yesterday when she had threatened to leave him and return home. At first, he had become angry, shouting that he didn't need her anyway. He said that this was his home and business now, and that he wasn't going back no matter what.

Later, he had become regretful, at least she thought so, when he saw her packing a suitcase.

"Don't be foolish," he said. "I'm not asking you to be in the store all day. Stay in the back and be a housewife. Watch television if you want. Just help out when it gets busy. In a few months when we'll have a few dollars saved, I'll get a man to help wait on customers, and you could stay home altogether. And when I say home, I don't mean here. We'll have a place in the suburbs."

She had forgiven him, promising to stay. Then he said he had a present for her, and for him as well. It was a little blue bankbook, a savings account, with fifty dollars marked as being deposited the day before.

"Watch it grow," he had said. "It's going to be our ticket to Florida."

She shivered now, thinking of the fifty dollars. That couldn't keep her warm. But the cold was something you could get used to, she guessed. The rats were a different story. She hated them, not only because of the harm they could do, but because she felt they were intelligent creatures sometimes capable of outsmarting man.

Listening during the day to stories by her customers of how the rats bit babies in their cribs, as well as children and adults while they slept, and then listening at night as the animals scampered between the walls, had made her even more fearful of them. Heretofore, she had occasionally seen dead rats on the streets but never a live one. Hearing them now and trying to visualize and associate their movements with their lifeless, squashed bodies only formed grotesque, nightmarish images in her mind. She even thought it was dangerous to kill rats because she had read in *Reader's Digest* an article which described how bubonic plague germs left the bodies of newly killed rats to jump on humans.

Although Allan had admitted staying awake one or two nights because of the rats, he and Simon had laughed when she said she was going to stand guard duty during the night and try to catch naps the next day. Her husband had said if that would make her happy, let her be happy. He wasn't going to take turns watching. He worked too hard to do without a lot of sleep.

She didn't want to tell them she was afraid one of the rats might bite Allan's face. Didn't one of the customers say a rat once crawled in a boy's bed and nipped a piece out of the penis? A fine thing. If either Allan's face or his penis were damaged, he might not be able to find a nice girl to marry.

How terrible for Allan this life was. No nice friends he could meet. No Jewish friends, she thought as her head nodded with sleep. Only *shvartzers* here. How was he going to marry a nice Jewish girl?

Her grip on the broomstick loosened and her chin touched her chest. Maybe she could rest her eyes just for a minute before checking Allan's room once again.

A few minutes later, she awoke with a start, and then began to nod her head again. Soon she arose, thinking that maybe she could go to bed, after all. It would be warm there. Maybe the rats went to sleep already.

She heard Allan scream.

Allan was more terrified by the unknown weight he felt on his ankle than by the stab in his large toe. He shook his legs convulsively, drawing them up and down in the bed. Even before the scream ended, he felt the weight leave his bed and heard it land on the floor. Then he heard the running steps of his father and mother coming from the other room.

"What's the matter?" his father shouted as his mother switched on the light.

"Something bit me."

"A rat!" His mother shook her head with fear. "I knew it. Where did it bite you? Come on, quick, don't be ashamed. Tell us."

"Let me see." His father leaned over the bed and shook his head. A small flap of skin hung loosely over a gash which barely dripped blood. It looked as if Allan had stepped on a small but sharp piece of broken glass.

"Into the bathroom, quick. Before it becomes poisoned," his mother said, pulling the blanket off and holding him by the elbow. His father stepped back, still shaking his head.

"Take it easy. Relax. Nothing to get excited about. Just drop a few drops of the disinfection thing in it."

"Don't tell me how to handle this," his mother shouted, feeling guilty about her failure to stand watch. "You just tend to the store's business."

"Look, Sarah. It's three o'clock in the morning. I don't usually tend to business at this hour."

She began to cry. "That's all you care about, the store. We're attacked by rats and the roaches share our food. What do you care? As long as you save money. Do me a favor, take the damn fifty dollars in the bank and spend it on an exterminator."

"I need to pay them good money to set traps? I'll do it myself."

Allan got up and limped slowly to the bathroom. He stepped only on the heel of the injured foot, sticking the toes up awkwardly. He closed the door so he wouldn't have to listen to them, but he heard anyway.

"Why was I crazy to come here with you? Who needed this?"

"Don't start that again. Who's keeping you here anyway? You want to go home, go home."

"I thought you said this was my home."

"This is no joking matter."

[99]

"Sure it's no joking matter. It's a tragedy, a shame, to take a young boy and a woman to live in the jungle of crazy *shvartzers.* Oh, my God! I should have had my head examined."

Allan heard her burst anew into loud crying. Annoyed by their squabbling during his moment of need, he accidentally spilled half of the bottle of benzalkonium chloride on his wound. He waited for it to dry and then carefully wrapped a bandage around it. He laughed to himself, thinking that he looked like one of those cartoons about rich men with gout who had a mountain of bandages around their big toes.

"Where's Allan?"

"In the bathroom, where else?" she answered.

"Then why don't you take care of him instead of screaming at me all night and all day? Let me tell you, I don't need that kind of treatment."

She ran from the room into her own bedroom where she slammed the door. Immediately, however, she reopened it and rushed to the bathroom. "Allan, open up. Let me see what it looks like."

"The door's open."

She went in quickly and examined the bandage. "Take it off. You're going to the doctor." She raised her voice. "I just don't care what it costs. I don't give a damn."

"It's okay, Mom. It doesn't hurt."

"You're going to go, and that's that. Do you want it to get infected? Do you want rabies?"

"Don't throw a scare into the boy," his father said

from the hallway. "You're not going to get a doctor at three in the morning. We'll see how it looks in the morning."

"Even if there's nothing there, he's still going."

His father, unwilling and too tired to accept the challenge, nodded. "Okay. Let's get back to sleep."

Back in his room, Allan inspected it for rat holes. There were none, not even in the closet, so the rat must have come in through the door, he thought. He knew it was Dracula. It had to be. What other rat had the nerve to do what it did? He shut the door and returned to bed, deciding to leave the light on.

Sleep could not come. First because his renewed and strengthened hatred of Dracula made him restless and then because his uninjured toe began to twitch, as if inviting and even daring another bite from Dracula. He visualized the rat looking at him from the doorway, grinning in a human-like way and waiting patiently for him to fall asleep once more.

The nerve of the little bastard, Allan thought. He could forget all of its other trespasses, but not this one. To jump in his nice warm bed, where he was snuggled between a clean white sheet and a blanket, and to rub its long, naked, scaly tail and its oily fur up against his body, and then bite him, that was the last straw.

Dracula had to die. He would buy fresh rat poison and more traps on the way home from school.

His bitten toe began to throb. He tried thinking of other things—school, the gang—before his mind turned to

Mother Matthews. He fell asleep thinking of taking off her clothes, piece by piece.

"Here comes the gypsy," Farber said, looking out the window. He was pleased, for Sarah would now spend a happy hour or so gossiping with Mother Matthews, whose long black hair and sparkling eyes, more than her occupation as a fortune-teller and psychological counselor, earned her the sobriquet.

The Farbers usually spoke in whispers about her, repeating some of the rumors that they had heard, especially the one that she slept with men for money. It was for this reason that Farber could not help but enjoy watching his wife try to hide her displeasure whenever he had to help Mother Matthews carry parcels home.

Whenever she came into the store she would leave a small pile of pamphlets on the counter advertising her services. None of the customers bothered to pick them up and Farber threw them out at the end of the day.

Sarah, in spite of her doubts about Mother Matthews' morality, had become quite friendly with her. Although she told herself she didn't believe in fortune-telling with either palm reading, crystal balls, or tea leaves, she was brought up on Jewish mysticism and found it difficult to laugh as her husband did at Mother Matthews' psychic services.

Frequently, Farber found the two women huddling over the counter, with his wife's mouth ajar as she listened to stories of the spirit world. Sarah tried to wheedle free prognostications from Mother Matthews, but the medium

[102]

countered with an invitation to visit her premises for the "proper spiritual environment." This Sarah refused to do, not so much for the few dollars it would cost, but for the teasing by her husband which she knew would go on for a long time.

"It's a God-given talent ah possess, Miz Simon," she had said. "Can't learn it in no books. You either has it or you don't. Ah didn't learn it in no school."

Farber waited until Mother Matthews came in now, said hello, and walked out to leave the ladies alone. When he returned later, Sarah was hanging over the counter.

"You must have had lots of interesting experiences, Mother Matthews."

Farber now chose to clean the meat showcase. He looked through the glass at the shapeliness of Mother Matthews, holding her coat in her arms. She was always dressed nicely, he thought, always with high heels and tight dresses with low bustlines. He could smell her perfume from where he kneeled and knew it would pervade the store for a long time after she had gone.

"You gets to meet all kinds of people. Some good, some bad. Ah tries to help each and ever one of them, irregardless of race, or if they's drinkers, or got monkey on them. Sometime they sex life is not of the best. Come on up with me, Miz Simon. Maybe ah can help you, too." She winked and looked in Farber's direction.

Sarah's porcelain-smooth skin broke in a grin, and she giggled. Farber stood up. He laughed too, caught up in a warm but harmless flirtation with the woman. "I understand you give advice to the lovelorn, Mother Matthews."

[103]

The word *mother* came hard for him. It was almost as if he had to say *father* to a priest. In Mother Matthews' case, his stumbling over the word did not stem from religious inhibition but from the fact that she did not look like a mother, certainly not like any of the fat mothers on the block. It was a joke that she played on herself, he thought, like an elderly man who likes to be called *junior* by his friends.

"Sometimes if they needs it, Mistah Simon. Maybe you need it." She smiled lewdly at him, and he felt a sudden flush in his groin.

"Maybe," was all he could mutter, blushing, and quickly changing the subject. He asked her how well she knew General Tammu.

"That trash that were in here the other day? He use to be a pimp and numbers man. He dangerous, too. Cut a man up once and was in jail. Yeah, just sliced that man like you slice that baloney."

Farber pledged to keep a knife handy under the counter. Maybe a gun instead. He hadn't used one since the army, twenty-five years ago, but he'd learn.

Just then Allan walked into the store and blushed when he saw Mother Matthews. She looked at him and smiled with teeth that were large, white, and even.

He glanced slyly at the curve where her hips unleashed themselves from her waist. As with all the colored women he saw, her legs were proportionately thin with a compensating backside which was extra large and round. But she was lighter and prettier than the other women.

His heart jumped when she moved to the spot and

[104]

remained there. Walking briskly, he told his parents, "I'll be down in the basement cleaning if you need me," and flew down the steps.

Below, he pulled a string to switch off the light, plunging the basement in darkness, except for a barely perceptible beam of light which seeped through a small hole in the old wooden floor above. Quietly and quickly, he placed one soda crate after another in a pile on which he stood. He pressed his eye against the hole.

Above appeared round, fleshy stalks surrounded by an umbrella dress which kept the peak in a mysterious, exciting darkness. He closed his eyes tightly, opened them, and squinted. Soon the top of the stockings became visible. Each was tied in a small knot at the border of flesh and cloth.

A minute universe of motes of dirt and dust swirled through the hole and brushed against his eye. He blinked, rubbed his eyes, and returned to gaze long and hard at her peak of darkness. He saw nothing.

Biting his lip, he carefully made his way down to the floor and then ran back upstairs for his father's powerful three-battery flashlight. He stumbled in his haste to return but did not hurt himself.

The flash of light funneled through the hole and up into the dark umbrella, followed by his intent gaze. A bristly mound, covered by pale underwear, came into view.

Of a sudden, his eye met the distant face of Mother Matthews, peering down like a giant at the hole. He switched the light off and waited anxiously in the darkness.

[105]

He dared not move and barely breathed. Then he heard his father call him.

Farber added Mother Matthews' bill in a loud, clear voice while writing the figures on a paper bag. One thing he had learned as a grocer, he thought, was the ability to add quickly out loud.

"Put it on the book, Mistah Simon," Mother Matthews said.

As usual with almost all of his customers, he reached under the counter for the book, a notebook segmented by names of the customers on credit. Each customer had his own small notebook into which the charge was placed and then written in the grocer's master book. That way, Gittelson had once explained, each party had a record and no additions or erasures could be made without one or the other party knowing about it. Never give credit without the customer's book, Farber was warned. On paydays, the customer came into the store and paid his bill after charges in his and the grocer's books were added, compared, and marked off as paid.

Farber sighed. There haven't been many paydays, however. If only he could take money in exchange for groceries. You bought, you paid for it on the spot. In the supermarkets they did it. No credit. Cash on the barrelhead. That was the way to run a business.

He began to pack the bags, soon filling both of them. The bulbs of scallion with their stringy hair waved from the corner of one bag, and Farber thought that they looked strangely like some sort of sex organ. He looked at Mother Matthews to see if she had the same impression, but

the woman busied herself with rearranging a box of breakfast cereal and two rolls of toilet paper in the other bag.

"I'll get my boy to help you." He called Allan.

Did she know about the hole and see the light? he
wondered.

He followed her at a pace's separation while she
walked slowly to her building which he had passed many
times on his way to school. Her second-floor apartment had
four windows plainly visible from the street. The two windows directly above the doorway held an outline of outstretched palms under which were PALMIST and ADVISOR.
On the other window was the face of Christ enveloped in
a moonish ring which made the picture look like a long-
haired man in a transparent space helmet. Next to it the
figure of Mary prayed with folded hands.

Over the entrance was a large sign, its writing balanced between a Christian cross and a drawing of a candle
burning inside a five-pointed star.

MOTHER MATTHEWS

SPIRITUAL HEALER AND ADVISOR

EVERYONE WELCOME

NO ONE TURNED AWAY

NO APPOINTMENT NECESSARY

Now he was behind her as they climbed the stairs. He
stared, hypnotized by her buttocks, weaving up and down,
almost machinelike in their precision of movement, yet
animalistic in their quivering motion. He wanted to bite
them.

She stopped suddenly when she reached the top of the

first landing and his face collided with her soft, fluttering mass.

"Whoa, young man. Slow down. This is where ah live."

Inside her apartment he smelled the unmistakable odor of burned candles and an insecticide.

"On the table, sonny." She looked at his face. "Shouldn't really be calling you sonny, should ah? You pretty big. Big enough to have a woman."

He turned his face away as she laughed. "Whoa. You shy? That no way to be. Here, take this."

She held a dime out to him, but he only stared at it.

"Never saw no Jew who ever turned down money. Here, come on. Take it. It yours."

She laughed loudly again. "Tell you what, little white boy. You don't think you earned this. Okay. You help me unpack the sack and you take the dime. Okay? That all right with you?"

He nodded, not for the dime, but to do something for her. She watched him scoop the groceries out of the bag and then suddenly she snatched from his arms a box with an unmarked blue wrapper.

"Hey, that personal. You know what that is?"

"Yeah."

"What?"

"Sanitary napkins." Curiosity one day had forced him to sneak a box off the shelves and unwrap it in the cellar.

"But what it for?"

He looked blankly at her, knowing but not wishing to tell.

"That to plug up the flood of another mothah. Mothah

[108]

Nature." She laughed and held the dime out to him. "Come on, take it. It won't bite." He reached for it and she clasped her other hand on his. "You like me, don't you? You look at me all the time. You want me, you can if you want to."

He saw that her body was the color of coffee ice cream, and felt that she was soft and warm, and smelled her talcum powder and perspiration. Her pomaded, straight black hair also smelled sweet, and he saw frontiers of grease which had oozed down from her hairline. She enveloped him with her body. He loved her color. He despised his own, dull and commonplace with no mysteries to hide.

Later she asked him, "Allan, how long you gonna ride me?"

"I don't know. What time's it?"

"You been here a hour. You daddy gonna give it to you on you pink behind."

"He doesn't touch me." He thought for a moment. "Say, you found out about the hole, didn't you?"

"What hole?"

"You know."

"Only hole ah know is the one you plug up all afternoon. You better go. You come back, again. Ah let you. You know why? Because you really something. You know how many times you pop on me? Four. Four times you Jew juice swished me. Four times in a hour. Man, that great. But you young. How old?"

"Sixteen."

"You daddy tell me fifteen. Wait till you thirty. Time you thirty all you can pop is one a night. But you come four

[109]

times in a hour. That show you. Never send no man to do a boy's job."

The insurance agent explained with a drawl why his company could not reimburse Farber for the robbery by the high school students.

"Well, it wasn't really a robbery. Let's not call it that. It wasn't a holdup. There was no threat made. No weapons involved. It was duplicity, pure, plain, and simple. We don't cover sneakery. We run into it all of the time. Two of them'll start an argument and fight in your store. You worry about your equipment and stock and try to stop it. A third man goes behind and swipes the dough. Happens all the time." He shook his head with finality. "I just can't see how we can pay you on your claim."

"Robbery is robbery, mister. I just got through paying you a hundred and sixty premium. Now . . ."

"Read the contract, Mr. Farber. Your claim now is for about forty dollars. Why, that's nothing. Forget about it. Count it up for experience. Besides, next time you want to file a claim, you'd better first report to the police. You never called them, you know."

Soon after the agent left, Jimmy came in and listened to Farber's story. The breadman grimaced, smacked his lips, and nodded his head knowingly before he gave his opinion.

"You got to tell yourself that you don't exactly have the diplomatic set of Washington, D.C., as your customers. You got the worst shit, black or white, in the asshole of the city. Next in line for being the biggest pile of shit is the

[110]

insurance companies. But I guess you learned a lesson."

"Yeah, you know," Farber agreed. "We close up now and use the side window."

"No, no, no!" Jimmy shouted. "That's not what I mean. I mean, next time that happens, file a claim that they threatened you and took your money. Then sit back and collect."

"I can't lie to the police."

"What do they know? You can never get any witnesses around here. Last week a grocer on my route was robbed of two hundred bucks and pistol-whipped in a store full of customers. Not one of them says he saw it. They were all looking at fly shit on the ceiling."

"A lie's a lie. With my luck, I'll probably lose out on the insurance and wind up in jail for lying."

"Look, when you're threatened, you don't remember what they look like. Tell that to the police. Tell them all of them look alike to you, anyway. It's the only way. Or else you'll be selling apples on the corner."

Farber shrugged his shoulders, examined Jimmy's bread bill, and paid it. "Say, why was the man pistol-whipped?"

"Because he was white, that's why. He gave them his money without trouble. Told them to help themselves to the register. But he was a white man, and they hate whites. It wasn't enough just to rob him."

The breadman shook his head and, without saying anything further, left the store to permit Farber to wait on two young men who had entered.

Farber felt a slight shock. He recognized one of the

[111]

youths as Fat Nasty. Still burning over the insurance, he wondered whether to say anything about it, and possibly cause new trouble, or just ignore the past incident. It had cost him enough time and trouble. He decided he wouldn't start anything unless they did.

The youths, the second one much smaller than Fat Nasty, looked impatient and annoyed.

Negroes, Farber thought. They all looked the same. Not their features, their expressions. They were, what was the word? Sullen, that was it. He had hardly even seen a Negro who had come into his store who wasn't sullen.

"What's it to be, boys?"

Fat Nasty, carrying a tattered briefcase, spoke. "We collectin' contra-bution for the Black Liberation Movement. You down here for twenty-five dollar." He held his palm straight out over the counter.

"What?"

"That right, mistah," the other one said. "Store people got to give more."

"I'm sorry. I can't afford anything. Not even a dime."

"You take money from black people and can't donate to a worthy cause?" the second boy asked.

"Sheet," Fat Nasty said. "You got my hard-earn money, man."

"What do you mean, your money? I earned it. I worked hard for it. What the hell nerve you got."

"Give you money back to the black man you stole it from," Fat Nasty grumbled. He came up close to Farber, almost as close as they do in the movies where a small

[112]

screen dictates false proximity of the characters, making them stand bare inches apart.

"I'll tell you what. You donate the money you stole from me. All right?"

"Sheet," Fat Nasty said, glancing at the other youth.

"What money, Fat Nasty?" his companion asked.

"Sheet. He lie. He don't care nothin' for the black man. He hate us."

"That's a lie. I always cared for the Negro. I used to give money when I could afford it." Farber dug far back into his memory. "You heard about the Scottsboro boys? I gave money for their defense."

Fat Nasty's eyes narrowed. "Who they?"

"A bunch of Negro boys framed down South."

"Fuck them. And fuck you, too." Saying that, Fat Nasty turned around, but not before digging into his briefcase. He brought up a paper and tossed it on the counter. "Dabba, dabba, doo. We get you, too."

Farber stiffened. He watched them leave and then looked at the paper, cheap, rough, and thin to the touch.

It was a poorly mimeographed cartoon of a bald, hook-nosed man with Stars of David sprinkled on his suit and dollar bills hanging out of his pockets. The man was pictured choking a young Negro in chains.

She had told him to come back in half an hour and he did, after having walked several blocks. He returned in time to see the client she had said she was "reading," a man who noticed him waiting in the hallway and laughed.

[113]

Mother Matthews, riding high on exuberance, greeted him cheerfully, telling him to wait a few minutes until she could eat something.

"Been busy all evenin'. Today payday for those who got work. And most of those been to see me for consultin'." She left him in the living room and returned shortly, munching on a sandwich. "Sit down, white boy."

She sat but he remained standing. He tried not to look directly into her eyes since he felt he did not belong with her and was imposing on her time.

"Well, if you ain't gonna sit at least say somethin'. Don't just stand there like a stump a dead wood."

He shrugged his shoulders and attempted to smile, but his facial muscles were frozen into an expression of guilt and forbidden expectation.

"Ah knows what you want, Allan. You want a fix. You need it now and ah'm the fixer." She gulped the remainder of her sandwich. " 'Stead of me stickin' you with dope, you want to stick me. You see, ah got you hooked by givin' a free sample a pussy. Ah knew you be back in a few days when you be feelin' strong and stiff but you don't want to beat it around youself in the dark 'cause you had the real thing and it just ain't the same like it is with you hand."

He blushed, but then relaxed. The major burden of explaining why he had come was lifted. Still, however, he could not understand the cold tone of her voice. It wasn't the same, soft kittenish purr of the woman who had taken him into her warm self just a few days ago. He now feared that she would send him home.

"It gonna cost you, boy. You want it, you got to get five dollars."

He was not disturbed. "I'll have to come back. I don't have it with me."

"You know where ah'll be."

Outside in the hall, he stood for a few moments. The idea about giving money to Mother Matthews to rent her body filled him with an alien joy. He ran down the stairs and into the street.

Two dollars were in his pocket and about two dollars in coins were in a drawer at home. He remembered seeing a quarter and a dime on the kitchen table. He'd take the rest from the register and come back before it got too late.

He awoke early while his parents still slept, got out of bed quickly, and ran down the stairs without bothering to put on slippers. Not wishing to make any noise that would frighten away an imminent catch, and because the store-room floor felt icy to his bare feet, he tiptoed swiftly and quietly.

In the middle of the store a trap lay overturned, with the baited cheese gone. Dracula had sprung the trap and got the cheese without being caught, or hurt, Allan guessed, looking at the neck-snapping square of steel dug deeply into the wood without indication of its force having been broken by a rat lucky enough to escape.

Another trap nearby, likewise flipped over, clutched in its vise the crushed body of a small rat. Its open mouth, baring sharp, pointed teeth, and its facial protuberance made the animal look remarkably like a shark. Despite the catch, the trap's bait was also missing, and Allan immediately blamed Dracula for stealing the dead rodent's cheese.

As usual in the morning, black rat droppings were scattered all over the store's floor, counter, and even on the keys of the cash register. Chewed-up remains of bread rolls and cereal boxes would have to be thrown out, along with about four or five loaves of bread which bore the jagged evidence of rat gnawing.

Allan examined the damage, carefully avoiding stepping with bare feet on the rat pellets. It bothered him that one rat, no doubt Dracula, had taken random bites, just enough to ruin or contaminate many foods instead of feasting upon one.

The entrance of his father, already dressed, brought curses and new threats to do something about the rats. His father threw the damaged goods in a trash box and then turned toward the traps.

"Allan, pick up the good trap and save it for tonight," he said, shaking his head as he gently nudged the other trap with the dead rat. "I don't know whether to fix this before or after breakfast."

"Fix what, Dad?"

"The trap. I've got to lift the spring and get the rat out. Separate it. The trap goes in the trash and the rat in the garbage can or else the trashman will complain."

"Maybe the garbage man'll say the rat should be picked up by some dead animal department."

"That's the least of my worries. They told me to keep garbage and trash separate." He lifted rat and trap by the wood and daintily held it away from his body as he went outside to the yard.

Allan, eating breakfast later, daydreamed of lifting the spring-iron on Dracula. The boy gulped his food as he pictured the animal lying dead and bleeding heavily from its shark mouth.

On subsequent mornings, using new traps, he and his father caught many rats, none of them Dracula. The animal avoided the traps, or kicked them until they snapped, stealing the baits. The old master seemed to know poisons, for they were shunned. At times Allan couldn't help believing that Dracula ate the lethal pellets which had no effect on the devil, invested in the form of a rodent.

Tammu, a bit more disheveled than the last time Farber had seen him the day after the window-breaking, ambled into the store.

"Greetings, fellow minority member."

"What's yours?" Farber said brusquely, eager to hold the man to strict business.

"What's mine? America is mine, but I don't have her." Tammu watched the grocer's stern face and shrugged his shoulders. "All right, then. Mine is the prerogative of giving you another chance to donate to our cause. Everybody has given except you. I don't think it's fair. Fair to neighborhood solidarity, to my people from whom you make a living, and to yourself as an honest individual."

"Everybody wants a donation! Why don't somebody take up a collection for me? Listen, I work hard for my money, mister. And so far I got nothing. Everything's going out and nothing's coming in."

"Business could pick up, you know. Give me a donation and I'll lift the black boycott against this store."

"So I'm being boycotted? I didn't know that."

"It's a regrettable but necessary move."

Deep anger filled Farber. "How long's this been going on?"

"A couple of weeks."

The grocer's peal of laughter had a bitter, sarcastic ring. "Business is the same since I bought the store. Lousy. Boycott or no boycott."

"It could be better. One hundred percent better."

"How much do you want?" Farber asked, his question more out of curiosity than a willingness to give.

"Just twenty-five dollars. And then twenty-five more per month afterwards."

"Drop dead."

"The Black Liberation Movement is prepared to increase its boycott activities against you. We may even set up a picket line."

"Black Liberation? That slob thief Fat Nasty works for you? You tell him the next time he peddles that anti-Semitic stuff here it'll be the last time he'll be able to walk."

"I wasn't aware that any of my officers caused you inconvenience."

"Some officers! They want money, let them go work for it. That goes for you, too."

"Yes, like you do. You come into the black ghetto to bilk the poor. Then you'll go back to your Jewish stronghold in New York or Florida with money taken from the blacks."

[118]

"Listen, big shot. Where do your blacks get *their* money? They either work for it, like I do, or they sit home and collect relief checks from my taxes."

"Hold on." Tammu raised both arms in a sign of surrender. "I'm not denying your right to earn a living. All I'm saying is that I think you ought to return some of the fruits of your exploitation to benefit our community. Don't think the blacks don't know that Jews send lots of money to Israel, a foreign country. How about some of that *gelt* to help your black American brothers?"

"I can't even afford to give money to Israel."

"Even?"

Farber turned around in an effort to drive Tammu from the store by ignoring him. He began to straighten some cans on the shelf, turning them with their labels face frontward. Tammu, also silent, was oblivious to the storekeeper's attempts at expulsion by silence. A few minutes later the grocer, realizing defeat, spoke.

"If you got nothing to buy, get out."

"I didn't come in here to buy anything. You know what I want. Now, come on. Don't reflect the cheapness of your race."

Farber picked up a can, turned, and slammed it on the counter. It bounced off, narrowly missing Tammu's foot. "What right you got to talk like that, you black piece of shit?"

"What right?" Tammu shouted back, matching the grocer's expression. "I'll tell you. The right I earned getting bullets in my ass when I fought Mr. Hitler while you and your kind were making money back home." He rolled up a pants leg and showed a deep, light-colored scarred

[119]

scoop where his calf muscle ought to have been. "See that? One of my rights I earned. Want to see the rest?"

"I wasn't exactly sitting around doing nothing . . ."

"The way I see it," Tammu interrupted, "is that I fought to save you Jews."

"I said I wasn't just sitting around. I had it in the South Pacific." Farber shook his head. "What am I telling you this for? What difference does it make? Who are you . . . a nothing . . . that I have to justify my right to live and earn a living? With all your misery and starvation, you *shvartzers* still got time to hate the Jews. Do me a favor, hate outside the store. I don't need your trade here. Your lousy dime soda."

To emphasize his point, Farber picked up the knife he kept under the counter. He waved it in front of Tammu. "Out!"

The Negro, amazed, moved backward slowly toward the door.

"And one thing more," Farber said, "you or Fat Nasty bother me again, or break my window, I'm not gonna bother with the police. I'm gonna go right after you."

Before the door slammed shut, a cold draft blew against the grocer's perspiration-soaked face.

When Farber finished paying his bills at the end of the week, he saw that his checking account and cash on hand were almost depleted. He shuddered in the knowledge that the utility bills plus one note, Quinn's, remained unpaid.

What am I going to do? he wondered, fingering the

[120]

checkbook and reexamining his figures. They were correct. The checkbook, do I really need one? It's a dollar a month service charge plus ten cents a check. What am I crazy or something? How else could I pay the bills, by postal money orders? They probably cost the same. Sending cash by mail isn't safe. The charge for a checkbook is only three, four dollars a month. But I've got to cut back somewhere.

He rubbed and scratched his itchy hands. He noticed a redness on them and thought back to how his hands were always chafed and rough when he worked as a carpenter in the cold outdoors. For a moment, he wished he were back working with wood and nail, having no worries and making good money.

A few moments passed before he realized that he was not going to be able to meet the payment to Quinn. He stood up, ready to go upstairs and awaken his wife, but sat down again in the knowledge that tears would be her only contribution. Only his brother could help him now.

I'd rather do the molding and hang doors for a six-floor apartment building than go see him. Even stand in the store forty-eight hours straight and then clean the walk-in with a toothbrush and a bowl. To ask him for a thousand dollars is just like someone asking me for fifty dollars, which I don't even have to spare now.

Farber had no doubt that Benny would give. The problem lay in the physical act of going to New York and asking him face to face for money. He also knew that he couldn't pass Gladys' muster, her probing questions arising out of personal curiosity rather than of true concern, her insistence that he be their house guest, and her urgent persistence that he "eat something."

Benny's ways were something else. After gaining entrance into Benny's office above his main store on Lexington Avenue, there would be the expensive cigars proffered, and then the invitation to have a seat, as if the cigars served to remind him of Benny's position while the chair was but a mere formality which even a poor tailor could furnish.

They would talk about the family before clearing throats while they searched in vain for something else to say. When they did speak, the buzzer and intercom on Benny's desk, like poor punctuation and badly irrelevant parenthetical exegeses, would continually interrupt their sentences.

Farber went over in his mind the course the conversation would take.

"So what brings you to New York, Sy?"

"A little vacation."

"And Sarah and the boy? They're not good enough to come with you?"

"Well, it's not really a vacation. Business."

A pause, a long one, and Farber would see on Benny's face the knowing look why the trip was made.

"How much do you need, Sy?"

"I don't need anything."

"Cut the shit. You're my brother, ain't you?"

Benny never cursed in front of his wife and son and two daughters but spiced his language when among friends and other relatives. After dinner one time, while digging in his mouth with a toothpick and sucking and blowing food particles, he had gently admonished Farber for saying "damn it" in front of Gladys and the children. "I want to make sure the kids get on the right boat," Benny had said.

Farber finished the meeting in his mind by shaking his head, as if to clear the stage for the next scene. They would be on their way out for lunch, or to Gladys' dinner, when Farber would sigh, close his eyes, and then open them. "Okay, Benny. Never could hide anything from you. I'll pay you back as soon's I can. Just a few months. A thousand. Not even that. Five hundred."

No, Farber now decided, he wouldn't visit Benny. He'd write a letter, instead. But what could he say in a letter? How would he start and end it?

Dear Benny, he dictated to himself. Just a few words to let you know we're okay. Not too many complaints except that we need a few bucks to carry a couple of notes that piled up on us all of a sudden. I wonder if you could spare a few hundred dollars for the time being. Maybe five hundred. I would get it at the bank but I don't want to bother with paperwork and red tape. You know what I mean. Let me know soon as you can. Give my regards to Gladys and the girls. How's Michael doing these days? You must be proud of him.

He'd end the letter by joking how he was hit unexpectedly the first of the year by all sorts of licenses and taxes. Beer and wine license, one hundred seventy dollars. Cigarette and patent medicine licenses, eighteen dollars. Cooperative and franchise tax, forty. And the grocery license, forty-five.

Regards, Sy.

He'd write the letter now and he wouldn't tell Sarah. Things were bad enough.

His hands began to itch again.

The itching awakened him. He looked at the clock. Three fifteen. In another two hours he'd have to get up and go to the market. He closed his eyes tightly, trying to fall asleep again, but the constant itching kept him awake. Cursing, he arose and went to the bathroom.

He saw that the rash on his hands had spread to his arms, creating huge red welts with pinkish valleys between them. He soaked his arms in warm water for a few minutes and returned to bed.

"What's the matter?" Sarah asked.

"I broke out with something on my arms."

"Let me see." She snapped the light on and held one of his arms to examine it. "You'd better go see a doctor if this doesn't clear up by tomorrow."

"It's nothing. Go to sleep."

The physical discomfort and burning teamed with thoughts of money and Benny to give him a sleepless night. By early morning, he drifted off to sleep only to be shaken by the alarm clock.

Some of the welts were gone, but the redness remained and he still felt a slight itching. See, it was nothing, he told himself, thinking that he wouldn't have to pay money to see a doctor. In the afternoon, however, both of his arms puffed up to become pink balloons with dark red patches. He called for an immediate doctor's appointment and returned several hours later.

"Well, Simon, what did he say? The arthritis again?"

"Nah. I waited two hours for him and then he spent two minutes with me. How should I know what he said?" He put on his apron, saw that it was too dirty to wear, and threw it on the floor. "That son of a bitch!"

"Allan will hear you."

Allan, upstairs reading, listened carefully.

"An allergy. I'm supposed to be allergic to something in the store. He said it could be something I'm touching that I never handled before."

"Don't tell me you can't be a grocer anymore. Did he give you any medicine?"

"Ointment. He said for me to try and find out what's bothering me. I could have stayed home and saved the money."

"Something you never touched before? At least it's not arthritis."

"That's right," he said, leaving the kitchen for the store when the bell rang. He returned a few minutes later. "A lousy pack of cigarettes. I'm supposed to make a living from that. One cent profit. It pays to run for it?" He turned to look back at the store. "I never touched any of this stuff in New York."

"Sure you did. Potatoes, tomatoes. Meat. Everything."

"I never saw pigs' feet until I came here."

"Let me do the waiting on pigs' feet for a while."

"Nah. I told you I didn't want you in the store unless it was necessary."

"It's necessary."

"I'll wear rubber gloves," he said.

[125]

The next morning the day's first customer was also the first to ask for pigs' feet.

"Now?"

"Yeah, Mistah Simon. For breakfas'. It make good suckin' on the toes."

Farber, his stomach rolling, pulled on the pair of rubber gloves, opened the jar, and pronged a foot with a fork.

"Mistah Simon, you looks like a doctor goin' to operate."

"For sanitary purposes," he answered nervously, wrapping the foot in waxed paper.

The customer looked warily at Farber's inflamed arm, exposed between glove and shirtsleeve. "You got some sort of disease on you hands?"

"No, no. I use the gloves for purposes of cleanliness."

"Looks to me like you got some sort of disease."

"Don't be foolish. Anything else?"

"No, thas' all. How much?"

"You know. Fifteen cents."

The customer whistled. "Went up, huh?"

"It's been fifteen cents." He rang up the purchase and watched the customer leave. "Sarah," he called, "I don't want the gloves. I think you better handle the pigs' feet for a few days."

Although he had not touched the pigs' feet for a full day, the blotchiness remained. Even if he didn't touch it, he thought, its aroma could still come to him through the air. The doctor said it was an allergy. Hay fever comes through the air, why not pieces of pigs' feet?

Feh, he said to himself. How could they eat that tasteless fat? He remembered that he had never tasted it, himself, so how could he say it was tasteless? Still, it was tasteless. It had to be.

In the evening he announced to Sarah and Allan that he would no longer buy pigs' feet for sale.

The third day after its appearance, the rash seemed to clear concomitantly with the disappearing number of feet in the jar. Mindless of the lotion that the doctor had prescribed and the fact that Sarah was called to spear and wrap each foot, Farber considered the healing something just short of a miracle.

Tired and sleepy at the end of the day, he wondered whether God was rewarding him for refusing to sell the feet. He sold a quarter pound of ham to the last customer of the day and promptly closed the store.

If the itching is religious, how is it that God isn't punishing me for keeping and selling ham? And what about pork?

Immediately he felt a quiver of an itch zooming from the wrist of one hand to the length of the arm.

No, it's not a religious thing. It's medical, an allergy. What am I, a granddaddy from the old country to think these thoughts? Wait till Sarah hears about this! It doesn't make any difference. I'm better now. Besides, I've got more important things to think about.

It had been three days since he had mailed the letter but he still hadn't heard from his brother.

After his father closed up and went to bed, Allan stealthily entered the store. He dipped his fingers into the register and lifted quarters and dimes which he dropped into his pajama shirt pocket. He guessed he took about three dollars which, with his two-dollar allowance, would be enough for Mother Matthews.

The meat showcase, lit up during the night to discourage burglary, cast a light directly on the jar of pigs' feet. Remembering his father's difficulty, a new excitement filled Allan, as great as the act of stealing money to have Mother Matthews. He returned to his room with a pig's foot in his hand.

Allan stared at it with suspicious awe, knowing that eating it was forbidden to him under Jewish dietary laws. His father had suffered wounds by touching it, according to what he had overheard them talking about. He wondered whether an angel of God had murmured some incantation over the feet to make them strike his father for the blasphemy of dealing with them.

For a full minute he stared at the foot before rolling up his sleeve. Holding the fat, ruddy foot like a wand, he rubbed it gently on his hand, and then his arm. He had to know whether it held some strange power to injure a Jew. The worst that could happen was that he'd develop a rash like his father. But, he thought, his father touched it to make his living. He was doing it to test the will and power of God, just as God had tested Abraham. Yet God could get angry and cause his hand and arm to wither and fall off.

He quickly opened the window and threw the piece outside, shivering as the cold night air struck his warm body. "Let Dracula have it," he said under his breath.

Flat on his back in bed, staring at the ceiling, he recalled a fairy tale about a prince who came across a sobbing woman. When asked what she was doing, she replied that a giant who held her captive had told her to make a pie of a small child for supper.

"Don't worry," the prince said. "I have a young pig you could put into the pie and the giant would never know the difference." And the giant never did, for the flesh of the pig is much like the flesh of a human. At least the story said so.

Maybe because of the similarity, Allan thought, God forbade the eating of pig. But why only to Jews? Why not Irish and Negroes, too?

He lay restlessly, unsatisfied with his test of faith and the might of God. Moments later found him back downstairs, holding a small drinking glass and a thin piece of paper.

A few minutes' wait was rewarded as he swooped down on a cockroach and placed the glass over it. Next, he slid the paper between floor and victim, enabling the transport to the jar of pigs' feet. Carefully, he unscrewed the top of the jar and dropped the insect into the mass of flesh and liquid.

The roach swam in the vinegar and juice and headed for a mountain of pink, shiny meat which protruded like an iceberg from the waters. Suddenly, however, as if shot, the insect stopped and spread out its transparent brown wings. A moment later, it lay still, dead.

Allan breathed deeply. He thought of killing Dracula this way by tossing the animal into a huge vat of slippery pigs' feet and bubbling, boiling vinegar.

[129]

With an edge of the paper he retrieved the insect and threw it and the glass into a trash box. Feeling better, he knew that there was something really unwholesome about pigs' feet. Why else would the cockroach die?

He thought of the vinegar and of the possibility that it could have killed the roach. If so, why didn't it bother humans who used the stuff all of the time? He made up his mind to try again, using another roach and a fresh bottle of vinegar, uncontaminated with pigs' feet.

In bed again, his mind turned to the next visit to Mother Matthews. She ate pigs' feet. He saw her buy some. It was turned into her body flesh. Did he commit a sin by screwing her? Was the screw a bigger sin than touching her pork-flesh?

The letter from the insurance company came on fine, thick white paper with raised letterhead of the company's trademark, an eagle with wings outspread and talons outstretched. Typed with nonconnecting cursive letters, it briefly stated that his robbery insurance was being canceled. A check for one hundred and twenty dollars, representing the remainder of his annual premium, was enclosed.

Jimmy, whose counsel he sought, called him stupid. Then the breadman cursed the insurance companies.

"Those no-good bastards. Didn't even give you a thirty-day notice of cancellation, eh? Just like them. They're out to make money, not give it away. They didn't even give you a chance to get new insurance."

"It's no use anyway. I tried to. I couldn't. No company's giving around here." Farber paused, picked his elbows from the counter, and rubbed them. "Maybe that's why they didn't give me time to get new insurance. They knew it's a waste of time. First the window insurance and now this."

Jimmy looked over his shoulder before he spoke. "Missus in the back?" He watched Farber nod. "I'll tell you," he said in a whisper, "when it comes, it won't make any difference even if you did have insurance."

"When what comes?" Farber returned the whisper.

"The blow-up. The riots. Niggers with guns. When the stores get hit, the companies won't pay. They'll say it was no riot, it was a insurrection. It wasn't stealing, it was looting. Let me tell you, there ain't no policy covers insurrection and looting. Nobody's claim is worth a damn."

Farber shrugged his shoulders. "It's not the riots I'm worried about. It's the burglaries. Twice in two weeks they broke in on me. Sarah doesn't know. I keep it from her. I'm down first in the morning and cover up. I can't afford the losses no more."

Jimmy mimicked Farber's shrug unintentionally. "Let me tell you a story. There's a mom and pop store on my route. Nice elderly Jewish couple. They paid in premiums thirty years. Then comes civil rights and crime. Two, three big holdups in a row. The company paid, then canceled. I'm telling you, nobody's out to give money away."

A customer entered and jokingly asked Jimmy where the fresh breads were. The deliveryman picked up a loaf of yesterday's bread from the front bin and placed it on the counter. Then he turned to Farber. "I've got to run. You owe me three eighty."

"Hey, wait a minute," the customer said to Jimmy.

"Ah want a brea' di-rek from you. Wholesale. Gonna save me some money."

"Don't sell retail, buddy," Jimmy said. "You just got to break down and let Mr. Farber earn his profit of two whole cents."

"Sheet," the customer said, plunking down two dimes and a penny.

He stormed out as Farber shook his head. "They begrudge you a penny. Like you're stealing from them. They lose dollars playing the numbers. Throw away money on dope and drink. They rather throw the two cents down the sewer than let you make profit off them."

"Listen," Jimmy said, picking up his basket, "what can you expect from a nigger?"

The cold winter continued, hurling down from clouded skies hard snow which remained until it turned blackish green. On some days, occasional sunshine competed poorly with blasts of wind that beat unmercifully against the face like a stick.

The first of February, she thought, and only another month or so before spring will come. It'll be warm and maybe they'll have enough saved up to move. He promised her that.

She turned toward his sleeping body and watched his nude and uncovered torso heaving with each breath. Even when asleep his relaxed muscles bulged with strength. She remembered how handsome he looked when dressed to go out; the cut of his suit accentuated his physique, making

[132]

shoulders broader, chest deeper, and waist narrower. Many times at weddings and banquets, she proudly stood next to him to show everybody that she belonged to him, the only masculine-looking man in a hall of overfed, pear-shaped men.

She got up eagerly, vowing to surprise him this morning by making his breakfast before he went to the market, but without knowing the reason, she felt that something was wrong before she descended the last step downstairs.

A trail of coins ran from the register through the storeroom and kitchen. She followed it with her eyes out the back door where she could still see brown pennies on the snow leading to the adjoining alley. The back door had been jimmied.

With her husband, whom she hastily called, the coins were picked up and an inventory made of stolen goods.

"A few cartons of cigarettes," he said. "Maybe a couple bottles of beer. Nothing else."

"Call the police," she ordered, rubbing her cold hands under a man's pullover she wore.

He didn't answer.

"Aren't you going to call them?"

"You know it don't do no good. I called them last week this happened. They didn't even bother to come down."

"Last week? Why didn't you tell me?"

"A couple boxes cigars and a case of beer. I didn't want to worry you."

"Worry me!" she gasped. "They could kill us in our sleep and you don't want to worry me."

[133]

"Nobody's killing nobody."

"You're going to call and get us a burglar alarm put in. And that's final." Although he nodded his head in agreement, she stormed into the kitchen and began slamming pans and plates as a warning that she wasn't going to change her mind and that he better not, either.

When he came in for breakfast, she was reading the morning newspaper. "They killed another grocer, Simon," she said, without bothering to look up.

"Oh, no! Everything happens at the same time."

"Look here." She held the newspaper up for him to see. The story was on top of the page.

2 YOUTHS ESCAPE AFTER SLAYING
NORTHWEST GROCER IN HOLDUP

Next to the column was a photograph of a white woman being consoled by two colored women, one of whom had her arm around the shoulders of the white lady. All three were crying, the tears of each plainly visible on their cheeks.

"A Northwest grocer, David Rubin, fifty-six, was shot and killed in his store last night during a holdup by two youths," Sarah read aloud. "Police said the two raced out of the store, jumped into a green car, and sped away toward the downtown area."

Farber breathed deeply. "That was Rubin. Yeah, I knew him from the market. I saw him yesterday and asked him how business was. A nice Jewish man. The bastards."

"It says he was shot in the right temple. I don't know why they had to speed away. Nobody runs away from a crime around here. They walk away. We're just fair game around here." She allowed a few tears to fall from her eyes before she continued. "It isn't worth it. Nothing is."

"What isn't worth it?" he played along.

"You know. Our lives. Why can't you be a man and admit you made a mistake?"

"Because it takes a man to see things through. Nobody'd finish nothing if they'd be stopped by bad luck. And what's my mistake? You agreed, too. You signed the papers."

"Sell the store, Simon."

"I'm not giving up because some guy breaks in or someone got shot in the head. I bet Rubin tried to fight it out, that dumb son of a gun. Not me. I'd open the register, stand aside, and invite them to take to their hearts' content." He suddenly recalled what Jimmy had warned. Always keep fifty, sixty bucks in the till especially for the holdup man. Why not ten or twenty? Farber had asked. Jimmy had laughed. Don't ask foolish questions, he said.

"Yeah," Farber continued, "I'll let them help themselves."

Sarah looked at him curiously, not wanting to disbelieve him, yet not totally believing him.

Her change of expression heightened his attack. "Honest to God. To hell with them. I wouldn't raise a finger. Not even a pinkie. As for the alarm company, I'm calling right now." He noted a pleased look on her. "What

[135]

else you want me to do? Get a bulletproof vest for my right temple?"

She laughed and then they heard someone knocking on the store door. They peeked around the storeroom door and saw an elderly woman they didn't recognize as being from the neighborhood.

Farber shouted, "Open in half an hour. Got to go to the market now."

"You-all open?" she replied.

"Might as well," he said to Sarah. "We could use the money now as well as later."

The woman shuffled to the counter and peered into their faces. Her toothless mouth opened. "You-all new around here, ain't you?"

Farber, relieved that the stranger had come just in time to help end the argument, smiled. "We've been here for more than a month. Where've you been?"

Later, a salesman from a burglar alarm company smacked his lips as he figured with pad and pencil the area to be covered and the number of doors and windows. "If you include the upstairs," he said, "it'll run you two hundred fifty-nine."

Farber held the side of his face and shook his head. "Forget about it."

"We'll even throw in free as a bonus of no charge a mirror. You can see the whole store in it from the register." He pointed to an area on top of the walk-in refrigerator. "Put it up there."

"What can you see?" Sarah asked.

"You really can't see too good in it, but it has a psychological effect on the niggers."

"I can't afford it," Farber said.

"It's a pity," the salesman, who had thick, downcast features, clucked. "But I'll tell you, we got a installment plan."

"I'm already on half a dozen plans now. One more might be the end of me."

"These burglaries will be the end of you." The salesman closed his pad with more force than was needed. "An electric alarm system is part of every business these days. Think about it."

As soon as the salesman left, Farber rushed out to buy pulleys, chains, wire and bells which he used to build a crude but intricate alarm system, using his skill as a carpenter. The front, rear, and side doors and all of the windows were meticulously rigged with belled wires. Lastly, he constructed a removable fence, which, he explained to her, would take seconds to set up nightly before they went to sleep.

"It looks like a barbed wire fence in wartime," she said. "I don't think that's enough. That'll tell us someone's here, maybe, but what's going to keep them out?"

"One thing at a time, Sarah." He glanced at his watch. It was close to midnight. "I've got to clean up for tomorrow. Why don't you go to sleep?"

"I think sooner or later you'll have to put in iron bars on the windows and iron grates over the doors."

[137]

"It's a fortune. A fortune."

"Jimmy says we also ought to get the windows, next time they're broken, to get them fit with cross-hatching so that the panes are smaller. Maybe they won't break all of the windows when they throw a rock. It'll be cheaper, Jimmy says, to replace a couple of squares."

"Jimmy doesn't have to pay for it," he replied, annoyed. "A window like that costs a couple-three hundred dollars."

She knew that a fresh argument would ensue if she continued this line. Instead, she stood up, yawned, and said she was going to bed.

So now it's traps for humans, she thought. Every night she listened to the rat traps being sprung and turned over, a sound which sent shivers through her body. She no longer cried during the nights, and sleep came more easily as fewer and fewer rats were caught. Thank God. There were less of them.

She climbed into bed, lay thinking for a while about a house in the suburbs, and then feigned sleep when her husband came. After his snoring began, she listened in earnest for the bells. At times she thought she heard them tinkle, and in her mind she saw the dark figure of a man brushing the wires aside as he came through the window. She followed him through the store as he picked up cigarettes and placed them into a large sack he carried over his shoulder, and then she watched him dump small change out of the register. Soon he came to the stairs, shining his small flashlight on the wire-and-bell fence. Did she hear his footsteps now? He began to climb up the steps, and

[138]

carefully stepped over the wires. Yes, she heard his footsteps.

She decided not to wake her husband. It could be her imagination and he'd get angry. Silently, she got out of bed and tiptoed to the door where she could listen more effectively. Not a sound. She snapped on the large light in the hallway, knowing that if there were a burglar she would either see him or hear him after he were frightened away by the light. Still nothing. There was nothing.

Shaky and sweaty, she returned to the bedroom. She couldn't go on like this, she thought. It's like living in an armed camp. They could be slaughtered while they slept. She couldn't go on living in constant fear during the day and throughout the night.

Later she fell asleep, but awoke shortly, sobbing from her nightmare of being raped and cut up with a knife. She stayed awake for a long time and one of her thoughts was that maybe her husband would see how bad she looked and she'd tell him why. Maybe then he'd buy bars for the windows and iron grates for the doors.

She fell asleep remembering the words her husband had said to her just before she went to bed, such a long time ago.

"If you're going to come down early, be careful not to trip over the wires."

"Yesterday was payday," Farber announced to Sarah. "I'm going to collect." He waited for an objection from

[139]

her but none came. Maybe she now realized the importance of money, he thought.

He knew it was a job he'd hate. It was bad enough delivering groceries to their dreary homes reeking with filth, hurrying to fulfill his invited invasion of their environment.

His own surroundings, the shelves, whose emptiness reflected the fullness of the credit book, now occupied his eyes. He didn't need the shelves to remind him that he barely took in enough cash that week to restock them. Trickles of money came in only from the students and a few customers with steady jobs.

"Yeah," he repeated, "that's what I intend to do. If they don't pay at least something on account, we'll cut them off. No more credit." His anger escalated, more for his own sake than hers. He needed resentment as an incentive to collect.

"They got money for everything else. For the chain stores. For gambling and drinking. But when they're broke they come to the corner grocery." He sighed, took the apron from around his neck, balled it up, and tossed it on a chair.

She looked at him with an expression showing that she wasn't listening to anything new. "Be careful," she said at last. "Don't look for a fight." She watched him nod and grunt as he shoved the credit book into his coat pocket. "Maybe I ought to go with you."

He smiled sarcastically. "What for? The amount of money I'm gonna collect only needs one person, maybe a midget, to carry it."

Icy blasts of wind belied the near arrival of spring and made Farber button up his Mackinaw as he trudged aimlessly for a few minutes. He stopped, leafed through the book with gloveless hands until he came to the name of Mrs. Hobson. Her address was the closest. She lived in a four-story apartment house, condemned but never evacuated by the tenants or destroyed by the city.

He entered, followed by cold drafts which whipped through the missing lobby door and did little to dilute the stench of urine and cabbage permeating the hallway. Closer to her apartment door, a familiar odor touched his nostrils, reminding him of the marketplace. In the market, it was accompanied by other smells and sounds. Here it was out of place, whatever it was. He closed his eyes and sniffed, still uncertain of the odor.

Mrs. Hobson opened the door and peeked out atop the safety chain. When she saw Farber, she unhooked the latch and gingerly stepped outside, closing the door quickly behind her, but not before a new wave of the smell entered the hallway, along with recognizably throaty murmurings.

Chickens, he said to himself. God almighty!

"Got to be real careful else they get out," she said.

"What'll get out?" He wanted her to tell him.

"Mah chickens. They be scurrying all over the hall and maybe run out the street."

"Oh," Farber nodded understandingly. He looked at her enormous brow ridge and the cute fish-shaped plastic curlers which swam in a black, woolly ocean.

The curlers, he thought, they wouldn't help. Who would want to make love to her? Now he examined her lips, suddenly realizing that they looked pink only because they were surrounded by her coal-color skin. Maybe the others, too, really didn't have pink lips. It was the contrast that made them pink. And then there were their teeth, even hers, clean, bright, large, and evenly shaped white teeth. How could they have such teeth when they never even bought toothpaste?

It was again the contrast, he humorously decided. Take those teeth and put them in a white man and they'd probably look crummy and yellow, like his own. He guessed he looked ugly to them, with his thin, mean lips, long, narrow nose, and narrow eyes. His skin, like a transparent sewer top, showed blue-green scraggly veins.

"Well, Mrs. Hobson. I almost forgot what I came for."

"Ah'd invite you in, Mistah Simon, but ah'm afraid you step in they do-do."

"What?"

"They not housebroke, you know," she laughed. "Ah don't keep them long enough to teach toilet trainin' so they do-do all over mah floor and ah cleans wonst a week."

He shook his head in amusement. "How many chickens do you keep?"

"Fifteen, eighteen. Ah raise them and eat what ah cain't sell, or what the rats don't kill and eat."

"You mean the rats get into your apartment?"

"They don't have to get in," she said in a loud, angry voice. "They already in. Ah got to watch them. They hidin' under the bed, the stove, everwheres. They devils. Comin' and killin' mah chicks."

Farber shifted his weight and pulled out the book. "Mrs. Hobson, I came to collect. The balance is seven dollars ninety."

Her eyes widened in surprise. "Oh, Mistah Simon. Ah don' have no money, now. Ah 'spect ah will, come two, three days. Ah see you then. But ah got nothin' now. That why ah ain't been shoppin' and ah be eatin' chicken three time a day."

Farber bit his lip. A bad sign, he guessed. When you don't get anything from the first one, you probably won't from the rest. He bade her good-bye, after she promised he wouldn't have to come back to see about the bill.

"Jesus be mah witness," he heard her words ring in his ears.

The Akers family lived in another apartment building with a hallway strewn with trash and animal waste. Dirty words and slogans covered those parts of the wall where the paint hadn't peeled or the plaster hadn't crumbled. A stray dog, startled by Farber, shivered and huddled closer in a corner. Its head bent low and the tail hung so long between the legs that it almost reached the underside of its chin.

Akers, a laborer when he wasn't drunk, had about six or seven children. Farber knew that one daughter, Bernice, had been arrested several times for prostitution. She was a pretty girl with a light complexion and could almost pass for Spanish or Italian, he thought. Maybe even Jewish. But no, her look was too wild, too vulgar.

Mrs. Akers answered his knock. She wore a heavy overcoat and wool slacks. Farber thought that he caught her on the way out.

"Why, hello there, Mistah Simon." She opened the door wide to let him in. "Come on in, heah. Make youself at home."

"Ah," he murmured, "thank you. Is the mister in?"

"Oh, no. He lookin' for work. He got lots of mouths to feed," she said, pronouncing mouths as mouth-ess. "Anything ah can do?"

"Well, I came to see about the book."

"Well, you come right on in, Mistah Simon. That's been on mah mind, too. Strangely."

I bet, he thought. "You're more than three weeks overdue. Fifty-seven dollars."

"You come right on in, Mistah Simon."

He followed her inside. She was a big-boned woman, and had white hair on the sides of her head. She wore a pair of old eyeglasses which sat on the edge of her nose, almost two inches away from her eyes. One bow was broken off but the frame was held to the ear by a piece of looped string.

All of her children inside the one-room apartment had their coats on. One boy, about fifteen, light complexioned like his sister, sat on the bed. Farber had not seen him before, nor another youth, slightly older, who had a moustache. Their sister was not in, but there were two toddlers whom Mrs. Akers had brought into the store many times. It suddenly occurred to him that she was too old to have such young children.

A large double bed with a mattress that looked as if it had never seen a sheet shared the room with a dresser, on which several candles of various lengths burned. Other equipment included a kitchen table, and a two-burner oil stove which leaned against a wall caked with grease and dirt.

"My," Farber said. "Your whole family's here."

"They got no place to go."

He looked at the two small children. "Twins?" He knew they weren't; they looked nothing alike, nor had she ever mentioned to him that they were twins, but he wanted to appear friendly and not only interested in money.

"Oh, no. Jeffrey's almost three, and Noonie, he about two and a half."

The two boys stood on chairs trying to catch crawling roaches on the kitchen table. Mrs. Akers looked at Farber watching them. "Don't you pay them no mind."

The boys were too close in age to be hers, he thought. Maybe she adopted one of them.

She answered his question. "Jeffrey and Noonie mah great-grandchildrens."

"What?" She was pulling his leg, he thought. "I don't believe it."

"Oh, no. Ah'm too old for that stuff. They mah grand-

[145]

children's childrens. Frazier and Samuel here is mah grand-childrens. Same as Bernice." She introduced the youths, who averted his look, glaring at the floor between them and appearing uneasy at being revealed to an outsider.

Farber shook his head. "Your grandchildren? But where are their parents? Your children?"

"Oh, they around," she said, her face without expression. "Ah see them, now and then. They hep me once in a while. You see, ah'm the legal guardian of mah grand-childrens and mah great-grandchildrens."

She raised her chin when she said legal guardian, as if proud of a title someone, a minor welfare department functionary, had bestowed upon her.

"Now ah know what you gonna say, Mistah Simon. Mah grandsons here too young to have childrens. Well, Frazier, he almost sixteen, but Samuel, he almost seventeen. He the one who the father of Jeffrey. Bernice the mother of Noonie."

Farber tried an understanding smile, but he failed. He glanced around the room and refused to think about their sleeping arrangements. The bed was large enough for her and her husband, but what about the rest of them?

"When do you expect Mr. Akers back?"

"Oh, he be lookin' for work."

Farber knew that their use of *be* meant that an action was being done on a daily basis. "Mrs. Akers, I came to collect on the book."

"Ah know that when ah see you walkin' comin' up the street from the window. We ain't got no money. They cut

[146]

off the gas. Soon the light. We ain't got no heat to keep warm. Cain't afford the oil for the burner. It broke anyway."

"Why don't you get it fixed?"

"It belong to the apartment. Ah'm not gonna spend no money on it. Let the Jew landlord do it."

Farber creased his forehead, deciding not to say anything. Her misery was enough.

"Why don't you call him and tell him to fix it?"

"Ah don't know his number."

Farber looked at the youths. "Can't you boys help your mother . . . your grandmother out?"

"Got no dime for no telephone," the one with the moustache said, pouting.

"Are you looking for a job?"

"Ah'm sick. Ah got back pain," the boy answered.

Farber looked at the light one, who, expecting the same question, shot his eyes first to his brother and then to his grandmother before resting them on Farber. "Ah cain't find no work. They won't let me quit school."

"Now, Mistah Simon," Mrs. Akers said, "don't you worry none about no money. Mah son-in-law, Frazier here's daddy, well, he promise me he gonna send money. And we 'spect a check any day now from welfare. Top that, mah husband, he not here now 'cause he went to collect unemployment."

"He's not looking for work?"

"Ain't no work, now."

"Mrs. Akers, I've got to pay rent and gas and light

[147]

bills, too. And I've got to stock up. That costs money."

"You get it. Soon's we do."

Farber nodded and turned to leave. Outside, his mind drew pictures of the tenement of his youth, when he and Benny used straw mattresses on the floor next to the bed of their parents. At night they piled whatever they could over themselves, blankets, coats, even sweaters and trousers, but still they were cold. Their meals were potatoes and black bread. There were no welfare checks, unemployment compensation, charity money. And there were no drunks, and no three-year-old great-grandchildren living with one of their parents and great-grandparents.

In the newspapers he remembered occasionally seeing stories about four generations, showing the three mothers and child sitting on a couch and staring at the camera. Here there were maybe four generations living in every other house. Married and unmarried, what difference did it make with them? he thought. The moustache, too sick with his back pain to get a job, but healthy enough to jump a girl and make a baby. And the other one, to busy doing nothing to find work after school.

The next name in the book was Jackson, who lived two houses away. Perry Jackson was a laborer, huge, with thick slabs of beef for shoulders and a waist as thin as a young boy's. He was a soft-spoken, gentle man, who usually came to the store directly from work on paydays with his boots dripping mud and overalls stiff from perspiration. Eight to ten children always ran around him, screaming for candy. Farber had thought they were neighborhood kids pouncing on a kind man, but he soon learned they were Jackson's own.

Olivia Jackson, a dark, brooding woman whose wall-eyes never seemed to blink, often told Farber how wonderful life would be if she had only one child instead of thirteen. All he could reply was that he wished he had more than one.

He clucked his tongue with shame now as he knocked on the door of the Jacksons' frame house. Someone had vandalized their front porch. Freshly fragmented and sharp, unpainted wood remnants bore witness to being recently chopped up.

"Good day, Mistah Simon. Cold weather we havin'."

No more dilly-dallying, no more time-wasting, he thought. "Is the mister in?"

"Oh, *no,*" she said in a way indicating that Farber should have known where her husband was. "He's lookin' for firewood. You see that busted-up porch? Ah do that for firewood when he not around to get me some. He fix it in springtime again with new lumber. But evertime it get cold, that porch is like a woodpile." She beckoned him to enter. "Mistah Jackson, he come back soon."

He didn't have to count to know that all thirteen of the Jackson children were in, wrapped in blankets and huddled around a wood stove with an open lid which ejected wisps of smoke and firelight. The children ranged in age from a girl in her middle teens to an infant she held in her lap. Like mute animals they sat, strangely quiet for children, with glazed and sad eyes. They looked disappointedly past

[149]

Farber, as if hoping that he had forgotten the groceries outside the door. Soon their gaze returned to the firelight. Atavistically, as if remembering a more hospitable, distant land, they stared at the light of their sun, letting the grownups remain in a dark and cold world.

"Come on, childrens. Leave a place by that fire for Mistah Simon." She waved an arm but they scarcely moved, daring not to lose a favored spot.

"Oh no, Mrs. Jackson. I've got to go."

"Mistah Jackson, he be back soon."

"I just came to see if he could make a payment on the book."

She shook her head slowly, picking up and clutching a child whom she held close to her bosom, as if to provide a barrier of innocence between her and Farber. "We give you if we had. Mistah Jackson, he goin' back to work soon. He tell me that just this mornin'."

A feeling of nausea spread through him and his face turned a dull crimson. Was this what he was going to listen to the rest of his life? He looked around for a quick escape, and settled on the children. "Very nice children you got there."

She wouldn't let him go. "Sometimes I wishes they was dead."

"Oh, come now. Stop it."

"They is hongry. And ah ain't got nothin' to give them." She shook her head, and Farber could see the tears. "You stay for supper, you believe me then. You know what we eat? Sugar sandwich. That's old stale bread that ah sprinkle sugar on then wet it under the water faucet. And then we eat it slow, real slow."

He remembered his own boyhood, his hunger, breakfasts of hard, black bread and stale cheese. He tasted them now, and they hung in his throat, choking him. "Don't worry, Mrs. Jackson. As long as I'm in the store, you're not gonna go hungry. You pay me when you get money."

She unleashed a new issue of tears. He wanted to dash out and run until he came to a place where the sun shone on green grass blowing in a soft breeze.

"Good-bye, Mrs. Jackson. Your husband will soon find work. I know it." He left quickly, glumly pushing the book further into his overcoat pocket. His frustration disappeared momentarily when he compared himself to a doctor who couldn't take money from a poor family. Yet he shuddered at the prospect of telling Sarah, of returning to them later, and of collecting from the many others on credit. No more today, he decided.

He approached the Akers' place again. Frazier and Samuel stood outside now, idly tossing a knife at a wood fence. They ignored him as he passed by.

He couldn't understand them, all of them. They just seemed content to sit around and do nothing, like an animal who knows it's trapped in a cage but just sits there in grouchy acceptance. There was a helplessness, maybe a laziness, he thought, which they transmitted like a disease among themselves and their children.

What would he do if he were in their place? he wondered. There was no work to be had, of that he was sure.

[151]

And how could he think of cleaning house or paying bills on time when his own survival would occupy his mind full-time? He couldn't blame them.

In the spring, things would be better. Even the warmth of the summer with its shafts of bright sunshine would make the shabbiest basement apartment seem livable and would drive to the outdoors the wrecks of human furniture who now shivered in unheated rooms.

It was a lie, he told himself. The spring wouldn't change anything. The dirt yards in front of their houses would remain hard, like cracked pieces of stone and sand. What would it take to make their earth live again and grow tomatoes and cucumbers?

What did he have that they didn't have? What chemical made him want to work like a horse, and to deny himself luxuries? He wondered if his disease were any better or worse than theirs, yet he knew that because of their failure, he would be a failure, too.

Allan laid his head back against the pillow, closed his eyes, and drew his knees up as he felt a new beginning of the now-familiar intermittent soft tickling and razor-sharp throbbing ache in the head of his penis. He knew his curling movement would be useless and in a few minutes he'd have to press down on it with both hands to lessen the pain.

He opened his eyes, staring at the ceiling and wondering why he had decided to hide whatever he had wrong with his sex organ. For days he had been wiping away secretions with toilet paper and secretly washing his underwear so that his mother wouldn't see the stains. He had diagnosed it as a cold in the penis, because of the whitish-yellow mucus which dribbled from it just like it oozed from someone's nose during a head cold.

The pain when he urinated worried him the most. He tried not to go as often, saving it until he could no longer hold back and then letting go with heavy breathing and murmured cries while he braced himself with one arm against the wall. It felt as if someone had shoved a lighted match into the opening and screwed it deep into the canal.

Having diagnosed his case, he treated it by taking warm baths and drinking hot milk to burn the cold away. After a week he became too tired and listless to continue. The cold hung on. At the end of the second week he asked James about it.

"Cold in the stick? That ain't no cold. That the ol' clapadapperdoopie. Man, you got the clap. You BVD huggin' the VD."

Allan smiled in frightened disbelief. The clap was something everybody joked about, even the kids in New York. Nobody but old bums and whores ever caught it. "You're kiddin' me," he managed to say in a level voice.

"It burn you?"

"Yeah."

"When you piss?"

Allan nodded. "White stuff comes out, too."

"Clapadapperdoopie!" James shouted, laughing and clapping his hands. "But don' you worry. It better than the syph. The syph, you toes drop off and then you fingers and

[153]

then you cock begin to shake laik a spider twistin' around a mothah fly in the web. And then it get real hard laik you gonna get you last screw for the last time but that ain't the cause, 'cause then it fall right off laik a icicle off the roof. In the clap, you turn white like a white mothah." James hesitated, looking at Allan's feet. "I mean if you black. You piss turn white and you blood turn white. Everthin' turn white on you, then you go blind and all you see is white laik you got you head deep in the snow."

Allan's stomach whirled. "I better go see a doctor. My father's gonna kill me when he finds out."

"You father don' have to know. You go to the clinic. It free and nobody know you. Jus' say you name somethin' else."

The clinic was in a ramshackle elementary school. Crumbled slate steps led from the front of the building through a green wooden door and a dual-painted hallway, green on the bottom, topped by dull white.

He followed the signs to a small, windowless auditorium filled with hard benches without back supports. The place emitted a strong odor of perspiration, stale, but also fresh from four women, a man, and two children who sat waiting. A Negro nurse sat bored at a desk near a door.

As the nurse and the patients stared, he approached the desk with a feeling that he'd be turned away because he was white. At one point he began to regret coming, and stopped to turn and leave, but the nurse snapped a question at him.

"You from around here, boy?"

[154]

He nodded.

"Give me your name and address and family doctor," she said, reaching into her desk drawer to pull out a mimeographed form.

He hadn't thought of an alias and for a moment, panicked. "I don't have a family doctor," he said, remembering that James had warned him to swear poverty. "I can't afford it."

"What's your name and where do you live around here?" she shot back impatiently. "There's hardly enough of the doctor's time to take care of the real sick and poor people around here."

Now it was a matter of principle. He wasn't going to give in without a fight, even though she was right, and he knew it. "But I live around here and I'm poor, too." He gave an address next door to the store's and then thought it would have been better to give one a block away from where he lived.

"And your name?"

"James Ferry."

"Do you have any identification?"

"No." To hell with it, he thought. If she'd turn him away, he'd steal more money and then see another doctor on the other side of town.

"What's wrong with you, James?"

"I got these pains in my side." He couldn't possibly tell her the truth.

"Okay, James. Have a seat. The doctor'll see you when your turn comes up."

The youngish, black doctor had an outsize jaw but soft and gentle eyes. On his short white examining jacket which hardly passed his belt line was a nameplate which bore DR. THOMPSON. Allan thought he heard a slight gasp when the doctor greeted him.

"Ah, you're white?"

"Yes, sir."

"You live around here?"

"Yes, sir."

"You're a rare bird." He paused to readjust a rubber hose attached to a sink. "Sorry I don't have a chair for you. We're supposed to let the patients in and out. Three to five minutes. Well, what do you think is wrong with you?"

"I think I've got the clap."

Without saying a word, Dr. Thompson got up and reached into a cabinet from which he produced two slivers of glass. "Pull down your pants and skin 'er back."

"What?"

"Pull your pecker back and then press forward. I want a specimen."

Allan did as he was told, hesitatingly dropping some of the secretion onto the glass which was held under his penis. The doctor covered the slide with the other glass and left the room for a few minutes. He returned smiling.

"Boy! I didn't even have to look under the 'scope for this one. It's a textbook case. You've got it all right. The old gleet. Bad blood. How long have you had the drip?"

"About a week, I guess."

"Why didn't you come in sooner? This thing's tougher to get rid of the longer you wait." He continued without giving Allan a chance to answer. "How'd you get it? From a drinking cup?" He laughed. "Toilet seat?" He laughed louder. "What's your name?" He pulled out a cellophane-covered syringe and two small bottles.

"James Ferry."

"That's what your paper says but you don't have to lie to me. With your face and expression and New York accent I'd say your name's more likely to be Jerome Farbstein."

Allan blinked, dismayed at the closeness between Farbstein and Farber. He jutted his lower lip forward to stop it from trembling, but he could not hide his wounded stare.

"Even your circumcised pecker gives you away. Now what's your story? Come on. I've got to file a monthly report on how many people I treated for VD. I don't even have to mention your name, Master Farbstein."

"I'm from New York," Allan said in a low voice. "I was visiting relatives in Virginia and hitchhiking my way back when I really did sit down in a bathroom." He knew that the doctor couldn't disprove this.

"Look, cut the nonsense. Give me the name of the girl. Is she from around here? We've got to catch her before she spreads more bugs. I won't tell her you sent me. If she won't come here, I'll go to her."

Allan, disgusted with himself for falling into a trap, also grew frightened at the prospect of an outraged Mother

[157]

Matthews getting some sort of revenge on him. He wasn't afraid of her physically. The worst thing she could do was to tell his parents.

"You don't tell me and I'll have to see your mom and dad."

"I didn't say I wasn't going to tell you," Allan said, watching him approach with the needle. "She doesn't live around this neighborhood." He felt the trap lifting, remembering that this was a local clinic, and the doctor probably wouldn't concern himself with an outside matter. "She lives in Virginia, across Chain Bridge."

"Turn around and bend over the table. I'm giving you a double dose of penicillin in your pink ass just because you waited so long before seeing a doctor. You allergic to the stuff?"

Allan shook his head. He decided not to ask the doctor if some could be spared for future emergencies.

"One in each cheek. The same thing tomorrow and probably the next day." He dabbed the skin with alcohol-soaked cotton and plunged the needle in, repeating the process with another syringe. "Where did you say she lives?"

"In Virginia. Near my friends."

"I thought you said they were relatives."

"Well, yeah. I made friends near my relatives."

"Mr. Farbstein-Ferry, the girl you screwed is probably laying a hundred other guys, giving them gonorrhea. It's bad enough you got a dose."

His mind became a battleground. Scenes of a court-room in which he was on the witness stand protecting an

[158]

innocent friend competed for space with images of him in uniform undergoing enemy interrogation.

"Have it your own way. If you come back here with the same strain of gonococcus I'll know it was the same girl, and I'll turn both you and her over to the cops for aiding and abetting the spread of disease. Now get out of here and come back tomorrow. Yeah, and you'd better wash your hands after you piss. Don't play with yourself. Drink a lot of water and don't drink alcohol. Not even wine tomorrow night at the Sabbath dinner. You understand?"

He went to the cabinet, this time for a rubber glove. "Wait a minute. I want to see what your prostate looks like. Bend over."

The gloved hand went into Allan, making him shriek, break out into a sweat, and think that this must be the way a virgin felt the first time. It hurt.

"Quiet! The people out front'll think I'm shoving something up your ass, or something."

Allan groaned with pain-pleasure when the hand came out.

"Hurts, doesn't it? Let that be a lesson to you. Next time you come in I'll put both hands in there and clap." He threw his head back and laughed. "Clap! That's great." He looked at Allan's pained expression. "Don't you get it?"

Before sending Allan away, Dr. Thompson wrote something on the mimeographed form. "Boy, you really are something. Can't even remember your lies. I see here that you gave the nurse a local address." He shook his head and grinned.

A hot flush overcame Farber when he looked out the window and saw the black Cadillac with the familiar yellow and black New York license plates circling around.

It was Benny.

His brother's car with its overly thick tires went around the corner but Farber spied Benny and Gladys during the first spin. They hadn't seen him, that he knew, else they'd have stopped and got out, sheepishly smiling and waving their arms with forced enthusiasm.

It had been a long time since Benny had sent the money. Farber never acknowledged its receipt, and hoped that Benny wouldn't write and mention it. Sarah still didn't know about the loan. He didn't want to see his brother now.

Farber guessed that Gladys had asked to circle around the block a few times to see the likes of the neighborhood. The knowledge she acquired would be spent later on her friends, whose minds and bodies were shaped by cookie cutters in the form of hair stylists, owners of weight-reducing clinics, and original dress designers.

As for her mind, it bored him to listen to her talk about her literary club which discussed the great works twice a month, on Wednesday afternoons. A campaign to improve Benny had begun and ended with an unsuccessful attempt to discourage him from sucking and blowing on his teeth after a meal. They had reached a short-lived compromise when he agreed to use toothpicks, which proved to be an unsatisfactory substitute for breath and tongue.

Farber grunted as he watched the car slow down and

stop. He bet with himself that Gladys would remain seated, unwilling to get out until Benny opened the door for her.

Benny strode out in front of his car, examining the store's exterior. He appeared to be thinking, but Gladys' annoyed rapping on the windshield and pointing to her side of the door made him race to her.

Farber greeted them and made an enthusiastic show of calling for Sarah and Allan. Soon they were all seated around the kitchen table, with Farber nearest the door, ready to jump into the store when a customer entered. A coffee pot steamed on the burner.

"Oh, please don't bother, Sarah," Gladys protested unconvincingly. "We just had dinner downtown. At a very nice place."

"Just some coffee," Sarah said.

Benny shook his head. "Can't stay long. We gonna try to make Miami with one stopover. How's that for driving, Sy?"

Farber shrugged his shoulders. His brother's energy and motivation showed up everywhere, even in vacation driving. He pondered how he might get Benny alone and beg him not to tell Sarah. But what about Gladys? Suppose she knew and might let the cat out of the bag?

"Boy, I'll tell you. Those Cadillacs may cost a few pennies more, but they're sure worth it. Twelve, fourteen hours a day. You hardly feel it. Drove all the way down with one arm on the back of the seat. Just shows you what good living can do for you."

Benny, in spite of his dark and expensive-looking suit,

still looked apelike with his long arms, protruding brow, and thick chest. His voice glowed with power. "Yeah, we're a little late for winter, we had a terrific busy season, and we decided better late than never, so we decided to go down South for a few weeks. Get some Fountainebleau tan." He looked over at Allan and then playfully slapped the boy on the shoulder. "You know what that is, Al?"

Everyone followed Benny in laughter until Gladys spoke. "What a fine-looking boy he's growing up to be. You know Michael's already sending out applications to medical schools." She patted her dyed blond hair as a gesture of controlled pride. "But we only want him to go to the best. An only son's an only son, you ought to know that, Simon."

"I'm even willing to donate money to the school he decided to go to," Benny said. "I figure that just the tuition is hardly enough to keep the school in the black. They got all sorts of expenses, overhead."

With his brother, the conversation always turned toward money, Farber noted, wondering when the blow of revelation would fall on Sarah. Benny looked at him curiously, and Farber guessed it was now coming.

"So how's business with you, Sy?"

"Making a living."

"Working hard, eh?" Benny said, trying to be sympathetic, but the question grated Farber. He resented Benny's attempt at an understanding wink, since he knew that it meant *in case you need any more money, you know where you can get it.* Maybe it also meant *don't worry about what you owe me.*

[162]

"It's a tough piece of bread," Farber said.

"I wish the three of you could go down South with us. Right now."

"Don't make me laugh, Gladys," said Sarah. "We can't even get to a movie these days."

"Too busy making money, eh?" Benny smiled.

The bell rang and Farber gave thanks silently that he could escape for a few minutes. When he returned, they were discussing Allan's future. Gladys continually crossed and uncrossed her sticklike legs, indicating annoyance on her part.

"You'll be sorry later on," she said, looking at Sarah. "Suppose he begins to talk like one?"

Benny, prompted by Sarah's worried look and the entry of Farber, and wishing to establish an important opinion, wrinkled his brow and shook his head. "Worse yet. Suppose he decides to marry one of them. Huh, Al? You wouldn't do such a thing, would you?"

Allan, his chin resting on chest, shrugged his shoulders. He made no attempt to hide his boredom.

"Now the thing to do," Benny continued, "is to ship him to New York. I can't see any percentage him going to school with niggers."

"You shouldn't talk like that in front of the boy, Benny," Farber said.

"Why not? The truth's the truth. Why hide it? If you face things square in the face, you'll be a success in your personal life. I find this holds true in business, too."

"We could send him to a private school, but that costs

[163]

a lot of money." Sarah glanced toward her husband to see if her statement met with his approval.

"Money's no problem," Benny said, looking down at the floor, head turned slightly, and winking again so that only Farber could see the gesture.

"Just another few months or so." Farber patted Allan on the head. "Right, Allan? Now, why don't you go do your homework? Upstairs."

"I finished. I want to go out tonight."

They watched silently as Allan climbed the stairs. When he was out of sight Farber spoke. "You sure you don't want to eat something before you go?" He hoped that would remind them they were in a hurry.

"Don't change the subject, Simon," Gladys said. "This is a serious affair. You can't raise a boy like that. Where's he going now? With white or black friends?"

"Just let me help you again," Benny pleaded, his arms outstretched in what he hoped was a dramatic pose. "Forget about what you owe me. You can't go on like this, living in a rat trap grocery store. Nobody works like this in America anymore. Maybe twenty, thirty years ago, but not now. I'm a businessman, I know. Nowadays it's the chain stores. No more penny candy and loaf of bread. Times have changed. You're living in the past."

"Benny, take it easy," Gladys said. "You're supposed to be on vacation."

"He's my brother," Benny shot back at her. "Do you mind?" Lusterless eyes shifted to his brother. "Sy, I'm trying to help. Don't you read the papers? The *shvartzers* are taking over the ghettoes, the small businesses. You're not that simple that you don't know that."

Farber stared fiercely without saying anything for a few moments. "You can't forget that you helped me, can you?" he said softly, and then, with voice escalating, added, "If you think by lending me money you can also give me advice, forget about it. Your money I'll give back when I can. Your advice you know what you can do with." He picked up his jacket and left the kitchen, slamming his way through the store and into the street.

An early April drizzle picked pleasantly at his face as he tried to condone and justify his outbreak. The sound of his footsteps in the night air provided a dialogue with his thoughts.

Him and his goddamn money. Help me again, huh? Benny can't forget favors he does. That's why he's so good in business. Why should I tell him I'm in business because I can't work anymore? That's not his worry. As far as he's concerned, I'm in business because I want to be.

The walk relaxed him and he returned later. Benny and Gladys were gone and the store stood dark and closed. He ate a small dinner by himself and said good night to Sarah, who went to bed complaining of a headache. Grateful that she didn't bring up Benny or the loan, he decided he'd repay her understanding by taking her out to the suburbs as soon as he could to look at apartments.

Feeling better, he reopened the store and kept it open an hour after usual closing time to make up for the time lost walking the streets. The cash register recorded that he took

[165]

in seven dollars and twenty-three cents during the extra hour. Figuring roughly at about eighteen percent profit, he found that his net gain came to about one dollar and thirty-two cents.

What about extra electricity? he thought. And wear and tear on the body? A dollar and thirty cents an hour. He made five times that much as a carpenter.

He told himself he didn't feel like sleeping so he might as well stay open just a little bit longer. Since no one came in, he thought he wouldn't waste time standing around waiting. The empty soda bottles could be placed into their respective shelved crates.

He worked hard, stopping only to wipe away the sweat which built up along his neck and face. When he was through, he collected a number of bottles of companies with which he did not deal. He or Sarah had accepted the bottles inadvertently during the busy hours, and tomorrow he'd take them to a store which carried the brands. There were thirteen bottles. That made twenty-six cents, he thought.

Finally, a customer came in. He wore a dark mask and held a gun.

At once he felt a weakness in his legs and a hollowness in the stomach. The gun's so tiny it looks like a toy, he thought. It could kill, even though it's so small, not like a bomb or a tank.

He stared, hypnotized by the end of the barrel, paralyzed with expectation that at any moment a charge could come screaming out of the muzzle to end his dreams, the store, his life.

"You're holding me up, mister?" he asked, hoping that perhaps he had misjudged the man's intentions, but the gun burned into his mind. Its dark gray metal formed a menacing complement to the black hand with tightly clenched knuckles showing the white of bone.

The man snickered. "Turn you ass around."

Hiding the nose and shape of the eyes, the shiny mask and exposed skin reflected the fluorescent lights of the store.

Farber subconsciously wished to hide from the danger. He escaped by staring at the man's face in amazement that it really shone. No wonder they're called shines, he thought.

"I said turn you ass, mothah."

Farber turned and heard the man walk behind the counter to the register to ring it open. Next came the sound of paper money being crumpled, and then coins being scooped up and dropped into a cloth sack. He listened to their muffled sound as they hit the bottom of the sack. Some dimes and quarters fell on the floor and rolled toward Farber's shoes. He felt like stepping on them or pushing them aside under the counter before the man could notice. They'd then be in a safe place for Allan's education and for the retirement in Florida, he reasoned in his helpless temptation.

"Mothah!" The man stomped in anger and kicked the dropped coins without bothering to pick them up.

Turning his head slightly, Farber eyed the sack. It held Saturday's cash gross, about one hundred and fifty dollars. The paper and metal, whose bumpy outlines he could see

[167]

pushing against the thin sack, represented his work, the cleaning and stocking, waiting on customers, going to the market, buying and selling and trading and sweating.

The mask stood between them. He couldn't reason with or appeal to a faceless figure. The gun was merely a tool for threatening, but the mask gave license to take for nothing. What gave the mask the right to do this? To gain the fruits of his labor?

With a lightning move Farber ripped away the mask. Dazed by his audacity, the grocer pinched the mask between thumb and forefinger at arm's length, like a young mother holding a wet diaper.

Stupid, crazy, he called himself. The man could kill me now. A look into the man's eyes in an effort to learn what was in store revealed only fear and surprise.

The man's features grotesquely sat on a thin snake neck. His nose appeared swollen, a misshapen, cartilage-less mass with wide nostrils forming a complete umbrella for obscene, thick, strawberry lips. A thin, wavy moustache rode the ridge of his upper lip, which now curled into a snarl.

"Mothahfucker!"

Farber saw a blur in front of his eyes and then felt a sharp pain tearing at his forehead and the back of his head. His eyes refused to focus and in a moment he felt the hardness of the floor slam against his face.

Pistol-whipping, the papers will say, he thought. He was crazy for pulling the mask off. What would he tell Sarah? He'd explain, he reasoned in the stupor of pain, that he did it for the principle, not for the sackful of money. But

[168]

who pulls masks off for principle? He could have at least fought back. In the same moment he had used for the mask he could have just as easily torn the gun from the man's hands or hit him on that pulpy nose.

A rough tugging at the back pocket of Farber's trousers told him that the man had thrust a hand inside to get at the wallet. But after the man had done so, his back straightened, his feet moved a few inches, position changes which lost him leverage for an easy pull-out of his hand. Nervousness interfered with cool thinking as attempts to extricate the frustrated, doubled-up fist failed.

With one hand holding the weapon, the bandit pulled and pulled to free the other, almost lifting Farber from the floor. They were the tar baby and the rabbit, or like two dogs stuck tight with haunch-to-haunch togetherness after frenzied copulation.

The panic-stricken thief, handcuffed as though through greed to his victim, acted as if the God of the grocers had finally visited His wrath upon him. He screamed curses and continually lifted his head to look over the counter in fear of seeing a customer or the police enter.

Farber missed the spectacle, more concerned with protecting the base of his skull with clasped hands against new blows expected to rain down at any moment.

Finally, hand retrieved, the bandit fled.

Farber heard the running steps of the holdup man, the opening of the door and the ringing of the bell, and then hard shoes against the pavement which seemed to say, Tammu, Tammu, Tammu.

[169]

That's right, he thought. Tammu was behind the holdup. It didn't matter whether it was to get money for his crackpot organization or to torment me. The fat *shvartzer* was behind the mask, pointing the gun, and holding the money sack.

Rage enabled him to stand up. He leaned against the counter and glared at the open cash register, its empty drawer hanging out like a dog's tongue on a hot day. Despite the closed door, he could still hear the rapid footfalls on the wet streets mocking the name of Tammu.

Farber walked unevenly until he reached the street, then ran stumbling in the direction in which he thought the bandit had gone. Soon he gasped for breath, as the muscles in his legs cried for a halt.

The running sounds faded into the stillness of the night, broken by the noise of an occasional automobile passing by. He stopped running, the clack of shoes now only an echo in his mind.

"Bastard!"

The shout in the direction of the disappeared bandit reverberated in the empty hallways and filled apartments of the neighborhood, long inured to similar cries in the night. No satisfaction accompanied the shout, and he returned wearily toward the store.

A painful throbbing in his head made him touch and then squeeze his forehead. His hand came back covered with wet and sticky blood. In his other hand he saw that he still held the mask.

[170]

Three girls passed by, swinging their high-arched buttocks under light and tight raincoats. Like bullfighters with
capes, they rustled the coats, hoping to attract the boys. The
girls varied in complexion. Two had milk chocolate brown
coloring while the skin of the third glowed with daffodil
brightness.

"Where you goin', girls?" James called out.

"To the school dance," the light one said, turning
around. Her skin, drawn tightly over high cheeks, and her
narrow slit eyes gave her an oriental look.

Allan quickly decided that she'd easily win the prize
for being the most beautiful girl he'd ever seen. She's like
a flower, he thought, noticing that she looked at him, not
James or Ferry, certain that she thought he was also a light
Negro. He wished he were.

"Come on, let's go," James said.

They followed briskly a pace behind the girls. "You
care we come with you?" James continued.

"Admission is twenty-five cents," the flower said,
looking behind once again at Allan.

The boys closed the walking gap. "What you-alls'
names?" James, their spokesman, said.

"I'm Yolanda," the flower replied. "She Jeannie and
she Sherelle," she pointed. "What you-alls' names?"

"James, Ferry, and Allan," Allan said. "I'm Allan.
What school dance you-all talking about?" He'd go too, he
thought, knowing he was entitled as a member in good
standing of James' gang.

They joked and teased one another, still not pairing

[171]

off, until they came to a school whose gym kept open late Saturday nights to cater to dancers. Girls outnumbered boys, the wallflowers sitting on folding chairs which ringed the dance floor. Phonograph music blared from two loudspeakers which perched awkwardly on ceiling rope in the gym's front and rear. Multicolored ribbon streamers, some wide enough to look suspiciously like toilet paper, flew from the same rope and from basketball hoops on either side of the court.

The hustle of entrance detached Allan from the group. He wandered for a few moments before he saw his friends dancing, but no sign of Yolanda. Minutes later, he spotted her, sitting with the wallflowers. Anxiety crept into him as he watched the approach of a tall youth whose skull structure made a black death's head of his face. Allan watched with relief as she shook her head slowly at Death's Head, smoothing out her pink, flowery dress in front of her.

Passing dancers stared unblinkingly at him. Distracted from his pursuit of Yolanda, he surrendered to them by pushing his lips out, snapping fingers and rolling hips to the beat of the music. He wondered whether he looked like he belonged. When the summer comes, he thought, he'd spend a great deal of time in the sun.

Halfway across the court from her now, he observed possessively from the corner of his eye while waiting for courage to be thrust upon him. Of a sudden, he accidentally caught her eye but then, in a bashful, speedy movement, he cast his eyes downward, immediately despising himself for doing so.

Allan remembered seeing in a movie a guy caught in the same situation, but who kept staring at the woman until she smiled in return. At least, he thought, he could have done the same thing. Better still, he could have moved his eyes away slowly after she had noticed him. That way she might think he was suave and cool.

His cheek facing her felt warm, and he guessed that she eyed him now. If he didn't ask her to dance now, someone else might, he reasoned, and she'd be lost to him. It was now or maybe never.

Allan braced himself, pushed his shoulders back, and made his arms hang an unnatural several inches away from his hips. He had seen movie stars who played tough Western heroes stand that way, and now he walked toward her, swinging his arms wide away from his body, as if he wanted to avoid striking two gun holsters.

Face to face in the light of the gym Allan thought her looks even more beautiful than in the defect-hiding darkness of the street.

"Yolanda, would you care to dance?"

"Yes, thank you," she said proudly, tilting her head to give her an aloof appearance.

She had a pleasant voice, he thought, guiding her to the floor. He didn't know how to dance, his awkward stiffness aggravated by a fear of pressing close to her. As he lifted her arm, and as she placed the other arm on his shoulder, he could smell her sweet perspiration, the odor leavened by a white talcum powder which he could still see. She probably didn't use underarm deodorant or perfume, he thought, not really caring about her smell, because she was pretty and warm. Neither he nor she spoke until the music stopped and he led her back to the same spot.

"Everbody lookin' at us," she said. "We the lightest ones here."

"Yeah."

"Allan, you know you hair is real straight." She came closer to him. "And you eyes is green, ain't they?"

The better to see you, my dear, he felt like saying, thinking about the wolf jumping out and Little Red Riding Hood seeing that he was a white boy. By way of response, he shrugged his shoulders.

"Hey, whitey!"

The fury in that word struck at his insides, enfeebling him, almost making him totter and drop like a dead autumn leaf. He wanted to shout, no, it's not true, I'm not, but all that came was a gurgle meant to be a denial. He had been called in the past by his fellow whites a kike, a sheeny, and other names which brought up fists and fights. But then, a Jew he was, and wanted to be. How could he defend his race now, when he was trying to deny it?

He turned to face Death's Head. "Me?" In one word, he tried to sound nice and placating, and in one glance surveyed the room for James and Ferry. He could see neither. He saw, however, the startled look in Yolanda's eyes. Now she knew.

"Out, whitey. We don't want no white mothahs here." Death's Head flicked a finger toward the door, his muscles

[174]

and veins bunching and popping like grapes on vines.

Allan looked at Yolanda. She glared with hate, not at Death's Head, but at him. He had deceived her. No, he thought, it wasn't that, but because she just hated whites.

"Ah catch you white tail here once more, ah'll whup it good," Death's Head said, stepping aside to let him pass.

He walked slowly toward the door, not bothering to find his friends and tell them of his shame. Only the dancers close to the disturbance knew, and only they followed him with their eyes as he left. Much later, under a moonless sky, he arrived at the store, dark and closed. He entered the side door of the building.

Upstairs, it was quiet, and he went into the bathroom. From the mirror his white and pale face bounced mockingly back at him. He rubbed and squeezed his cheeks as if he expected the pallidness to gain in color and intensity which would spread over his body.

His mind wandered and he imagined being a little white boy found homeless by Negroes. They raised him to become one of them, just like in the movies when a white son of dead pioneers was raised by Indians and later fell in love with an Indian girl. They'd nick their wrists with an arrow, holding them together to exchange drops of blood and thus become one in love and life.

Eyes closed, he held a wrist out to touch Yolanda's but sighed when he felt nothing and reopened them, blinking several times at the splotches of blood on the bathroom floor. He looked at his wrist and saw no break in the skin.

The drops led to his parents' bedroom, where he

flicked on a light switch and found his father lying on a scarlet-stained pillow. His mother, awakened by the light, began with a scream which gradually decreased in intensity to end as a low moan.

The store seemed to be always busy. While the old credit customers bought and paid immediately, the hard-cash ones who drank countless bottles of soda pop and continuously bought dime and quarter items appeared to increase in numbers and their purchases.

The money seemed to flow in. Several times during the day he had to shovel his hand into the till, lift out a stack of bills, and put it into a paper bag which he kept underneath the cash register. A dirty rag stuffed on top of the bag served to mask the money against possible thieves.

He seemed to work out a schedule, beginning with the store closing for two hours after lunch. The first hour he traveled to and from the bank to make a deposit. During the second he rested so that he'd be able to stay on his feet in the evening.

He seemed to learn new business tricks. Special sales printed by hand with red letters on white pasted on the windows greeted the neighborhood. He began to sell dry goods, which showed a good profit. In order to make room for hosiery and underwear, he got rid of the penny candy, a nerve-wracking bother which drew little profit but scores of noisy, thieving kids.

His profits soaring, he thought of hiring help. Sarah busied herself in their sunshiny suburban home. Allan, however, out of school for the summer, proved to be a great help after he had learned how to cut meat, and draw and quarter chickens.

Although he seemed to work harder with the increased business, some of his chores became lighter, as when the soda and beer companies began distributing throw-away bottles. No more was it necessary to worry about deposits, argue with strangers bearing bushels of bottles which they had purchased elsewhere, and sort and stuff the bottles in the wooden compartment cases. He decided not to hire anybody and to save the money instead.

Then he sold the store and bought a black Cadillac with thick tires and drove it to Florida.

He awoke with a start, reaching out blindly to snuff out the clock's alarm. He felt the bandage on his head and smelled the antiseptic.

A dream, a dream, he said softly to himself, his head aching unbearably as the events of the night projected rapidly on the screen of his closed eyelids.

The holdup man and the beating. Allan awakening him and the hysterics of Sarah, who insisted on calling an ambulance, a doctor, the police, even an agent to sell the store. At one o'clock in the morning, yet. His objections, saying he was all right, and when that didn't stop her, threatening to lock himself in the bathroom and see no one at all. They compromised. Okay, call the police, he said, thinking that didn't cost money. But no doctor. The police came, wrote, and left. Another Saturday night holdup. Sarah bandaged the head.

[177]

He had promised her he'd remain closed today but the store had to be opened. There was no money to pay the bills. Sunday the chain stores shut their doors, making it the only day for the small businessman to open his.

He sat at the edge of his bed, already too tired to take a hot bath to discourage the hemorrhoids which threatened like a man's angry fists before attacking. He had stood on his feet too long yesterday, he thought, looking at his legs. They're getting thinner. They look like an old man's, smooth and hairless. He sighed as he examined and pressed the blue veins which broke the whiteness of the skin.

A nice, thick pair of white socks, that's what I need. They cost about a dollar or maybe two bucks a pair. What difference does it make what they cost? I'm not going to spend the money anyway. Profit from the sale of a lousy loaf of bread is two cents. I'd have to sell a hundred breads to make enough to buy a two-dollar pair of socks.

The socks, thick with rayon and cotton and wool, would warm his feet and help to insulate them against the hard floor. But he thought also of the one hundred breads being passed over the counter, and of the jealous glint in the customer's eyes when the twenty-five cents rang on the register. Many times Farber felt like saying, look, all that's not profit. I'm not making twenty-five cents. Only two.

But *shvartzers,* what did they know?

No, he'd wear his old regular socks, torn in some places, but still serviceable. He could do without a new jacket, about fifteen hundred breads, and a soft drink with his lunch, five breads.

[178]

Sarah stirred and opened her eyes, sitting up to stare at him for a few moments before she spoke. "How do you feel?"

He pulled on a sock. "Could be worse. I'm already late opening the store."

"You deserve a day of rest. At least, today, with your head all bandaged up. Even the lowest of the lowest ditchdigger doesn't work seven days a week."

"Arguments before breakfast even? You'll wake Allan."

"Did you see what time he got in last night?" When he showed no reaction she breathed deeply and reached for her robe. "I'll make you breakfast."

Downstairs, they ate silently, avoiding each other's eyes, and staring into the coffee as if it held the secret to their future. Several times he opened his mouth to say something, to tell her he had to make some changes in running the store, but her sad, tired face stopped him. Only when he arose to rinse his cup did he speak.

"We can't go on like this. They're stealing and robbing us blind. All of them." He walked around the kitchen, stopped at the table, and put his fist on it. "I'm gonna get back at them. I'm gonna steal from them on the scale. A few pennies here, and a few there. It'll make up a bit for the losses."

Sarah shook her head. "So you penalize the ones who pay for the ones who get without paying. It doesn't make sense, Simon."

"It makes sense when you understand that the ones

[179]

who pay would love to steal if they could, too."

"Stealing because someone else steals just isn't right. If you don't have money, Simon, you don't have money. But if you're not honest, you've got nothing, no ideals. If you got ideals, you'd at least have something."

"So I got ideals and no money." He groaned humorously. "You know, it's easier to make money if you don't have ideals. I don't even know if I could cheat those people. I don't know whether because it's wrong, or because I'm afraid I'd get caught."

He put on his apron. "It couldn't be wrong because they'd be absorbing my losses. The big stores do it. Everybody cheats a little. Only I don't. Sarah, do you know what I think? Gittelson cheated us on the guarantee. That's right. What stopped him from sending in his friends and relatives to make the thousand-dollar guarantee?"

"They were all colored who came in. No whites."

"So he couldn't give them a few bucks and tell them to keep the free groceries as a bonus? Anything to get rid of this store. He could have also rung up two dollars on the register for a fifty-cent sale when I wasn't looking."

"The cash matched the register receipts."

"So he dropped in the extra dollar and a half. Anything's possible with a crook. What's a dollar and a half when you're getting rid of a lemon?"

"Ah, so the chickens are coming home to roost."

"What?"

"Never mind," she said. "Maybe it was because of the

Christmas holiday that they were able to meet the guarantee."

"We can't live from Christmas to Christmas." He looked at his watch. "I've got to open."

"Go. Your business is calling you." Her voice had a bitter, sarcastic ring.

A new policy is what's needed, he thought, scanning the street traversed by a few families on their way to church. Come what may, he'd have to tighten and toughen up. Don't blame the recession, the break-ins, the stealing, the credit losses. Maybe it's bad management. Maybe I'm not a businessman and don't have what it takes. What does it take?

The first customer asked for a can of pork and beans, marked on the shelf for thirty-eight cents. Farber asked for forty-two and waited for the whistled complaint, but the customer paid and left.

That's it. Charge more on Sundays. Keeping open wasn't just for their convenience. Let them pay for it. Other stores that open on a twenty-four-hour and Sunday basis do it.

"So who's cheating, anyway?" he said aloud to no one. "I'm not putting a thumb on the scale and I'm not short-weighing. So I overcharge a penny here, a penny there. Why not? They think and say I do anyway, even if I don't. But I'll just do it on Sunday."

My God, he thought. I'm going to have a nervous breakdown, talking to myself like that.

[181]

He looked around the store, wondering where else he might economize, save, tighten up and cut back. The credit's the main thing. What if he could charge interest for the credit? The big stores do it, so what's so terrible? He'd have to talk to Jimmy and the boys at the market about that.

The second customer, a youth who walked on the balls of his feet, making his already high, protruding buttocks ride higher on long pin legs, ordered a box of cereal and a loaf of bread.

Farber rang the purchase up and shoved the items into a bag. As an afterthought, he removed them and replaced the bag on a shelf. "Here you are."

The youth stared incredulously. "What happened to mah bag?"

"You don't need no bag. They're already wrapped."

"No they ain't."

"Sure they are." Farber tapped the cereal carton and squeezed the cellophane wrapping of the bread. "See?"

"Sheet!"

"Bags cost me two for a penny. I make a lousy two cents on a loaf of bread. How do you expect me to make a living if I have to give you a bag for every piece of crap that's already covered?"

"That your problem." The youth grinned maliciously, picked up the goods, and headed for the door, where he turned and shouted, "Cheap Jew sheet!"

Farber ran after him, almost stumbling over Mrs. Hobson, who entered and blocked the way at the door.

"You sure in a hurry for church this mornin'," she

smiled, delight on her face from tweaking a Jewish man. "Jesus can wait."

Farber's anger occupied his mind. He watched the boy run like a track star until an alley enveloped him. Only then did the grocer turn toward Mrs. Hobson, not conscious of what she had said.

"How are you doing there, Mrs. Hobson?"

Disappointed, she replied, "All righty."

"How them chicks of yours?" he asked, more interested in knowing whether she came to pay something on account.

"Gettin' along nicely." She placed a bottled quart of milk on the counter. "This here's sour."

He thought, why should I accept it? He'd only have to argue with the milkman tomorrow and maybe or maybe not get some money back on it, depending on the mood of the deliveryman. Yesterday he'd have taken it without question from Mrs. Hobson, but today's a new policy.

"How come it's half empty? Took you that long to find out it's no good?" He laughed. "Maybe you drank half of it two weeks ago and found it in the back of the refrigerator this morning. Huh?"

He watched as she shrugged her shoulders. He'd be damned if he was going to take it back. Maybe it wasn't milk at all but white powder she mixed with water after drinking the milk.

"Sorry, Mrs. Hobson. All my milk's fresh. I don't know when you bought that. You haven't been in the store for the last few days."

[183]

"Got it from Miz Simon when you wasn't here."

"Wait a minute. I'll call her."

She grinned like a bashful schoolgirl and left, saying nothing further but leaving the bottle on the counter. He picked it up and put it aside. Tomorrow he'd return it to the milkman and maybe collect on it.

Why not? I'd have given her the money but she already owes me a small fortune. Might as well get something back on it. He made up his mind not to accept so readily stale bread or rotten produce from customers eager to return them. He wasn't running a department store.

He shook his head with disbelief over how he used to give away for nothing paper bags to customers who asked for them to sack school or work lunches. Stupid, stupid. But no more.

His new policy, maybe it'll work after all.

I'm learning, give me time, he begged himself, now convinced that he had what it takes.

Allan, faced with guilt about not being around when his father needed him the most, and aggrieved that his friends had deserted him at the dance when he needed them just as badly, skipped going with James and the gang and spent the next day after school helping in the store. Later, he did his homework in his room at the window where he could overlook the store front and watch out for suspicious characters.

As he studied, or peered into the street below, Yolanda come to his mind, not the last image of her twisted face, but a smiling portrait of their first contact. He felt his body stirring for her, and then for Mother Matthews, whose likeness superimposed itself over that of the girl.

Picking up his pen, he began writing in his school notebook.

Dear Dr. Thompson,
You wanted to know who gave me the sickness I had when I visited you. It was a lady, Mother Matthews who lives at 1223 Parkway. Please don't tell her it was me who wrote.

After reading the letter twice, he added:

I am the white boy who visited you last week.
James Ferry

The next day after he mailed the letter to Dr. Thompson in care of the clinic, he changed his lookout point so he could see Mother Matthews' apartment house by watching from another, more advantageous window of his room. She lived nearly two blocks away, but he was certain he'd be able to spot an official-looking ambulance from his window.

School dragged on endlessly for him. He told his mother he felt sick the following two days and moved his bed next to the window. Suppose he had missed the doctor the first day while in school? he wondered. Suppose they don't even bother to send the doctor down? Dr. Thompson did say they were very busy. Or maybe they'll just send her a letter telling her to come down to the clinic, and she does, without any fuss.

It soon occurred to him that Dr. Thompson might drive an unmarked car in order to remain anonymous, or some other doctor might go instead. He scanned every face that came near the apartment and then gave up, realizing he wouldn't be able to tell a strange doctor from one of her customers.

Allan made vague promises that he'd never visit Mother Matthews again, not so much that she made him pay money, but because he could never go to a whore who had other men all of the time. It was like eating food that a stranger bit off and chewed for you. Maybe even swallowed and then upchucked.

Reassuring himself that he didn't write Dr. Thompson to seek revenge on her, he thought that it would be terrible if she weren't treated, for her sake as well as for innocent victims of passion, such as Yolanda and himself. That's it. He couldn't go to Mother Matthews and then see Yolanda because he might contaminate her.

He returned to school and passed by Mother Matthews' apartment house on the way home. A truck with *Washington, D.C. Department of Public Health* on its paneled door stood at the curb.

Good, he thought. That's in case he'd ever want to go back to her.

Quickly, Sarah covered her clothes with a bedspread and listened again. No, it was the rain on the roof, not footsteps.

For the third time in two days she laid her clothes on the bed, sorting and arranging, trying to determine which

[186]

would fit in her suitcase and what would be needed for a long stay. Spring and summer wardrobe, for sure.

Wardrobe, she repeated to herself. A word she hadn't heard in a long time. She'd been a virtual prisoner during the long winter, afraid to go out, taking a cab whenever she went shopping or to a movie. Yesterday, she had visited the hairdresser at the beauty parlor after hibernating for almost five months. Hairdresser, beauty parlor, two more distant terms.

She had decided to salvage her appearance since seeing Gladys weeks and weeks ago, but the shock yesterday of what the store had done to her, plus the terrible attack on her husband by a holdup man, made up her mind to do something more drastic, like leaving him.

The mirror in the beauty parlor reflected listless eyes, ringed with deep depressions of darkness. Her once ivory skin showed sallow, with many new creases all over and the few old ones cut deeper. Gray hair cried for dyeing.

Was it possible that fear and worry could do this to her in so short a time? she wondered. Possible or not, she'd had enough.

He tried hard, but their world was falling all around them. Nobody worked like this anymore. In that same rare trip out of the neighborhood she had visited a supermarket, surprised that she had almost forgotten what they looked like and overwhelmed by the selection, the array, the neatness, and the low prices. Benny was right. Simon is living and working in the past, like a man with a spade trying to work against a steam shovel.

[187]

Surly with recent memories, she took a restless turn around the room, thinking of his frustrations which made her the victim. He'd get up early to go to the produce market, but stay there talking with his cronies long after he was supposed to open the store. That chore was left to her, in spite of the fact that he had promised not to ask her to help unless really needed.

It was as if postponement of the store's opening relieved his frustrations. If the store was such a torture, why didn't he sell out? At last, she thought, the chickens were coming home to roost.

She gathered her clothes in a pile, undecided what to do with it. The suitcase protruded from behind a closet door, while her bureau drawer gaped open, as if begging for return of the clothes.

If she didn't leave now, she would the next time he picked on her in front of customers. He knew where everything was because he constantly shifted stock during dull periods to keep himself occupied. When it got busy and she'd help, he seemed to gloat at her inability to find things. And when she'd finally ask, he'd point and gruffly remark in front of everybody, "Don't you know where anything is around here?"

The store was doing it to him, turning a good and gentle man into a tyrant, of that she was convinced. Yet she could forgive most anything, but not lying. Well, no, it wasn't exactly a lie. He withheld information, like about the first burglary and then about the loan from Benny. That money was already eaten up by the store.

[188]

How much longer? Lies and promises. Trouble after trouble. It will all end with them going back with their tail between their legs.

The good things were few. The cold weather passed and most of the rats were dead. His arthritis had cleared up, but would return, she guessed, if he'd ever go back to carpentry. The bad things were many. The holdup and attack on Simon, the day-to-day fear, and the lousy business.

And now, the trouble with Allan. She had seen him at the register when he thought no one was looking. Also, money disappeared from various places, the kitchen table, her bureau, even her pocketbook. He stole for the *shvartzer* gang he belonged to. She had proof. Didn't she also find in his drawer anti-white literature? Yet she couldn't tell her husband about it until she had a chance to talk with the boy first.

Allan needed her, and she'd take him along with her. For that matter, Simon needed her, too. She resented the idea within her mind that she only went through the motions of leaving him just to show herself that she still had some fight, some rebellion left in her.

A worry that she had become more apathetic and willing to accept his words and promises, mostly because there was nothing else, made her frown. Well, she had something else. Her departure.

Checking the bureau to see what else she might take, she found the bank book he had given her. A finger ran over and then rubbed the fifty-dollar figure, the one and

[189]

only deposit listed, as if disbelieving the eyes that the money was still there.

Warm air blew in from an open window and brushed against her cheek. Summer, already here, she thought, replacing the book. She could always leave, and she would, she decided, if things didn't pick up within the first few weeks of the warm weather.

He waited across the street from the front entrance of the school, his chest heaving as he sucked air to catch the breath lost from the twelve-block jog-and-walk from his own school. As he had done yesterday, he skipped the last hour period, history, in order to arrive at Yolanda's school before it let out for the day.

He didn't even know her last name. Maybe she had told him, but now he couldn't recall it.

Yolanda. What a strange name, so unlike the names of the girls back home, the Susans, Judys, Deborahs, and Sandras. Yolanda. The name conjured visions for him of things Spanish, foreign, and exciting.

He was convinced that she wasn't angry at him for lying about being Negro. She just had to look angry because everyone was watching them. During the first few minutes it had looked as if she really liked him, of this he was certain.

Although he nodded hello to Negro girls at school, he never had enough nerve to sit down at the lunch table with any, or to walk home with them. When James and Ferry were with girls, he usually kept away, except that one night of the dance. At school, the girls at first treated him with

[190]

cordiality only because of curiosity. When he became less of an oddity, they turned cool and distant.

Yolanda was the only one he had approached, the only one who allowed him to like her. He was glad she went to another school which made it easier for him to daydream about her being his girl. He knew that if she were present during the day in the hallways of his own school, she'd become like the rest of them.

Standing behind a tree and car so that he wouldn't be conspicuous, he wore a cap pulled down to his eyebrows, forcing him to lift his jaw so that he could see. Yesterday he had also made use of the cap and a tree but had watched from the rear of the school. She hadn't passed, and he wondered whether she left via the front entrance, or was absent that day. He had even waited more than an hour, until four o'clock, when the students who were kept after school for disciplinary reasons were permitted to leave.

A bell rang.

Seconds later, they streamed out of the double doors, boys and girls, equally shouting and pushing their way to the head of the crowd. They rushed to leave the building, as if to escape a fire. Forearms parallel, they shoved forward like football players until they were several yards from the doorway and well on the sidewalk, where they stopped pushing and broke up into stationary groups, chatting, laughing, and calling to each other.

The girls carried books. The boys did not, and used their hands either to plunge them deeply into trouser pockets or to hold cigarettes.

Soon Yolanda appeared, swept along for a few mo-

[191]

ments like a leaf driven by the wind in a street gutter. She stopped, waved to several students, two boys and a girl, and then joined them.

Allan flushed and immediately drew closer against the tree for fear that she might see him, but then just as quickly stepped out in the clear, worried that she might not. He wanted to do something to attract her attention, to run, to jump, even to pick a fight with one of the boys who accompanied her.

She strolled with her friends in the direction away from which Allan had come. He followed them, readjusting his cap, miserably conscious of his color, yet assured that he passed as a light-skinned student. He had a book with him and imitated what he believed was the Negro boys' typical walk, the bobbing and weaving and the striding on the balls of the feet.

Now only several yards behind, he fixed his eyes on her, intensely jealous of the two boys, one of whom occasionally touched her, on the arm, shoulder, and once or twice, on the waist. They laughed loudly, singing, and then playing a modified hopscotch in which they jumped on one leg trying to avoid the lines in the pavement.

Presently one couple peeled off to go down another street, leaving Yolanda and the remaining youth, who wore a windbreaker. Allan couldn't see what his face looked like but he hated him nonetheless.

They passed another block. Allan dropped farther behind them since other students thinned out, leaving three others on the street besides Yolanda and her friend. Anxiety remained with Allan, who expected her to glance back and see only him.

His heart throbbed irregularly for a few moments when he saw them grasp each other's hands, but he was relieved that the hand holding proved to be a farewell, for the boy crossed the street and entered a building.

She was alone.

He stalked her cautiously, not daring to catch up to her because she'd then know he had followed her. He hoped that she wouldn't at any moment go into one of the dilapidated apartment houses that made up the street. Worse still, she might even turn and confirm a gnawing suspicion that she really hated whites.

As she crossed the intersection to the next block the idea came to him of running completely around the new block she was on and then meeting her face to face as she reached the corner. This way, he thought, he'd give the appearance of a chance meeting. He'd also be able to gauge her expression of either hate, like, or indifference, maybe even love, as they strode toward each other.

Although tired from traveling the long distance that afternoon, the prospect of finally being with her again through a clever maneuver on his part gave him renewed energy. He waited until she moved a short distance up the block before he raced to catch her at the corner.

His ears became a battleground as air slammed them while the frenzied pulsation of his heart reverberated against them from the inside. Faster and faster he ran. The flanks of his rib cage ached from running and his feet burned from two days of pounding sidewalks.

At the end of the third side of the block he stopped to catch his breath, not wanting to let her see him gasping and holding his sides. That would make him appear too suspicious, or unmanly, or both. He might be able to lie about his presence in her neighborhood, but he knew he'd falter in explaining why he had been running.

Straightening his back, he stepped to the corner and turned to greet her. She had vanished. He blinked hard several times before realizing that she had entered into one of the houses, but which one?

Allan, like a dog looking for its master, scampered down the street, peering into each doorway, searching for a sign he knew he wouldn't find, a dropped book, a torn piece of her green cloth coat caught on a sharp edge of a door, even one of her white kneesocks which could have been strangely lost. No sign betrayed her passing.

He scanned the last names on mailboxes in the hope that he'd be able to recognize hers, but all of the names were common, and unfamiliar in their familiarity. Then he wondered if he could knock on each door of the several apartment buildings.

Returning to the spot where he had last seen her, he swore that he'd come back tomorrow. No, he couldn't wait until the next day, he had to see her now, that afternoon, and he'd stay until she came out for an errand or to visit friends.

Allan waited until it became too dark to stand around. A new plan came to him as he turned to leave; he would skip all of his classes tomorrow and catch her on her way to school.

Neither his mother nor father questioned his leaving early for classes the next day. He arrived on her block with plenty of time to spare. As the minutes passed, his breathing became heavier and the tightness in his throat increased.

She came in his direction slowly, hesitating slightly when she recognized him. Her face registered anxiety intermingled with a tremulous curiosity. She motioned as if to avoid him by crossing to the other side of the street, but he anticipated her move and stepped quickly up to her, calling her by name.

"Hello," she replied, anxiously looking around to see if anybody watched them. "What you doing here?"

"Just passing through." Of a sudden, in spite of his forwardness in coming to her street, he became painfully shy in her presence. So much so, that he wanted to turn and run from her. He even contemplated asking her to do something he knew she would refuse, thus setting the stage for a mutually satisfying disengagement.

"How about skipping school?"

"You crazy, boy. What you want to get us in trouble for?"

"We won't get into no trouble. Nobody'd know the difference. The kids do it all the time."

She lowered her eyes. "No place to go," she said in an unconvincing voice which indicated an interest in skipping, if not sudden, near total collapse of her reasons for not skipping. "It too dangerous to mess around in the

[195]

park. Someone from school might see us."

What did she mean by "mess around," he wondered, as other students of all ages passed around them, throwing glances at him and his white skin. Excitement shot through him as he envisioned lying with her on the grass.

"We could ride the bus for a while, then we could go to the museum." He watched her expression change to one of eagerness. "It's nice there. I've got some money so we could eat out and have a good time."

"Only thing is ah got to mind my sisters when they come home from school."

"Okay," Allan said, now certain of his newly won prize. "We'll be back before three o'clock. We got all day."

They stood looking awkwardly at each other, until she pointed to the corner. "You wait for me at the bus stop. Ah'm gonna put mah books back."

Yolanda returned about ten minutes later, wearing the same pink dress she had worn at the dance. Allan's heart beat quickly with the victory. She had also put on lipstick, powdered her cheeks with a cheap rouge which caked like glacial scratchings, and covered herself with a perfume that made Allan after a few moments want to turn his head away from her and breathe fresh air.

"Come on," she said. "Let's get out of here before someone see us."

The bus, stuffy and hot, braked and hissed to a halt on Pennsylvania Avenue at a bus transfer point about half a dozen blocks from the museum. Allan puzzled over what was worth more to him, to sit next to her again on the next bus and feel the exciting tinge of warmth from her thighs, or to walk in the fresh air. She answered the question for him.

"Ah don't feel like catching no other bus."

"Okay, we can walk."

He searched his mind in vain for something to say, even though she didn't particularly seem to care whether they conversed or not. Mercifully, on the bus she had looked out the window while he sat on the aisle seat, staring ahead of him. The riders, all of them Negro, had not guessed that they were together.

Now they walked in silence for a few more minutes as Allan's mind blurred with panic to find a topic of conversation. He finally thought about the incident at the dance and, wishing to clear it up once and for all, as well as to end the embarrassing stillness, he asked her whether she minded being with a white boy.

"Not unless you do."

"I don't mind being with a white boy," he joked back, glancing sidelong at her face to see her smile. In truth, he thought, she was lighter than he. Their hair, although the same shade of black, differed only in texture; his, fine and silky, while hers was thick and strong, almost as crisp and tough as fibers of wool.

He again thought of the wrist and blood exchange scene from the movies as an idea came to him about Solomon and the Queen of Sheba. He asked her if she knew about the ancient lovers. She shook her head.

"Solomon was the King of Israel a long time ago," he

said, thankful for the first time for the many afternoons spent attending Hebrew school, yet determined now to establish an unbreakable racial link with Yolanda by embellishing the story. "He fell in love with the Queen of Sheba. She was Negro and ruled a Negro country."

Allan examined her face for favorable reaction as he related how the King of Israel, a Jewish country, had married the Queen, who bore many children, the ancestors of Jews today. Their countries, Negro and Jewish, had been united, he continued, explaining the reason why so many Jews were dark people.

"Did you know that Israel today is really on the African continent and that Jews in Egypt used to be slaves, just like the Negro here?"

She shrugged her shoulders. "So what? Where do that leave me?"

"Don't you know?" he whined with disappointment.

"Know what?"

"I'm Jewish."

"So what?"

Allan felt as if his speech had been wasted.

"You still a white boy. So don't make out that you better than you are."

To him, he had failed. It sounded as if his whiteness were a terrible barrier for her to overcome. He thought hard, trying to reason and make up excuses why she could like him despite his being white. What had happened at the dance was one thing. Surrounded by her friends, she had to act the part. But now, alone with him, she could speak and act without fear. But if she didn't care for him, why was she here? he asked himself, disturbed at the thought that maybe she felt it was better than being in school.

They became silent again, listening to their own footsteps on the pavement. Few people walked the downtown streets, being either at work or school. It was too early for most shoppers and sightseers.

Allan felt a sense of relief when they approached the museum and climbed its steps to the entrance between marble columns. Inside, a bored guard sat on a stool holding a device which he used to count visitors. He immediately snapped his head up when he saw them enter. An amused grin appeared on his thin face.

"Say, what're you kids doing outta school?"

Allan, stricken by the unexpected question, gasped, and spoke in a voice that stuttered. "We got an excuse from our teacher. You see, we're doing a special project. Visit here and make a report to the class."

The guard's grin widened as he thrust a leg out to prevent their passing. "Oh, yeah. Let's have a look at the note from your teacher."

"What note?" Allan said. "She didn't say nothing about a note."

"Can't let you in here without a note," the guard said, leering at Yolanda. "No telling what might happen to me if I did. Might even lose my job." He smiled confidently. "I've got to do my duty."

Yolanda's face twisted into a snarl. "You don't have to do nothing. All you got to do is push that button on that thing evertime someone pass. Sheet, Allan! Let's go."

She gripped Allan's hand and pulled him around the guard's leg. Startled, the guard remained seated, fidgeting with and palming his mechanical hand counter. Allan followed her meekly, not daring to look over his shoulder at the guard.

She, however, not content with her victory, fired another burst without turning her head. "Besides, we sixteen and don't have to go to school if we don't want to so don't give me none of you lip about no excuse from a teacher."

The guard growled something under his breath and shook his head viciously, but his defeat was total as he thumbed two clicks on the counter.

Allan, shaken by the exchange, noted that she had said more within the previous few seconds than she had during the past hour with him. He felt pride and satisfaction that his Sheba had fought and won a battle for him. Had he broken through her aloofness?

They wandered hand in hand into a hall displaying an exhibit on the races of man. Figures of wax, with red, brown, black, yellow, and white faces, and wearing many costumes, stared out of their glass display cases with the same vacant expressions.

As he looked down to see the soft hand still enclasping his own, he remembered words taught in school or read somewhere about the equality of man and the brotherhood of races. The term "darker-pigmented brethren" came to his mind. His heart, quickly filled with love, went out to all mankind, and to Yolanda. In a moment of ecstasy mixed

[200]

with humanitarian fervor and sexual love, he raised her hand and kissed the back of it. She responded by bringing his hand around to her lips.

Soon they found themselves in an alcove and out of sight of the few tourists who were also in the hall. Like marionettes controlled by an instinctive force, they embraced and kissed. He felt her shivering body against his, and then her warm and wet lips covering his own. Although he responded, he couldn't concentrate on her, afraid that someone might interrupt them at any moment. He had to say something that would temporarily break their ardor; words that wouldn't destroy it completely but that would postpone it until a better time.

"This is the first time I ever kissed a colored girl," he said, immediately thinking of Mother Matthews but then just as quickly eliminating her as far from being a girl.

She kissed him again, darting her tongue in his mouth with snakelike rapidity, and then whispering in his ear, "Too many nosybodies 'round here. Let's go home."

He hated to return to her neighborhood where the passersby would glare hatred at him for being with her. He wondered if she suffered to see whites stare at her unrelentingly. Then he remembered how she had handled the guard and felt sure she'd hit back at anybody, black or white, who tried to hurt them.

"Okay, let's go."

Emboldened by being the only passengers on the bus coming back, they held each other's hand, despite the white driver whose eyes pierced with grim inquiry from the rear-view mirror, watching them more diligently than the road ahead of him. Although the seat in front of them shielded most of their bodies and arms from the driver's eyes, Allan felt inclined not to press his thigh against hers.

If Yolanda became his girlfriend, he'd spend much time being aggravated by museum guards, police, bus drivers, and theater ushers who'd take little pain to disguise looks of displeasure and outright hatred. What would his parents think about Yolanda? His mother would probably argue with his father again about moving to a white or Jewish neighborhood. Her parents? He envisioned himself caught in a Romeo-Juliet situation.

Her apartment consisted of one small room and a long, narrow kitchen. In the middle of the room stood a bed and two smaller cots. On the wall, a bumpy, badly hung wallpaper, designed with the words CARTE DU JOUR and covered with drawings of menus, chefs with tall white hats, champagne bottles, lobsters, and the Eiffel Tower, covered space not taken up by two windows and a closet.

Allan, with scarcely enough room to move, felt uncomfortable facing a crucifix which hung crookedly near one Eiffel Tower. Still, he found it hard to take his eyes away from a muscular Jesus whose knees turned effeminately to one side like a girl's at a beauty contest. Inches away, on a shelf, a can of insect spray rested next to a propped-up photograph of two little dark girls with pigtails.

[202]

"Who are the two girls?"

"They my sisters. Ah've got to take care of them when they come from school."

"Until your mother and father come home?"

She looked toward a window. A slight frown creased around her lips. "My father went away for a while. My mother come home about seven o'clock. When Josie and Loretta come home, they usually play outside."

She asked him to take off his jacket and shoes and lie down on the bed. "Ah'd love to bring you slippers, but ah don't have no men's slippers." She removed her shoes and lay down beside him.

He touched her bare arm with a slight pinch. "Say," he smiled, "the color doesn't come off."

Now she rubbed his arm. "Ah'm gonna see if my color could come off on you so you don't look like the color of vomit." They laughed, and Allan had to bite his tongue not to say that his skin was slightly darker than hers. Soon they embraced, but only for a moment before she sat up and got out of bed. "You just can't put no trust in no man," she said, halfway into the kitchen.

Noises of plates, pans, and silverware being used filled the room. "What are you doing?" he shouted, vexed at her leaving so abruptly.

"Ah fix you somethin' to eat, Allan."

He entered the kitchen. "I don't want nothing . . ." Astonished by what he saw, he couldn't finish his sentence.

She held a spoon in a pan on the burner, moving her hand in a circular fashion as if stirring something. The

[203]

burner was turned off and there was nothing in the pan. "What are you messing around with? There's nothing in that pan."

She looked down at the vessel as if to dispute him, but only shook her head and sighed. "Ah just felt like doing that."

Allan wanted to lead her back to the bed, but he felt strangely guilty about doing so. Her childlike behavior made him reluctant to do anything but stand there, hoping and yet not hoping she would suggest the bed. He reached out for her but she took his hand and kissed it as she had in the museum.

In a few minutes' struggle her dress came off in his hand, revealing a wasp-waisted body the color of light red mixed with yellow. She wore no brassiere. Her nipples resembled nuts on a lump of butter. Her panties, too large for her and obviously her mother's, disclosed a good part of pubic hair.

"You want to fuck me but you better not give me a baby unless you want to take care of it and pay the bills."

Allan nodded, "Yeah, yeah." He tugged at his belt buckle but a noise behind him made him turn his head to see the front door open and the two girls in the photograph walk in, each carrying a book and papers.

"Josie and Loretta," Yolanda said unhesitatingly, "go in the kitchen for a cookie while ah gives this laundryman some dirty clothes."

The girls ran into the kitchen. Allan, breathless, whispered, "I better go, huh?"

"Yeah. Maybe some other time. Tonight."

"No, I got a meeting," he said proudly. "The Black Brigade."

"Okay, you come to me again. We be alone and ah let you do what you want to."

"Yeah, okay," he whispered with passion, but to him it sounded like instructions to an athletic teammate. He left before her sisters returned, but they didn't worry him as much as her playing with the empty pan on the shut-off burner.

Farber groaned as he kneeled to put away bottles and cartons of milk in the bottom of the meat showcase. When he finished, he remained on his knees and rubbed the stiffness in his neck.

Already creaking with old age, he thought. How could I work at a new life when the old one doesn't let me alone? He looked at his hands. They appeared to be larger, more knobbed and calloused than when he had worked as a carpenter. This is no white-collar job, he told himself. Unless you mean the white of the apron string around your neck. A clean, white apron put on in the morning turned grimy black by the end of the fifteen-hour day, except for the string.

Standing up, he felt sweat on his forehead. So early in the morning and it's hot, he thought, remembering that Jimmy had told him that Washington usually didn't have a spring. Cold one week gave way to heat the next, without much in between.

[205]

The sound of water rushing told him Sarah was cleaning dishes in the kitchen. Soured by the thought that she looked as if she had an argument brewing in her mind at breakfast, he decided against getting another cup of coffee from her.

A white man dressed in a business suit entered the store. He carried a notebook and a clipboard, and immediately Farber knew that he was an inspector, probably one checking on a new law that required seven specks of sawdust to each square inch around the butcher block.

Last week a city health inspector had demanded that Farber lay a fresh coat of paint on the ceiling of the walk-in since flaking paint looked like it might fall at any time onto some of the meat that hung on hooks attached to beams. The man had overlooked nothing. He ran a penknife along the wood in the meat section of the cooler and dug out gray, putrid pieces of fat. The wood ought to be metal, he said, citing a law. Then he ordered that a sink be put in near the butcher block to clean the knives, saws, and grinders.

But they're cleaned in the back, in the kitchen, Farber had retaliated, smugly triumphant that he had been able to trip up the inspector with so simple a reply. New ordinance says you got to have a sink in the same room, or no more than three feet away from the block, the man counterattacked, allowing himself a regretful smile. Farber had protested, saying that his kitchen sink was located right through the storeroom, no more than about twelve feet away. The man smiled again and wrote out a thirty-day

[206]

alteration and installation notice for the paint job, metal refrigerator lining, and sink.

The figure of the estimated two hundred dollars for the job swam in Farber's mind as he greeted the new inspector coolly. How much is this guy going to cost me? he thought.

"Mr. Farber?"

"Yeah."

"We've had a complaint that you're overcharging your customers."

"Let them go somewhere else," Farber said, surprised at the soft tone of his response in spite of the quick anger that built up. "It's a free country." He paused and reached for a dustrag to clean the shelves since he wanted to appear cool and unconcerned. "Who complained?"

"We don't see where that's relevant."

"Who are you?"

"I represent the city's consumer protection office. Now let me tell you something. We can't tell you what to charge your customers, but you can get a summons for misrepresentation."

"What're you talking about?"

"Like advertising. You advertise you sell something for twenty cents when actually you sell it for twenty-five cents, we can get you on that. Or there's an ordinance that says you have to post prices on the shelves and each item has to be marked."

"I don't advertise. Who can afford it?"

The man pointed to the windows, splattered with posters announcing sales. "What do you call that?"

Farber shrugged. "They're the same as the prices in the store." The man has no case, he thought, relieved that there would be no fine, or legal action, or expense involved.

The inspector said nothing but walked around, poking around the cans, looking for marked prices. He picked up a can of tuna fish marked in red with 2¢ OFF and a can of the same product without the sale label. "This says two cents off but it's the same price as the fish with the old label here."

"I charge according to what I pay for it. The manufacturer puts on whatever labels he wants, that's his business, but he still charges the same price to me. Am I supposed to pay out of my own pocket just because of the label?"

"Well, the manufacturer should pass on the savings to the grocer and then to the consumer, but it doesn't work that way. The grocer is stuck with a phony label. We try . . ."

Farber impatiently cut him off. "So what are you telling me that for? I got no control over that. Is that what one of my customers complained about?"

"Well, it's not one. It's a group"—he glanced at his notebook—"called the Black Liberation Movement. Now I know a lot of us are putting up with a lot of this type of organization lately, but we have to do our jobs. A complaint has been forwarded to us with a petition signed by about twenty-five persons."

[208]

Farber, at first bewildered, laughed. "I don't even have that many customers."

"The petition states that you overcharge on many items. And it has a list here of the products bought, the prices, and the dates."

"So sue me," Farber said belligerently, buoyed up by the knowledge that the inspector had no power to act. He fought an impulse to turn around and walk into the kitchen, leaving the man alone and looking foolish.

"We can't tell you what to charge your customers. But think of these poor people here. They can't afford to be victimized."

"What about me? I can afford to be victimized? Do you have an office that protects the grocer? You should. I pay taxes, too. More than half the block here. How come you don't investigate how they steal from me every chance they get?"

"Mr. Farber, losing your temper won't solve this problem. Now, you're doing nothing illegal . . ."

"So I charge them. I carry them on my back for weeks giving them food without money . . ."

". . . but you'll find that soon the competition of the stores with lower prices will get the best of you."

"Do the chains do that?"

"What?"

"Give credit? No, they don't. I have losses. I worry. So my customers have to pay a little more for the credit. Everybody knows that prices are higher in smaller stores. It's like combat pay. Do you know what combat pay is? It's when a soldier gets more money for being shot at. I've got to make it up somehow. This is the answer."

"Price gouging isn't the answer."

"So find me another answer."

The inspector breathed deeply. "I'll have to file a report of this. As you know, there's nothing illegal . . ."

Farber nodded his head, as if listening. He watched the man's mouth open and close, and then the fingers write with a pen in the notebook. Soon the legs carried the man out.

Losing his temper felt good. He'd have to try it more often. Maybe with the people who owed him money. From now on, he thought, remembering a suggestion that Jimmy had made, there would be a charge of a dime each time to cash their welfare checks. He wasn't running a check-cashing service.

"Simon?" Sarah's voice carried from the kitchen. "Who was that?"

He'd have that coffee, after all.

She sat gloomily at the kitchen table while he poured coffee into his cup and told how he had handled the latest city inspector. "A first-class *nudnick.* Do you want some coffee?"

"Simon, we've got to have a talk. It's important."

It bothered him that she ignored his question and appeared disinterested in his triumph over the inspector. He dreaded listening to what she thought was important. It was probably the moving to the suburbs. He decided to torpedo her argument before she began.

"I know what you're worried about. Florida is still a

little ways off. You got to work hard for something you really want. Make a few sacrifices."

"I'm not worried about Miami, Simon. Nothing could be further from my mind. It's Allan I want to talk about."

Comforted that it was Allan and not the store, and still cheerful over his rout of the inspector, Farber made an effort to be serious. "He's getting to be a big shot. He's been staying out too late every night." No big problem, Farber thought, despite the Negro school and neighborhood. Any boy could stand practical experience in knowing another race, but Negro schools lagged behind the white ones in the suburbs. Everyone knows that. One year or so in a bad school wouldn't hurt Allan, he rationalized.

"If we don't get Allan out of here he'll soon be like the rest of them," Sarah said. "Smoke marijuana, rob, steal, rape. Is this what you're working for?"

She caught Farber by surprise. He twisted in his chair and put the coffee cup down, trying to gain time to think. She tricked him into making a decision about a house by bringing up Allan's immediate welfare, he thought, deciding that silence was his best defense for the moment.

Sarah handed him several pieces of paper. "Look what I found in his drawer."

Farber tried to smile to minimize whatever importance they had, but he could not, immediately recognizing the mimeographed copies as being of the same cheap sort that Fat Nasty had handed to him months ago. He'd never forget that. He hastily glanced at the material, all of it violently anti-white.

"*Shvartzer* stuff. Black Liberation Movement. I see it

[211]

once in a while. So Allan picked up a couple of sheets he found in the gutter. So what?"

"His name is on it." She pointed to a column of print at the bottom of one of the pages. "See? Under where it says something about new members."

Farber shook his head. "It's crazy. A mistake. I don't understand how they let a white boy, a Jewish boy . . . where is he now?"

"Out. Where else? Who knows what he's doing now? Don't waste your breath on him. I tried. He told me nothing's wrong and ran out screaming like a wild Indian that he was late for a meeting and that I should leave him alone."

"Meeting? What meeting?"

"Who knows? That gang of his."

"Well, you can't lock him up in a cage like he was a canary. He's got to be out."

"In a neighborhood like this?"

Again, the store, he thought. "Another year, Sarah. Please!" He picked up his coffee and poured it into the sink, wishing to show her that he was too agitated to drink and that she had badly affected his mood. "At most, a year. Maybe even six to eight months we'll have enough to move out of here. I just need a little more time."

"Please, Simon. No more promises. I don't need them anymore."

"Don't you see," he continued, paying no attention to her, "an apartment or house will eat up most of what we earn now. And then there's the time it'll take us to get to and from the store."

[212]

"Allan's been stealing money from the register," she said abruptly, unable to hold back the weapon she had been saving. "I caught him. He's giving it to his gang. To Tammu."

"It's a boy's gang. Not the Black Liberation Movement."

"You just said the papers were from the Movement."

Farber, beaten, sat down. A matchstick on the table fell prey to his angry fingers. He lifted his head and unwittingly cracked the matchstick, subconsciously knowing that he wouldn't need it any longer.

"If you want to, we'll go ahead and move. If you want to stay at home all day, that's okay, too. I'll be in the store by myself." He realized but did not care that his words meant her main reason for moving was to avoid helping in the store. "I can manage by myself."

"We can't move so stop talking about it. I know it. But you can take care of what you have to take care of."

They looked at each other with wary impatience. Finally, he nodded his head.

"What do I have to take care of now?"

"Talk to Allan. But he won't listen, so you'll have to see Tammu, too. Tell him to keep away from our boy."

"All right," he said, happy to get peace, nevertheless feeling that he had succeeded in postponing again the business of moving. As far as Tammu was concerned, Farber thought, a chewing out was long overdue.

About fifteen boys sat crosslegged on the concrete floor under the big white X on the ceiling. For Allan, the meeting of the Black Brigade held the same thrill for him as the first he had attended long ago when James and Ferry introduced him as a boy who had just moved into the neighborhood. They accepted him as a light-skinned member.

As on the other meeting nights, when fire in a trash can suffused the shack with an eerie glow, Allan gazed at their faces and arms. He thought of how mysterious and masculine their brown and black skin was, shining in the firelight along with their yellow and blue and green shirts. He wanted to have their shiny black musculature, instead of his own white arms, flat with no sinewy definition.

Their hair was rough and matted, the way hair should be, he imagined, not soft, long, and fragile like a white man's, but strong, like a powerful animal's. He would take a jar of hair pomade from the store and use it to make his hair thick and kinky, he thought. He cursed his straight hair.

His own skin, what could he do for it? Buy a sunlamp, of course! He had seen one in the drugstore selling for about ten dollars. Better yet, he'd buy the special sun tan lotion which tans and colors the skin even without the sun.

James appeared in front of the group and clapped his hands for silence before pointing to the ceiling X.

"O mighty X, mothah of us all. We come to you to receive us. The Black Brigade."

Shouting and clapping immediately followed. "Black is best!" they cried out.

"Black, black, black was the color of my true love's skin," a boy sang.

[214]

"Black is beautiful," shouted another.

Reciting one by one, each stood up and said his piece, followed by hand clapping.

"Black earth is the best earth for planting and growing."

"Brown sugar don't cause no cavities."

"Blacker the berry, sweeter the juice."

Most of them stood now. Their expressions, restless against wideset eyes and flat, broad noses, showed anger and fearlessness. Their bodies, although motionless, seemed endowed with an animalistic ability to move with terrorizing speed and agility at a moment's notice.

James clapped his hands again as they sat down. "Ah got a important announcement. Let me have you undivided attention. Tonight, we got a special visitor. General Tammu of our mothah organization, the Black Liberation Movement."

Allan, suddenly uncomfortable, looked behind him to see if he could leave without being noticed. He knew of Tammu, having heard his parents speak of him with disgust and fear, while the boys in the gang came close to worshiping him.

Allan had seen the Negro leader many times in the neighborhood and didn't want to be around when he arrived, afraid that Tammu might recognize him and say something unpleasant. Again he glanced in the direction of the door, but it opened to frame the huge body of Tammu.

Accompanied by Fat Nasty and several other older youths, Tammu walked swiftly to the front. He squinted

[215]

his eyes at the boys for a few moments in the unfamiliar light of the fire before his rich voice rolled out.

"Brothers, good evening. I extend a warm arm of friendship to the Black Brigade."

Smiling and nodding his head to acknowledge their applause, he nevertheless cut it off by raising and shaking his arm in a gesture of impatience.

"Young brothers, the time will soon be here to establish our black independence." He peered around, now more accustomed to the light, and then sighted Allan. Scratching his forehead, he looked first with disbelief and then scowled. "I see we have a member of the opposite race here. Who let him in? I was under the impression that this was a black organization."

No reply came from either James or Ferry or anybody else. Allan felt betrayal in the form of silence enveloping him.

"Do you-all know what that thing is? He's a Jew, a member of a despised minority which is sucking the lifeblood of our black brethren. I repeat, who let that blue-eyed honky Jew devil in here?"

"He a member," James mumbled, relieving Allan from a paralyzing shock which rendered him unable to think or move.

"This is a black movement. There's no room for white in it. He's trying to pollute our race. I got a lot of people telling me what goes in this neighborhood. They tell me this white mothah has got a black girl."

They all turned to look at Allan, who sat newly immobilized, not even daring to look up at his tormentor.

"You keep your white mothahfuckin' hands off her!" Tammu thundered down with forefinger pointed at the boy. "Do you hear? We know what goes on around here. We catch you with her again and we're gonna circumcise six more inches off your Jew prick. Now get the hell outta here!"

Allan rose and walked toward the door, noticing that only his two friends, James and Ferry, kept their eyes downcast while the others gazed in unblinking enmity. Lousy bastard traitors, he thought. Why couldn't he shout back instead of being shamed and threatened into leaving like a dog? Why couldn't he turn around, walk up to Tammu and face the gang, reminding them in a strong, clear voice that Negroes didn't pay attention to the color of the eyes of the two Jewish civil rights workers murdered in Mississippi? But he could not.

He tried not to think about Tammu and James on the way home, and their presence in his mind came each time he thought of Yolanda. He made up his mind that he'd still see her. He'd show them he wasn't afraid.

A warm sweat glued to his tired body by the time he reached the side door of his house, which he entered, taking off his shoes before climbing the stairs.

"Allan?" his father called.

He didn't know whether to respond by shouting or whispering. If his mother were asleep, she'd have been awakened by his father's shout, but if she were still asleep, a reply by him probably would arouse her.

"Allan?" the call came louder. "Why don't you answer me when I call you?"

"Yes," he whispered loudly. "I didn't hear you," he lied, thinking that to be better than a long explanation.

The springs in the bed creaked as his father got off the mattress. "Go wait downstairs."

Back in the kitchen, he sat down and waited until his father showed up holding several papers.

"Where did you get this trash, Allan?"

Allan recognized the material James had given him. "At school. I found it."

"How come they got you listed as a member?"

Allan didn't answer.

Farber lashed out and slapped the boy on the face. His hand began to sting as he saw the flush come to the affected side of Allan's face. It bothered Farber that Allan did not let out a whimper, as if the sound would indicate the sin. Of a sudden, a feeling of guilt and self-hatred for striking Allan overwhelmed him, so he struck the boy again, in a blind, furious hope that the second blow might somehow justify the first. Still no sound came from Allan.

Farber listened for a moment to hear if Sarah were awakened by the noise. Then he forced himself to sit down on the other side of the table because he knew he could not trust himself not to hit the boy again.

"To go with the *shvartzers* is bad enough. But you don't have to lie to me, your father."

Allan, avoiding his father's eyes, refused to admit that the problem no longer existed since he had been thrown

[218]

out by the gang. He felt that such an admission would give his father a twisted sense of success resulting from the slaps.

"Keep away from the *shvartzers,* do you hear?"

"Where else could I go, Dad?"

Farber nodded more in futility than in agreement. His son had given him a punch below the belt, he thought. Worse than anything Sarah had ever said. Tomorrow he would think of something. Maybe next week.

He whispered to the boy to get to sleep, and then shuffled to his own bed to lay half awake until the alarm clock charged through him like an electrical shock, reminding him of the store which had now completely alienated him from his family.

The storefront office still bore the sign BLACK LIBERA-TION MOVEMENT in the window. Surrounding it were magazine and newspaper photographs of Negro leaders. Some of the clippings hung precariously, or had fallen to the window stage, revealing print and other pictures on the backsides. In smaller letters on another cardboard, *Gen. Tammu, Commandant* pressed against the door from the inside.

Although located only across the street from the store, Farber had never been near Tammu's office. He had often seen youths entering and leaving in varying degrees of military dress, some with all khaki clothes, some with garrison caps only, while others wore bloused trousers over combat boots. At times he had heard bugle calls vaguely resembling official U.S. Army bugling. Customers had told him that Tammu had converted the store into barracks of a sort.

Farber knocked loudly. He wished to establish a strong presence at the outset. A tall boy wearing a black beret perched uncertainly on a mass of woolly hair opened the door and told Farber to wait. Moments later the grocer was ushered into an office in which sat the General, whose desk had a missing leg for which several piled telephone books served as a transplant. Above him on the wall was a map of the United States with pins stuck in various cities, and with lines of thread connecting all of the pins to Washington, D.C. A battered bugle hung lopsidedly by its strap on a hook nearby.

"Don't tell me," Tammu said with an expansive smile settling over his fleshy jowls, "you're here to collect money for B'nai B'rith." He laughed, but squinted surreptitiously at Farber's hands, as if actually expecting to see a contribution, or perhaps a weapon.

He looked much older than when last Farber had seen him. His hair appeared whiter, more grown out, while the shoulders rose thick and massive above the desk, which hid his thick waist and broad hips and thus conferred upon him a deceiving V-shaped, circus strong man look.

"I came to tell you to leave my boy alone." Farber tossed Allan's papers on the desk top and stood belligerently glaring at the Negro.

[220]

Tammu glanced at them. "You seem to be always accusing me of something or other. I wouldn't waste this stuff on a white boy. Ours is a black movement."

Relieved that his task had seemed more terrible than it was, Farber nodded his head. "That's what I say. What do you want from him? He's not a colored boy. We're white people. We're not interested in your politics."

Tammu laughed loudly, quivering his dewlaps. Suddenly, he mimicked, "We're white people," and laughed again before studying Farber for a few moments. "Why don't you wake up, Farber?"

"What?"

"You're no more white than I am. You're a Jew. Like us, you have no free choice. You're a merchant like so many of your co-religionists, doing the job the white Christian created for you. Back when he said, 'Jew, you can't work in the professions, till or own the land, and you're not allowed to shit more than once a day,' you said, 'Suits me fine.' And he let you go into moneylending only because his church told him it ain't nice to make money from money. Nowadays, you're still spat upon by him, yet you suck his boots because you got a few more rights as his lackey."

Farber shrugged his shoulders. "Okay, enough already. There's . . ."

"Do you know something, Farber? You're not white. By white I mean the ruling Christian establishment. The trouble is that you Jews have a problem. Maybe just as big as ours. You think you can blend. We know we can't. You

[221]

think you're safe, but you're not. Look what happened in Germany. You assume protective coloration wherever you go, and you behave like the majority, and become educated, adopt the manners, and you think you've got it made. But when the chips are down you get it in the ass just like we probably will here. Only thing is that we know the kick is coming and you don't. You think that just because you've had it once, you're immune. But when you get it again it'll probably be the last of you."

Farber squeezed his eyes shut and then opened them. His laugh was hollow, gargling. "Mr. Tammu, you're crazy. Read the history books, the newspapers . . ."

"I've read them all. I've learned this country's built on racism. The Puritans and the lovable Peter Stuyvesant who thought Jews were devils. The slaughter of Indians. Restrictions against oriental immigrants. The Christian institution of slavery. The concentration camps for Americans of Japanese ancestry. And now genocide for the black man. And who's doing this to us? The polacks, the wops, and the bohunks. We built this land while they were still in the old country eating cow shit and fucking goats. We get nothing and they get the fat of the land just because they got a pink skin."

"Enough, already," Farber said with a groan of exasperation. "There's something else I want to talk to you about."

Tammu yawned. "I'm tired." He rubbed his eyes. "You want to talk about your boy. Well, I lied to you. He's really a member of the Movement. You want him out, pay for it. It'll cost you one hundred dollars for his membership card."

"You're talking crazy again. You and all your big talk about discrimination and equal rights. Look at me. I got rights in your neighborhood? You rob me, break my windows, and attack me. And then you say you got a right to move to a white neighborhood without being bothered."

"Who wants to live with you white crackers? What we want is our own state. Complete separation is the only answer. We can never assimilate so we must separate. Whites and blacks *are* different, regardless of what the liberals say. Our bodies smell stronger than yours. We're stronger physically and sexually."

Farber shifted his weight and made a motion toward the door. Tammu, sensing his guest's restlessness, raised an arm. "I even feel like I'm losing this battle of words with you," he joked. "I can't speak as well as you. My lips are thicker than yours."

"Yesterday an inspector . . ."

"We're twenty-two million strong and we don't want a stinking cracker, no good, barren hole like Mississippi or Louisiana. We want Arizona, New Mexico, and California."

Tammu continued, pointing to the map on the wall. "First of all, we need an army. That's where I come in. See those pins? Each represents a thousand men in strategic cities. I can muster an army of twenty thousand men right now. Next year that figure will be tripled. It's incumbent upon people like you who prey upon us to help us with our goal. We'll let you have your son's card for one hundred dollars, which will also cover your first month's contribution to our organization."

This time Farber laughed. "You've got a lot of nerve. My trouble is that I take you seriously. I'll tell you, for a hundred dollars that you'll give me, you can have him."

Tammu's eyes, dark and smoldering, reflected no humor. "I said I was tired."

"So who tells you to talk so much?" Farber sensed Tammu's displeasure. "Okay, I came to see you about something else. Your stinking boycott I could take. But how about laying off with sending inspectors? If you wanted to get even for the cops I sent to you, you're even."

"We will continue to press for our rights in the ghetto. The ghetto merchant and the slum landlord will be dealt with legally at first. If that doesn't work, there are other means."

"What're you talking about? What did I ever do to my customers but help them?"

"Nobody puts the touch on the black man like the Jews with their three hundred percent interest."

"You piece of shit!" Farber exploded. "Tell me, what do you do to deserve to live? Do you ever do a day's work? Did you ever say to yourself, I worked hard today? I earned my money? No, you sit there on your fat can dreaming of becoming a *shvartzer* Hitler."

Tammu did not answer immediately. A few moments passed before he spoke. "Spoken like a true, hardworking Joosh businessman. Joosh businessmen are always blood-

[224]

sucking blacks. Joosh. Juice," Tammu continued, playing with the words. "Yes siree. That's where we get the word juice. You get juice by squeezing. Who's always squeezing? The Jews. Hence, juice. Gotten by squeezing, the dictionary says. If it doesn't, it should say juice is derived from Jews."

Farber, holding fists up, rushed around the desk to Tammu, who jumped and scooted to the side where Farber had been. For a few minutes they raced around and around, stop and go, as Tammu managed to keep the desk between them. They were a grotesque distortion of a cartooned boss pursuing a pretty secretary.

Breathlessly, Tammu yelled, "You raise one finger and I'll call my bodyguards. And Fat Nasty," Tammu gasped, "do you know what he could do . . . ah, ah ah"— the breath spurted forth—"to you with just one of his fingers?"

A loud knock came from the door, pushed open by two men who struggled under the weight of a wooden box shaped like a small coffin. Tammu shook his head and motioned them not to enter.

"Not in here, goddamn it!"

The two carriers looked sheepishly at each other and put the box down to renew their grip. The lid had been pried loose and lifted up a few inches, high enough for Farber to see the box's contents, a row of rifles nestled snugly between white foam rubber. He turned his head away quickly, hoping that they didn't see him observe the weapons.

[225]

"Well, come on, goddamn it! Get it out of here!"

As the men left with the box, Tammu opened a drawer in his desk and pulled out a small revolver. "This will help keep you on your side of the desk. You tell anybody what you saw and we'll toss a Molotov cocktail into your bedroom. Our aim is especially good at three in the morning."

"You want me to be quiet you get off my back," Farber replied quickly. "You leave me and my family alone."

"Okay, get out of here." He pointed the weapon at Farber. "Just remember, this gets out and you and your wife and kid will burn alive in that store. We'll make you look like some of those Jew ashes from the gas ovens."

Farber moved forward again but forced himself into a state of calm when he saw the barrel of the gun. "Bastard!" he said hoarsely, turning to leave.

For a moment Allan forgot where he had agreed to meet Yolanda. His pace slackened as he wondered in which direction he ought to turn. Not his school playground, he thought, even though they had once met there shortly after the gang kicked him out. The danger of running into a member of the Black Brigade was too great in his neighborhood.

He had not yet told Yolanda of the gang's threats, which probably would be carried out if he continued to see her, yet she accepted without question or complaint the long distances traveled separately by them to places where they were unknown.

Snapping his fingers, he quickened his stride, remembering that tonight it was to be her playground. Although at times fearful of Tammu's threat, he enjoyed acting like a spy in the movies. He looked over his shoulder and stealthily checked each corner before entering an intersection.

The dreaded enemy, of course, was Tammu and the gang, while his parents, to whom he lied about his weekly wanderings, represented foes of a much less dangerous sort. His parents knew that he had left the gang and in their busied existence were quite willing to leave well enough alone, accepting his stories with a nod and hurried advice to be careful.

He now tried to recall how many different times he had made love to her since that whispered promise in her apartment weeks ago. The times quickly recollected the places to his mind—under the trees, the murmurs of love smothered by aircraft taking off and landing at National Airport; at the foot of a grassy knoll near the U.S. Capitol, where they overheard two passing men talking about "quorum calls"; and under a thick bush at Lafayette Park, where across the street, angry demonstrators with placards marched in front of the White House lit by floodlights in the night.

Now he walked hurriedly in the middle of the street, eschewing the dark sidewalks for fear of muggers. Already the April rains had left puddles in potholes scooped out by the cold and ice of winter. By autumn, the highway department would see that the potholes were repaired. The muddy scum of the puddles barely reflected headlights of passing cars or the streetlamps.

The streets familiar to him in the daylight assumed a strange look at night. Humidity was high, grasping automobile exhaust fumes with which it scoured his lungs after each breath. Nervously, he gingerly avoided the holes and automobiles, keeping a watchful eye for the Black Brigade.

A moving object spun out from under a parked car in front of his path, forcing him to jump back in terror. When he recognized it as a rat, he grew sick to his stomach. He thought of Dracula, still the uninvited and unremovable guest in the house. He dismissed the rat from his mind when ahead rose the high chain link fence of the schoolyard. Farther beyond, the huge school building stood like a square mountain.

Allan entered the unlighted yard through an opened double gate and quickly went to the meeting place, a concrete basketball court squeezed in a space between two wings of the building. From the moonlight he walked into the shadows of the building which enveloped him as he turned into the court.

An odor of perspiration filled his nostrils and almost made him gag. Sniffing like a cat, even to the point of nodding his head, he wondered how it was possible for the smell of sweaty, athletic bodies to remain in an out-of-doors place continually whipped and washed by wind and rain. It was as bad as an indoor gym.

He arrived about ten minutes early since he didn't want Yolanda to do the waiting in the dark. He also wished to have the advantage of the approached, the one who,

[228]

unseen, could gaze upon the approacher.

To pass the time, he hopped and skipped, dribbling an imaginary ball which he tossed through the netless hoop. Then he leaned against the basket pole and stared in the direction from which Yolanda would come. His body twinged with excitement and he shivered as he thought of feeling her, lifting her dress, and pressing against her.

Where would they do it this time? The grass, what there was of it, was wet. There was the mud. The concrete ground would be too hard, but she could lie on top of him, he thought. It could easily be done that way.

Suppose she didn't want to do it for some reason or another? He'd worry about that when she said no, not before. She had been too willing during the past few times to refuse now, even though her behavior at times was strange. He found it hard to forget how she had acted with the pots and pans. Right now, all that mattered to him, all that counted in the world, was to have her. His only worry was whether she would let him.

The crunch of heels against pebbly concrete shook his thoughts away. He narrowed his eyes but saw nothing in the darkness and became annoyed that his advantage in arriving first was of no use. Only when she called his name did he see her, wearing a black raincoat. For a moment her face glowed yellow and eerie in the light as a passing dark cloud unclothed the moon.

"You're right on time," he said.

"Where we go now?"

"How about right here?" He peered closely at her face to catch a sign of approval. If she looked unwilling,

[229]

he'd think of something else before she opened her mouth.

"Grass too wet. Mah bottom's gonna get wet."

"On the ground, then. We'll use your coat."

"Where *your* coat? We use that. Not mine."

"I didn't bring one." He went up to her and opened her raincoat, intruding his leg between her knees.

"Not standing up," she ordered. "Animals do it standing up."

They walked to the end of the court and to the wall of the building where she removed her coat and placed it on the concrete before they lay down to lift dress and open fly.

A chill wind blew some errant raindrops on his neck and scattered pebbles, as clouds completely covered the moon. From afar came the sounds of a racing car, a mother calling her child, and a bottle smashing against a hard surface.

He eased himself up and lay on her, spreading one arm and palm outward for a moment to adjust his weight. He felt something soft and rubbery with the outstretched hand, something he knew did not belong on the concrete. His fingers explored the perimeter of a shoe, a sneaker swollen and hard with a foot in it. With jumping heart and stilled breath, he advanced to feel an ankle and trousers.

"Mothahfuck," he heard a thick voice above him say.

The voice of Quinn still echoed in his ears as he waited for Sarah to come downstairs and help with figuring the bills. Although not unexpected, the long-distance call made him realize that he could not go on, even for another week, with the business. He'd have to give it up, declare bankruptcy.

He was two months behind paying the note to Quinn, and now the Irishman had sounded a threat over the telephone.

"I believe you, Farber. Things are not so good. That's why I'm calling you. Any other time I'd let you miss two, three months. But I'll tell you a secret. The money you borrowed from me wasn't mine. It belongs to a bunch who don't think twice about breaking some bones to get what they think is coming to them."

"What do you mean? What kind of business is that?" Farber had tried to be furious, uncertain whether Quinn was making a joke.

"The thing is, the bunch knows I'm not to blame. I put them off all I can. They know about you."

"Mr. Quinn, stop the kidding around. What kind of dirty business is that? What the hell's going on?"

"Don't be stupid, Farber. They want the money. In full. They're giving you until the first of July. That's the start of the fiscal year, you know." Quinn could hardly laugh at his own joke. All that came out had been "Heh, heh."

"But it's only about five, six hundred dollars," Farber had said, embarrassed that he couldn't remember the exact sum.

"They been known to work on bones for less than that."

"Now, look, Mr. Quinn, cut the shit."

"I *am* not crapping around. They're very impatient people. They want their investment back. First as a penalty for you, as well as me. There's only one thing they'll consider. That is if you pay twelve percent interest on the remaining six ninety."

"Six ninety!"

"Didn't you know that?"

"That much?"

"My loan, or rather, theirs, I was just passing it on, was for a thousand, payable one fifteen a month for twelve months. Figure it out."

Farber had felt dizzy. "I . . . didn't realize . . ."

"Twelve percent and they let you go. No further interest raise."

"You're a loanshark, Mr. Quinn."

"Heh, heh."

"You're a piece of crap. I'll get you your lousy money, all of it, by the first."

The dizziness he had experienced an hour ago now turned into a headache. He could feel time pressing against him, as if it were a subway rider trying to get around and exit.

Could Quinn's bunch be the Mafia? That lying shit. I don't even know if he's telling the truth. The point is, I still got to pay off, whether it's the Mafia or not.

"Ready?"

He jerked his head up, startled by Sarah's quiet entrance. "Yeah."

As on previous Saturday nights following closing of

[232]

the store, they added the week's receipts of money paid for stock, services, and other expenses. A side column showed payments on monthly notes, broken down to weekly amounts for easy figuring.

They next consulted seven pieces of paper recording the daily gross for the week. Farber obtained each slip at the end of the day, when he lit a match in the darkened store and held it close to the small window on the cash register. After he'd read the indicated gross and marked it on the paper scrap, he'd turn a lever, rolling the indicator back to a fresh row of zeros. In the morning the first coins and bills received would ring up numerals to replace the zeros.

Farber cursed to himself as he looked over the lists of his debtors. He couldn't count credit on the books as part of the gross since he didn't know when the customers would settle their accounts. It bothered him every time he thought about it, but even more so now. Why couldn't the Mafia break some of his customers' legs?

More than just a few times customers had moved out or disappeared without paying their bills. Even if he found them, what could he do? he asked himself. To go to a small claims court would be a waste of time, since they didn't have any money or property, or salaries to garnishee. He felt better in knowing that he had not given any new credit for the past few months and was slowly phasing out his old credit customers.

"Did you finish?"

Once again Sarah's voice surprised him. He pushed a stack of papers across the table to her. For some reason her recent habit of sticking a pencil behind her ear suddenly disturbed him. He thought she resembled one of those fat-legged, dirty-aproned, sexless women he saw plucking and selling chickens at the marketplace.

Farber watched sullenly as she checked and rechecked his figures, adding row upon row, using his pencil instead of the one on her head. He wanted to ask her why she did that, and then reach out to her ear and knock the pencil flying to the floor.

To keep busy while she worked he fumbled with the list of bills he'd have to pay by the end of the month. Quinn's notes were the first, having risen to the top priority position by dint of lack of payment for two months.

Should he pay the twelve percent and get a breathing spell or pay off the whole thing once and for all? The only way he could pay in full was to take another loan or get a part-time job. A part-time job? he thought. Don't be ridiculous. I'm working seven days, twelve hours a day now and still losing my shirt.

Sarah returned some bills and receipts to him. "These all figure up all right."

"Okay." He put the papers in a notebook and wondered whether he ought to tell her about Quinn's call. She returned his pencil and removed hers from the ear, but he felt no sense of relief, nor did he feel any satisfaction or pride in watching her work. Her eyes diligently followed the pencil up and down the columns, playing a pas de deux of staccato, symbiotic movements.

Both of them, he thought, working all of the time for

[234]

nothing. The rent was being paid, but not one penny was put aside for a better life. What was the trouble? There were heavy losses from thefts and bad debts, but these couldn't smother him altogether. Business wasn't that bad now with spring construction and an increase in buying. They were taking in more than eleven hundred a week now, excluding credit. Where was the hole?

Perhaps he mismanaged the store. He often thought about this possibility. The first year of business was the worst, he rationalized, especially for a man who was just learning. In the back of his mind, however, there was a gnawing feeling that he did not belong in business. The papers confused him. The bills, receipts, notes, the many taxes, licenses needed for selling, the little bits of paper with figures on them, the inspections by the sanitary people and tax people, the weights and measures investigators, and all sorts of municipal investigators looking for code violations of one sort or another made him wish that he had never come to Washington.

He was a carpenter. He was used to doing what he was told, and doing a clean, thorough job quickly and efficiently, and then forgetting about it and moving on to another job. He wished he were back in carpentry work, feeling the satisfaction of doing a hard day's work in the fresh air, being away from the stink and dampness of a grocery store, from the complaints and hatred of the *shvartzers,* and picking up a paycheck at the end of the week, with no worries about overhead. He always knew where he was as a carpenter.

Farber watched her finish adding the last column. An

apartment, that was out of the question, he thought. Bankruptcy was around the corner, not an apartment, or a house, or a life in Florida.

He could easily declare bankruptcy. Doing so wasn't so bad, he had heard. Nobody got shook up anymore about being a business failure. It happens all the time. First, you get a smart lawyer to file your case so that you'd pay less than fifty cents on the dollar. Jimmy had said that bankruptcy doesn't kill your future credit. You could always borrow more money to go into business. But who was crazy enough to go back into business after getting out of it?

The feeling now that he was a failure increased the severity of his headache. He was only good for manual labor, he told himself. When it came to thinking, or running a business, he was just no good. He couldn't even add a line of numbers correctly. That's why he always had to ask Sarah to check his figuring.

No, he decided. He couldn't go bankrupt. He couldn't go back to New York without a penny in his pocket. He'd stick it out. Things had to get better.

"Simon, we took in twelve hundred and forty-eight dollars last week."

He nodded knowingly. "The store is good, Sarah. It's the bills that are choking us." The store could carry its own weight, he thought. There were just too many bills to pay. If he could go bankrupt, he'd go back to work and maybe save enough money to buy a business outright without shark loans from Quinn or anybody else. He was drowning before he had a chance to swim.

[236]

The idea to work for a few weeks during the summer came so suddenly, and so favorably, that he announced it almost at the same time he received it.

"Sarah, I'm going back to work as a carpenter for a short time. I don't think the arthritis will bother me. The weather's pretty warm and I just won't knock myself out. I'll pace myself."

Her blank, uncomprehending stare made him speak louder, faster.

"Until we can get back on our feet. I could make five, six dollars an hour. This summer, as soon as school's out, you won't be so busy. Maybe Allan could come with me as a laborer and pull in some money for his own college."

"I'm not going to stay here alone," she hissed.

"Keep the store closed. Just open it when a customer you know knocks on the door. Lots of grocers do that."

"I'm not going to stay alone. There's got to be another way."

"There is. Go bankrupt." He hoped she didn't know that bankruptcy wasn't such a terrible thing. He told her how he thought that the store could hold its own and that only the heavy notes were killing them. When she still shook her head, he told her about Quinn and the Mafia.

Allan looked up to see a giant form looming over Yolanda and him. The moon reappeared and at once it reflected on the interloper's teeth, bared in a grin. Two other shadowy hulks stood next to the stranger.

[237]

"Well, ah do declare. What have we here?"

Allan recognized the deep, throaty voice as that of Death's Head. Thank God, he thought, Death's Head wasn't a member of the Black Brigade.

"Hello, Leroy," Yolanda said, not uncheerfully. "And good-bye. You got no call to be here pestering other people."

"No fuckin' on school prop-ty," one of the other hulks said. "The principal, he say so. He say it bad for the grass."

"It sure good for the ass," Death's Head, or Leroy, said. "Right, Yolanda?"

"Sheet," the girl said, standing up.

Yolanda's audacity surprised Allan, but he was even more amazed as to how the three youths were able to sneak up unheard and unseen. Their sneakers made it possible, he realized. All of them wore sneakers—not that they really needed the rubber shoes. They could wear iron boots and still glide along the concrete like deer on the range.

Another hulk clapped his hands and danced. "Uh, uh. They not doing it on the grass. They on the concrete and that's bad for the concrete. 'Cause if that boy miss the hole he make a crack in the concrete and that make the principal mad. So mad that he don't allow no more fuckin' for no-body, not even hisself. So you got to do it in the mud. That the law. But you break the law."

Allan, sweating and shivering, knew they were playing with him, torturing him with nonsensical talk the same way

[238]

they did when he had met Yolanda during the school dance. He got to his knees, hoping to make it to his feet so he could at least protect himself when their blows came raining down on him. He could already see himself crunched against the concrete like an insect, his face smashed by the hamlike muscles of Death's Head and his friends. A moment later, he was up, but he regretted it. Death's Head saw his whiteness and recognized him.

"Mothahfuck! It that mothahfucker white mothah!" Without warning, he swung out and struck Allan across the bridge of the nose, sending up red and white flashes across the boy's vision. Allan fell backward, and down hard on his back.

"Leave that boy be!" Yolanda shouted.

"Shut up, pussy," Death's Head ordered, "and lay down for some fuckin'."

"Ah'm next," one youth addressed Death's Head. The other spat and kicked Allan on the knee. "You stay right there, mothah."

Rape, it's rape. The thought came racing through Allan's mind as he clutched at the searing pain in his knee with one hand and held his bleeding nose with the other. He must save Yolanda. He'd fight all three of them, he thought, as he listened in vain to hear her cries of protest and screams of fear. The hard shock of his own fear gave way to a rage which choked and clogged his throat, a rage that diminished when he heard Yolanda's reptilelike hiss in the darkness.

"You all want pussy, okay. But you got to do it mah

[239]

way. All three of you lay down, three in a row. Ah'm gonna play you-all like a piano."

Allan closed his eyes and shook his head. That couldn't be her. It was a trick like the communists play when they imitated prisoners' voices to record confessions. But again, she spoke.

"Easy, Leroy. You gonna wear me down."

The package of emotions which filled him, the fear, anger, hatred, disbelief, now included abomination. She was a pig and a whore, he thought, listening to the animal grunts and laughter filling the air. His hatred of her surpassed that of Death's Head. She deserved to die. Better still, she deserved to be raped.

She giggled, she laughed, and she said, "Take it easy, mothah."

He told himself he was dreaming a dream like the ones in which nameless terrors pursued him while his legs moved molasseslike toward nothing but new and unknown horrors. But he ran, more to escape her laughter, her enjoyment, than for fear of his own bodily harm.

Before he arrived home he made a dozen promises never to think of Yolanda again, and never to have anything to do with Negroes unless he couldn't help it. He was through with them, all of them. One by one, they turned out to be—he searched for a moment for the right word— black shits.

Yet that evening he stayed awake, unable to expunge his experience by sleep. The remaining sediment of tension following his fright and close escape was made murkier by Yolanda's action. Again, there was something strange about her behavior, far more outlandish than the business with the pots and pans had been in her apartment. It distressed him that he couldn't understand why she had acted the way she had in the schoolyard, but he was certain of only one thing, the promise he made to himself never to see her again.

In the morning, scant seconds before awakening, he dreamt that Death's Head socked him hard against the shoulder. He opened his eyes to see his father shaking him awake. Then his father told him that they'd be working on a construction job as soon as school let out.

Sarah looked up when she heard the screen door screech open. A man with a green shirt and dark trousers reached for the knob and tried unsuccessfully to open the closed door. He pushed a second time, using his shoulder. Failing again, he looked through the door window by cupping his hands around his eyes to keep the outside light reflection from spoiling his view.

Sarah, not recognizing him, ducked back behind the meat showcase where she cleaned shelves with a rag and soapy water. Some way to run a business, she thought for the hundredth time since her husband had gone off to work. She didn't need his warning to keep the store closed during the hours he was away and to open the door only to regular customers that she knew.

It was crazy, but her customers accepted it without question and felt honored and privileged to be among the chosen few permitted entry. Many of the neighborhood stores, even the dry goods and hardware businesses along

[241]

the well-lighted and -traveled streets, kept a simultaneous closed-open schedule, especially at night. Customers could often be heard discussing how they were recognized and let in at one store but not another.

Sarah raised her head and peeked over the counter. The stranger now rapped on the door window while holding one palm like a horse's blinder alongside his face as he peered into the store.

She hoped he'd go away before a known customer arrived. It would be embarrassing to open the door and have to let both of them in.

The potential embarrassment soon gave way to fright in her mind. Suppose the stranger would ask her to wait on the regular customer first, saying that he had to think about what he wanted to buy? She'd know it was a trick, and shuddered at the thought of being left alone with the stranger after stalling unsuccessfully with the friendly customer in hopes the stranger would become impatient and leave. She swore she'd let neither customer nor stranger enter, and just hope that the customer would come back later.

The rapping stopped and she looked again. The man with the green shirt had gone.

It was a crazy way to run a business, she thought again. But this was a crazy world where the Mafia could hurt and maybe kill her husband for not paying off a note. How she and Simon could get involved with the Mafia, of all things, was beyond her. If it weren't for that, she'd be on a train right now heading for New York instead of trying to squeeze an extra few pennies out of the store.

No, that wasn't true, she told herself. Even if it weren't for the Mafia and her nightmares of police finding her husband's tied-up body in the river, with legs cemented in a barrel, she'd have given him one more chance to make a go of it. She believed that at least it was worth a try, but felt sorry that he had to work all day and open the doors at six o'clock after showering and eating. The money flowed in, but it was very difficult. Just a few more weeks, she promised herself, echoing the words of her husband.

Maybe the setup wasn't that bad, she thought. Maybe she could open the side window they used during the student rush hours and take in more money. But there wasn't that much trade during the summer day, at least not enough to risk a holdup or something worse by opening the window to all. Besides the safety factor, the closed-door policy enabled her to do housework, even though it meant running downstairs every time she heard a knock. She also had time to stock shelves and clean the store, chores she spared her tired husband from doing. She even found time to watch television or to read newspapers and magazines.

She picked up and washed the wooden frames used to permit water drainage from the bottom of the showcase. They'd probably dry better in the sun, she thought, carrying them through the storeroom and kitchen to the back yard. The sun and fresh air would also help remove from the frames the sour odor of stale meat, vegetables, and spilled milk.

Suddenly, hard, calloused hands seized her from behind, just like in her dreams. The frames fell from her hands on the yard ground as she turned to see a dark face and a green shirt. Only a dream, she thought. No sense in waking up her husband. He is so tired these days.

She felt a rough pulling on her apron and a hand moving hard on her knee and thigh.

Then she screamed.

Allan laid four short planks of two-by-eights on top of each other and hoisted the pile onto his shoulder. He began to walk but faltered as pain struck at his crotch, moving like lightning across a summer evening sky to spread up his groin and then to his hips.

Rupture, he thought, looking up to see Rosita staring at him from the toolshed. He couldn't put down the planks now, but had to walk to the building lift with them. Slowly he placed one foot in front of the other, but with each step a new sharp pain tore at his lower abdomen.

Rosita met him at the elevator. "Go work the second floor on the beams," the foreman said, pointing to the building.

Already a laborer stood on the ground next to the building, with workers on the first, third, and roof levels. Rosita, a finger plucked cowboy style on his belt, accompanied Allan as far as the ground laborer and then watched the boy enter the building and come to the second-floor window.

Rosita glared at his crew on the ground and roof and framed in the windows. "All them beams gotta be on the roof before tomorrow. Got a carpenter crew scheduled." he said in a throaty voice to the men, lined up like ducks in a shooting gallery. As if giving them a signal to begin, he gathered mucus from deep within sinuses and spat on the ground, raising a tiny cloud of dust which almost obscured the slime.

The ground man picked up a beam, weighing close to one hundred pounds, and handed an end of it to the man in the first-floor window, who pulled it in a few feet and, using the sill as a fulcrum, pushed down with arms and chest until the opposite end swung up to Allan on the second floor, where he duplicated the operation for the third-floor man. The hardest part was pulling the beam in through the window far enough in order to apply pressure to swing it upward.

With each pull-up Allan felt the pain like no other he had ever experienced. At times he thought that he heard the ripping of something inside of him, like the tearing of dry newspapers. Once he had read something in a magazine about ruptures. He envisioned a piece of round intestine getting larger and larger with each pull-up, pushing against the wall of his abdomen and trying to break through to come out as large as a baseball. No, it wasn't baseball shaped. It was long, as long as a snake. In his mind he saw his intestines spilling out from a hole in his body, dancing and squirming on the floor, a white bloody snake with no place to go.

He thought about quitting, right then and there, and just telling Rosita, "I quit, you wop." He'd better not say

[245]

wop. Rosita might hit him with the claw hammer hanging on his belt.

Allan couldn't quit, because Rosita might say or think that all Jews are soft and yellow. Didn't the foreman ask him on his first day on the job why he wasn't selling shoes or going to medical school? "Boy, you must really be a dumb Jew," Rosita had said. Allan had thought a while about that, uncertain whether it was a compliment or an insult and then realized that it could be taken as a compliment to the Jewish people—all of them were supposed to be smart, and so any Jew not in a profession or business must be dumb. He was glad his father was in business.

Allan didn't want to quit and let his father down by leaving now and subjecting him to taunts from the other carpenters about his soft son. Also, his father counted on the money. No, quitting was out of the question. The article never said anything about a rupture killing anybody.

No sooner had the last beam left his hands when Rosita yelled at him, "Git back on the two-by-eights, boy."

Farber, holding a saw, looked out of the window at Allan picking up lumber. He closed his eyes tightly and ran a finger along the teeth of the instrument, as if wishing to inflict some pain upon himself.

Now my son is involved in my failure. First Sarah, and now Allan.

He pictured Sarah working in the store, wiping the sweat from her forehead with an apron as she waited on customers and cleaned and did God knows what.

Sarah, alone in the store.

"Just for a short time," he had explained the night he told her he had made up his mind to go back to work. She had cried, even more so when he brought up the Mafia. Her tears had served to increase his desire to do something about their situation, although he felt not quite right about using a threat from the Mafia to serve his ends. He had no proof that they were behind Quinn, nor had the Irishman mentioned anybody by name.

And if that wasn't bad enough, he now thought, he had to go ahead and suggest that she keep the store partly open. "When you see someone you recognize, let him in if you want to. Lots of storekeepers do that."

He had known his "if you want to" fell just short of a request that she couldn't refuse, not with the Mafia breathing down their necks. At that time he had also thought that she could easily pull in several dozen dollars a day without strain or fear.

He opened his eyes again and watched Allan waver as he walked crookedly under the weight. The boy's just not cut out for that type of work, he said to himself, again rubbing the saw.

The other laborers were itinerant hillbillies, lean and wiry. Like monkeys, they had hidden strength in their thin, power-belying arms and shoulders. They laid four or more two-by-eights atop one another, and then quickly and easily snatched and hoisted the lumber to their shoulders. They knew exactly where to place the lumber so that it would be balanced evenly while they walked, some with their carrying arm locked over the wood while the free arm shot

[247]

straight out like that of a motorist signaling a left turn.

Farber looked at Rosita, standing with hands on hips and watching Allan struggle with three planks. The boy couldn't pick them up, much less carry them.

Just two at a time, Allan, Farber wanted to shout down. Just one at a time, Allan. He felt his throat drying as the sweat of his palms pasted hand to wooden saw handle. What does Rosita want from the boy? He can't do that work.

Farber stepped back from the window. But if he can't do it, why did I bring him here? I'll tell him to quit, tomorrow.

He turned to his own job, throwing a plank over a wooden sawhorse. He sawed furiously, elated as his knee, bent over half of the wood, transmitted vibrations of accomplishment as it felt the loosening and then the final severing of the plank. Perspiration piled on his forehead and ran down his arms. He felt strong and needed. This was his work, his only work. He didn't need the store. He wanted a simple life. You worked your eight hours, five days a week, and that was that. The arthritis, the hell with it. I'll dope myself up with so much aspirin I wouldn't know if I was coming or going. I'll get the work done.

"Farber, this here police officer wanna talk to you a few minutes," Rosita said. "So why don' you knock off?"

They stood outside looking in through the unfinished doorway without a door like actors in a poorly furnished high school set; Rosita with his old, tattered workclothes, and the officer, tunicless, with a summer, sweat-soaked uniform of dark blue trousers and a lighter blue shirt which he also wore in winter under a tunic.

Thoughts of guilt flashed through Farber's mind. The store—some kind of health-department violation? If that was true, it wouldn't mean a personal visit from a cop. Somebody's hurt. Allan. The boy got hurt. No, he didn't. I just saw him. Sarah.

"Mr. Farber?" the youngish officer asked. Without waiting for an answer or a nod, he continued. "There's been an accident. Your wife had an accident. We'd like you to come and identify her."

"What's the matter," Farber blurted out, "can't she identify herself?"

The police officer shook his head and looked down. "Look, you better come."

Rosita nodded his low-hanging head. "You better go with the officer. I won't dock you for knocking off early."

"Tell me, goddamn it! What happened?"

"I'm sorry to tell you she's dead," the officer said.

A scream rose within him but he could not release it. "Dead? She's dead? An accident?"

"Yeah. Somebody killed her."

"That's an accident?" was all he could say.

Allan sat beside his silent father as they sped along in the police squad car. His father had come up to where he had been working and simply said that his mother was dead. For a moment he had stood there looking as if his father had said, "Okay, let's knock off for lunch." Then he

[249]

reacted by thinking, who is going to wake me in the morning in time for school?

The police car ran over the curbstone, scattered a small crowd, and parked within a few inches of the door. Farber and Allan got out.

"All right, folks. Show's over. Go on back home to your television," a policeman shouted, leading the victim's survivors into the store, where they met the two other officers and a man dressed in a tight business suit.

"Better stay right there, sonny," the man in the suit said as he barred Allan's way into the stockroom.

He heard his father gasp and call "Sarah" over and over again until the sobbing choked off the calls. Suddenly he dashed around the plainclothesman, who made no effort to stop him.

Her dress was pulled up, showing plump, strangely white legs sticking out like those of a tattered rag doll in a trash can. The ashen grayness of her face was disrupted by the red of an open mouth and walleyes of death. On one side of her face was a bunched-up apron, the string of which was wrapped tightly around her neck.

He felt shame for her exposed parts and was thankful that at least her crotch was covered by part of the dress. He walked forward to her, wanting to cover her partial nakedness in front of the strangers. Then he saw her ripped and blood-stained panties lying near a dirty broom a few feet away.

"Get him out of here!" his father screamed at one of

[250]

the policemen, who pushed Allan gently into the kitchen and motioned him to go upstairs.

Allan tried not to think of what he had seen. He knew what had happened as soon as he saw her panties. But why did she have to die? Yolanda didn't die even after three of them got her. But Yolanda didn't fight and his mother did, he was sure.

He sat next to his window and looked down at the people, many of whom he recognized as customers. Watching them for a while, he rested his head on folded arms. Throughout the afternoon, since the arrival of the police, the crowd alternated in size, never below ten or above twenty. Soon a loud and familiar voice outside attracted his attention and he lifted his head. It was General Tammu.

"People are hungry in this here neighborhood," Tammu said, his voice sounding as if it came through a horn. "And when they get hungry, they'll do anything."

Everybody joined in by shouting, "Yeah, yeah," and "You tell 'em, nigger." One old lady repeated, "Amen, amen," as if she were in church.

"I'm leadin' this here campaign and I want you all to join me before things get worse 'cause people'll do anything when they get hungry."

Yes, Allan thought, even rip off the panties of women. He turned from the window and began to cry. "She's gone and won't be here anymore," he said aloud, almost loud enough for the people downstairs to hear.

[251]

Another police officer entered the storeroom and approached the plainclothesman. They whispered to each other for a few moments, watching Farber as they spoke. Then the plainclothes detective nodded to Farber. "I think we got a suspect, Mr. Farber. Let's take a look at him."

Farber, sitting on a chair, shook his head. "I want to stay with her."

"Look, Mr. Farber. This is important. This could be the guy who murdered her."

"What do I know about him? I couldn't tell you anything."

"You could tell us if you saw him before. If he's a customer that you got in an argument with. Lots of things."

Farber reluctantly stood up. "How do you know if you got the right man?"

"We picked him up a few blocks from here. He fits the description given by some customer of yours who called us after seeing him in your back yard."

"Lots of kids get in my back yard."

"This ain't no kid. He's got blood on his shirt and come juice on his pants. Come on, outside in the wagon."

The young man sat crouched on an iron fold-down bench in a corner of the police van. He leaned his head on a window, laced with an iron screen, through which a driver or rider in the front cab could look. He held his handcuffed hands awkwardly on his lap, lifting them up to wipe a running nose with a sleeve of his green shirt.

Farber saw blood on him. What right did he have in keeping her blood, part of her being, on his filthy body? He wanted to smash and crush his face against the screened window and watch the tiny fragments of flesh and bone filter to the other side.

"Did you do it, you black bastard?"

"Careful, man," the detective said, nervously eyeing the crowd being kept a few paces away by two police officers. "You want more trouble on your hands?"

The youth looked up and scowled. "Mothah, get outta chere!"

Farber put his foot on the first step of the two leading into the van but was held back by the detective, who grabbed the grocer by the belt.

"Whoa, Mr. Farber. You can't go in there."

Standing up, the youth waggled his clenched fists. "Get dese offa me. Ah take care of dat mothah."

Farber lunged forward again, lifting and pulling the detective after him up the steps and into the van. The first blow caught the youth in the Adam's apple, sending a choking cough from his lips. Farber struck again, and the youth slid to the floor and covered his head under fists and handcuffs.

"You stupid shit!" the plainclothesman yelled as he gained his balance. He glanced at the white face of one of his officers peering into the van along with a group of Negroes. "Close that goddamn door!" He barked at the officers. Next he snapped the inside lock on the door, moved over to where Farber stood, and pushed the grocer roughly toward the bench. Then he turned toward the Negro, picking up a foot and bringing it down on the

[253]

youth's head in such a way that the heel caught the handcuffs and dug them deeply into the skull.

Red blood, oozing out like drops of water wrung from a washcloth, looked unnatural and unclean against the black of his skin. The foot stomped again, this time smashing the bridge of the suspect's nose.

By now blood covered the floor and the shoes of the detective. It reminded Farber of visits to the chicken slaughterhouse at the market where blood, mixed with sawdust and dirt, clung to his shoes. A special trough of soapy water was installed outside for the benefit of grocers buying wholesale.

Moans from the youth made the detective smile at Farber. "It's okay. This thing's soundproof." He laughed breathlessly. "We don't usually get a suspect worked over by a victim. When they ask what happened to him, I'll just say you lost your head. You'll be in the clear. After all, he's just murdered your wife. You know what? They'll probably give this turd ten years with three years off for good behavior."

The detective rambled on, still breathing heavily, almost in rhythm with the gasps of the Negro. Farber buried his face in his arms, thinking, What do I do now? Should I contact an undertaker? I'll have to look for a Jewish one. What about a rabbi? Somebody's got to call New York for the relatives to know. I'm busy, maybe Sarah could. She's dead.

"You didn't tell me, Mr. Farber, if you ever saw this man before."

[254]

They returned to the store late in the evening. Farber paid the cab driver, who scurried to the trunk from which he pulled two suitcases.

"Hurry, Allan. It's dangerous out here," Farber said, overly cautious since the death of Sarah. He fumbled in his pocket for coins to tip the driver and for the key to the store. Even in the dim light of the streetlamp he could see the small cardboard sign on which he had penciled:

CLOSED ON ACCOUNT
OF DEATH IN FAMILY

That wouldn't impress them, he thought. Death, violent death by knife and gun, death by neglect, all were a normal way of life with them. He could have moved them more if he'd have written: Closed on Account of Hitting the Number.

With only one foot in the store, he reached behind the door window and tore the sign down. The transparent tape, weakened by a week of sun and heat, relinquished its burden without a struggle.

"Take the suitcases upstairs. I'll make a couple of sandwiches. Cheese?" He didn't bother to watch Allan nod. He put up coffee, took off his jacket and tie, and sat down heavily.

There was no more sense in thinking about Florida. Without Sarah, it didn't make any difference. The point now was to make some money fast, enough to go back to

New York and be able to send Allan off to a good school. Nothing else mattered. He knew the emptiness of life without Sarah would pass. It was a matter of time.

Time heals. Time will make me forget. Time will make me a rich man.

He wouldn't go back to carpentry and become a slave to a weekly check. He'd find a way somehow to pay off Quinn, maybe with the insurance on Sarah's life. Then he'd squeeze every penny he could from the *shvartzers.*

Farber suddenly realized that he hated them. He told himself that although he never really liked them before moving to Washington, he didn't fear or hate them as he did now. He had given money willingly many times whenever the union made collections for one or another Negro's defense fund. It seemed that some Negro was always being framed for some crime he didn't commit, according to what the union or the liberal do-gooders claimed. And the crime always seemed to be rape. They were forever being accused of raping white women. Where there's smoke there's fire. Maybe the accusers were right, after all, he thought.

He had seen the *shvartzers* steal what they could, scream the filthiest of words at him, and threaten his life several times.

They killed Sarah.

Niggers, that's what they are. He had seen mothers changing men while their children's diapers went unchanged. The good ones, where were they? He couldn't blame the white people from running when the *shvartzers* moved into a neighborhood. Weeds begin to grow, lawns die and become garbage patches, houses are neglected, and the neighborhood degenerates into a slum, infested with rats and vermin on stinking piles of trash and garbage thrown into alleys. Slums don't make themselves.

That they don't want to make better lives for themselves is one thing. But why should they want to stop someone else from bettering his own lot? He remembered indifferent faces which seemed to accept their life. The only thing they're not impassive about is committing crime.

Prostitutes, muggers, drunks, thieves, dope addicts, murderers. The police can't do anything about it. They're even afraid to come into the area. He remembered seeing a movie a long time ago. What was it? Yeah, it was with Charles Boyer playing some kind of a gangster in an Arab quarter, the casbah. For some reason of religious sanctuary, the police never went into the casbah to arrest him and the other thieves. Now the police were afraid to come into this area because they'd be chewed up. What did he want from the *shvartzers?* Being a Ku Klux Klanner wouldn't bring his wife back. How could he think about them when his wife lay fresh in the ground, rotting away minute by minute? "To keep from going crazy," he said aloud.

"What did you say, Dad?"

"Er, nothing."

"Got the sandwiches?"

Farber stood up. "Yeah, in a minute."

Sarah, rotting away. He remembered how she used to

[257]

run to the sink and wash her hands each time she handled sticky change from the kids.

Silently, tearlessly, with back turned toward his son, he cried.

The procession began early the next morning with Mrs. Jackson, taciturn and brooding, who shuffled in wearing old house slippers with backs bent forward by thick heels. Her house dress, several sizes too large, made her bulk seem even more massive.

"Ah come to pay mah bill and this here extra two dollars what Miz Simon lend me one day. She give me more, but ah pay later on that."

Farber stood silent for a moment. "She lent you money?"

"Yeah." She eyed him coolly, suspiciously, as if not trusting him with dollars his wife had given, but having no alternative but to pass them on to him by default.

Just a few dollars, he thought. It wouldn't hurt anything. I wish she'd have told me about it. I wouldn't have said no. I wonder if there are any more. She could have left some sort of record. Where could I look?

"That's okay about the rest of the money, Mrs. Jackson. Pay whenever you can." Should he ask? he wondered. "How much more did she give you?"

Mrs. Jackson glared in return. "You get it back."

He had a right to know how much more, he told himself, fighting a shame which began to creep into his consciousness. Sarah was a good woman. She cared for them. "Forget about the rest," he said.

Later, Mrs. Hobson, still wearing curlers in the shape of fish, registered as much sympathy as her deep-set eyes and enormous brow would allow. Her head turned to one side, while the corners of her mouth dipped downward. In her hand she carried a large bowl covered on the top with waxed paper.

"Here," she said. "For you and you boy. Ah made it from mah own chicken." A few tears gathered and flowed over the corners of her eyes.

The bowl was warm to the touch. Farber removed the waxed paper and breathed deeply of the aroma of chicken soup, thick and almost gelatinous with chunks of chicken and vegetables. "Thank you," he said, holding back his own tears while trying to think how he could ever ask her to pay her long-overdue bill.

On the following days they came to express regrets and sorrow—Jimmy the breadman, other grocers, and people from the market. Mother Matthews and many other customers seemed just as disturbed that the murderer was a black man as by the murder itself.

They're ashamed, Farber told himself. It serves them right. Refusing to listen to any more alibis and tongue-clucking, he closed the store at six o'clock, the earliest he had ever done so. He was tired, more tired than he had ever been in his life. Fatigue wracked his body, charging through it like sensations of pain.

Not bothering to check and empty the cash register or to do any of the usual nightly cleaning, he went directly into the kitchen to eat, more out of habit than desire. The food tasted chalky, no matter what it was, tomatoes and cheese or bread and butter. No, he wouldn't eat but go to bed instead.

Upstairs he heard Allan's radio tuned to blaring music. That's all the boy ever does, he thought, wondering whether the proper mourning period had ended and whether he should ask Allan to turn off the radio. He shuffled to his own room instead and lay down on the bed without taking off his clothes.

He thought of Sarah.

Her life insurance money had been quick in coming to him, and he just as rapidly paid off Quinn and a few other debts even though a sense of guilt had tightened around him like a noose. Even now he felt sinful for using the insurance benefit to pay for something which indirectly helped to kill her. He would build a memorial to her, he thought, or perhaps give money in her name to charity or to buy trees for planting in Israel.

Eyes closed, he drifted away in his mind from the sound of Allan's music. Presently he was aboard a ship, looking down into the dark waters. For a few moments all he could see was his own reflection. Suddenly lightning and thunder struck, illuminating the dark waters momentarily and enabling him to see Sarah struggling far below. Again lightning creased the sky and she reappeared. He jumped in, not so much to save her but to be with her, but he swam hopelessly in the dark, waiting in vain for another flash of lightning. He lost her.

"Dad, Dad. Wake up!"

He opened his eyes.

"You were having a nightmare."

He turned around, away from Allan.

"You ought to take off your clothes, Dad. You can't sleep like that."

He didn't answer. The lights went out and he tried to resume searching for Sarah. A dream, he thought, nothing but a dream. When the time comes for me to die, I'll find that my whole life was a dream.

A black iceberg appeared in the water. Who ever heard of a black iceberg? But no, he couldn't tell if the iceberg were really black because of the darkness of the night. Angrily, he chipped away at the black iceberg with a hammer and a nail. You can't do that, he told himself. Nobody ever broke up an iceberg with such lousy tools. You're a carpenter, you ought to know better. He continued working, however, even though he told himself to stop. Small pieces of ice flew in all directions, striking his face, entering his mouth, and even hitting his eyes.

He awoke by himself, his bed and clothes damp with perspiration. Unthinkingly, he got up and sat down on a chair by the bed.

[261]

Allan awoke to the noise of someone rapping on the glass window of the store. He looked out and saw several customers standing around by the door. A soda pop truck pulled up to the curb and the deliveryman got out.

"Mr. Farber not opened yet?" the driver asked one of the customers.

"He mus' be sleepin'," the customer replied, himself not yet wide awake.

Allan rushed down the stairs to the kitchen and found it just as he had left it last night when his father had gone to bed early. Usually in the mornings his father had water boiling on the stove and two fresh eggs on the table ready for breakfast.

He passed through the storeroom and into the empty store. Where was his father?

He didn't bother going down to check the basement. Its door latch fastened from the outside told him his father couldn't possibly be down there. Nobody was in the yard.

Upstairs, Allan thought, he didn't really look around upstairs. He found his father in a chair, head drooped, lolling grotesquely and eyes bulging open.

"Dad, what's wrong? You sick?"

His father muttered a low guttural sound, much like a foreign language badly received over a short-wave radio. His facial muscles twitched and his arms and legs trembled.

Frightened, Allan said loudly, "You'd better get to bed. You're sick. Don't worry about the store. We'll keep it closed." He cautiously approached his father, expecting almost anything to happen. "Come on," he said, taking an arm, "I'll help you into bed."

Farber permitted himself to be led, but when he reached the bed, he beat savagely with his hands on the pillow before trying to pull it down on his head like a helmet.

"I want out," he screamed. "Out of this cage! Don't keep me locked up!"

Almost as suddenly as it began, his outbreak halted. He slid into bed and closed his eyes.

Allan, too perplexed and astounded to do anything but cover him with a blanket, left by walking backward to the door. He returned a few seconds later and laid a palm against his father's forehead. There was no fever.

Now Farber wandered in an empty field with winter winds pushing at his face. In the distance he saw a house set against the sun, a dull red ember skimming low over the horizon. Closer, he saw that it was an uncompleted house still under construction, but it was not new. The wooden beams of the roof were dark and heavily creased with weather-worn lines. It doesn't make any difference, he thought, as long as I'm warm. He curled up like a dog and slept on the floor, only to be awakened by noise, perhaps the workmen returning.

"Daddy," Allan cried, shaking him. "What's the matter with you? Should I get a doctor?"

"No," Farber rasped. "There's no sense in it." God, he thought, was that my voice or someone else's? "Let me sleep," he begged.

Allan returned downstairs and made himself breakfast. He spent the rest of the day roaming, ducking every time he heard someone at the door. He hoped the customers and deliverymen would think the closing had something to do with the death of his mother. He knew, however, that they might think it strange that the store had been closed for a while, opened, and now closed again. A new sign would have to be made about closing on account of death in family and then pasted on the door where the old one had been.

Several cans of vegetables lay crookedly on a shelf; he straightened them before looking for other things to do to pass the time. For a short time he watched television until thoughts of his father's condition made viewing difficult.

There's no sense in calling a doctor now, he told himself, content to believe that his father would get well by tomorrow. Besides, if you'll leave things alone, they're apt to get better. Didn't his own painful rupture lessen to nothing?

Suppose his father was really sick and dying? A few tears came to his eyes. Now his father was dying and would soon be gone like his mother.

He tried not to think of his mother again, but he did, and fresh tears chased the old. He had promised himself not to cry anymore after having seen himself and others crying at the synagogue and cemetery. By sheer will, he had forced his black grief to become shortlived, to become a gray ache. But now he found himself slipping back into mourning.

He thought of the funeral, and the way he had day-dreamed during the services, just like he did at weddings and bar mitzvahs. He had paid attention, however, when the rabbi mentioned his mother's name and how she had suffered so much pain that God decided to relieve her of the suffering. Allan had felt like telling the rabbi that she wasn't in any pain and she wasn't sick. Then the rabbi had addressed him by name, looking directly at him. "Allan, your mother was taken because God needed her more than you did."

In the half year since moving into the store, he had seen little of his mother. He had been away with his friends, and she had busied herself in the house and store, but he had known her presence. His breakfast was made for him in the morning. His clean clothes laid out. A hasty admonishment was given now and then for staying out late, or not taking a bath, or not helping with any of the chores.

No, he just wouldn't think about her.

The next day he found his father, face leaden, eyes dull, staring at the ceiling. The blanket lay crumpled on the floor, and when he picked it up to cover and tuck it in around his father's shoulders, a strong odor made him rear back in half disgust, half fear.

He wondered what to do; wait outside for Jimmy the breadman and ask for advice and help, or go see what Mother Matthews could do. Who else was there? Perhaps he could call his Uncle Benny in New York. But Uncle Benny was too far away, maybe even in Miami now, and probably would raise cain why a doctor hadn't been called right away.

His father hadn't been sick very long, he rationalized.

Just one day and a couple of nights. However, it looked like it was going to be another day of his father's talking to himself and not eating.

Allan returned downstairs, picked up the telephone book, and flipped it open to the section marked physicians in the yellow pages. There were many names but he couldn't decide which one to choose, so he chose none, telling himself that he wouldn't know how to ask a doctor to make a house call, and the problem of paying the fee, of actually handing over cash to the doctor, would be very embarrassing.

He would take care of his own father, and the healing medicine would be food.

He didn't bother to dilute the condensed soup, heated in the can, thinking that it would be more nutritious without water. Propped up in a sitting position for spoonfeeding, his father, waxlike and drawn, cooperated, even though he sucked in only a few spoonfuls before beginning to mumble, gradually speaking louder and more coherently.

"I've got to go home before I go crazy here," he said, wringing his hands and cracking his knuckles, something Allan had never seen him do before. "She's the only one who knows how to take care of me. If I don't eat, she makes me eat."

Dreamlike, Allan returned the soup to the kitchen, spilled the contents into the sink and put the empty can in the refrigerator. His father is crazy, the thought came to

[266]

him, along with the burden of blame for not immediately getting a doctor who could have prevented the insanity or stopped it from getting worse.

Mother Matthews will help. Maybe she'll be able to look at his father and do something. She doesn't have the clap anymore. Dr. Thompson took care of that.

Dr. Thompson.

The number of the clinic he found easily enough, but he agonized over how to lure the doctor to come over.

"Dr. Thompson, you wouldn't remember me but remember the boy James Ferry you treated a couple months ago?"

"A white boy with gonorrhea?"

Allan breathed a sigh of happy deliverance. "Yeah, that's the one."

"Got burnt again? Come on over. We're open nine to five."

"No, no," Allan protested. "This is more serious and I need your help, or rather it's a friend of mine who needs your help who's sick and needs a doctor. You'll have to come over to his house."

"What about his family doctor? I just can't take cases out of the blue sky. I work for a clinic."

"Well, that's what I mean. He's got gonorrhea, too, but he's afraid to come to the clinic. So I wonder if you could drop by." He congratulated himself for remembering Dr. Thompson's obsession with people who refused clinic treatment for gonorrhea.

[267]

Allan gave him the address, explaining that it was over a grocery store so that he'd have to knock on the side door.

"He's your father, isn't he?" Dr. Thompson asked, examining Farber. "What's your real name?"

"Allan Farber."

"Well, Allan Farber, your diagnosis is incorrect. I could tell that without even looking at his member." The doctor held Farber's wrist for about half a minute, looked into his eyes, and pulled off the sick man's shirt to examine his chest, which he thumped, poked at with a finger, and massaged, before applying a stethoscope. He paused and then stuck a thermometer in Farber's mouth, holding his jaw open to prevent a glassy accident.

"Your father seems to be in a state of shock. He's got a rapid pulse rate. I don't know what else, and wouldn't know without a workup at the hospital. It could be something organic."

Farber, awakened by the thermometer, opened his eyes. "Who are you?"

"Dr. Thompson. Here to take care of you. You seem to be a little sick. Does anything hurt you?"

"Please let me go home. Sarah can take care of me." He closed his eyes.

"Who's Sarah?" Dr. Thompson asked.

"My mother. She was killed here a few weeks ago in a holdup."

"Murdered?"

[268]

"I guess so. Yeah."

"Your father has got to go to a hospital. Right away. It's hard for me to explain it, but I can't take care of him here."

"I can," Allan said, dreading the thought of sending his father to a hospital. How would that be done, with an ambulance or taxicab? What about all of the other details?

"No, you can't. Your father's got what you might call a nervous breakdown. My guess is that it was precipitated by your mother's death. He needs specialized help."

Dr. Thompson turned to Farber and shook him gently. "Mr. Farber, can you hear me?"

"Yeah," Farber replied in a low, almost inaudible voice.

"Do you feel all right?"

A long period of silence followed before Farber opened his eyes. His unshaven face remained frozen and blank. "What did you say?"

"We're going to have to take you to the hospital."

Allan sobbed. His tears spilled down his cheeks like rain on a smooth, round rock. "I could take care of him. I told you that. If he goes, I'll be left here all alone."

Dr. Thompson motioned with his head for Allan to leave the bedroom. Then he followed the boy into the hall, where he grasped his arm.

"Look. You said you could take care of him? Okay. You'll have to wash him first of all with a cloth or a sponge and soapy water. You're going to have to feed him and take him to the toilet and give him his medicine. I'm going to

[269]

let him rest in bed for a couple of days. If he doesn't show signs of improvement, off to the hospital he goes, regardless of your crybaby tears. Your father's health is a bit more important than whether or not you're afraid of the dark."

Allan nodded, wiping his face with a sleeve.

"I'm going out for medicine that'll make him feel better. And if I catch you crying around him again, I'll send you to the hospital with a broken ass."

He was the only one on the beach. The others, fearing the midday sun or wishing to nap after the full lunch at the hotel, had left around noon and would not be back until after three. He did not mind being alone, for it felt as if the sun were concentrating only on him.

Now a mirror came to his mind as he thought of the sun penetrating his body. He stood examining his naked body in the full-length mirror of the hotel bathroom. His hands, sundarkened, were no longer choppy with crevices. A thick band of whiteness on his hips separated like a no man's land the tanned skin of his torso and that of his legs.

It was funny, he thought. He took money from the Negro to get skin like the Negro. But nothing was given and nothing was taken. He had worked hard for everything, and the sand and sun were his reward.

The surf, sounding like the slow breathing of a sleeping man, sent its water gently around his heels and calves to lap lovingly at his thighs and buttocks. It cooled the sand-touched parts of his body, although the rest of him remained hot and perspiring. The water's coolness reminded him of the electric heater he had kept on the floor behind the counter. The heater toasted the side of the body presented before it, provided that portion was stationary long enough, about a minute, to get warm. The other side stayed cold.

A bell's tinkling made him open his eyes and raise himself on his elbows. He narrowed his eyes to keep the glare of the sun out as he scanned the beach for the source of the sound. At first he thought an ice cream vendor passed, but no one else was on the beach. Besides, the bell had a somber, mournful peal, unlike the loud, commercial ring-a-ding of vendors with their ice cream boxes strapped on their backs.

Looking out at the ocean, he saw a small sailboard which rocked perilously on the waves. A woman with long, dark hair sat at the edge of the boat, dangling her feet in the water and unmindful of the danger.

She looked like Sarah. He stood up and walked to the water to see more clearly. Yes, it was Sarah. There was no doubt in his mind.

He cupped his hands to his mouth and called to her, but the sound of the waves and tinkling of the bell smothered the call. Shouting her name, he trudged deeper and deeper into the water until it reached his chest, but still she did not hear him. He began to swim toward the boat.

When he lifted his head after a few minutes to see how far he had gone, the boat had disappeared. The tinkling continued, and now he could see that it came from a bell caged in a dome-shaped buoy.

[271]

Farber sat up quickly in bed. He listened carefully, hoping to hear some echo or reverberation of the tinkling bell ushering in the entrance of a customer.

I overslept. Customers are coming in, and here I am, sleeping. No wonder I'm losing my shirt.

He jumped out of bed, stumbling over the chair in the darkness before he found the light switch. The clock on the bureau read eight twenty. Outside the window, night gave no sign of retreating before the dawn, yet he thought the time to be late in the morning. In the store, the electric clock told him it was almost two thirty.

I must have been mistaken about the bell, he thought, both sorry and annoyed that he wouldn't be able to open the store for another few hours. He wanted to make money badly.

He turned the lights on, and became surprised at the unfamiliar sight of the store, as if he were seeing it after being away for a long time. A few things were not quite where they should have been, or not where they were when he left them last night. Last night? Why does it seem so long ago?

The floor had been swept and the canned goods on the shelves straightened. Three cartons of stock—soap powder, cereal, and cornstarch—which were delivered yesterday afternoon, he remembered, were now shelved. He had meant to put up the stock, he was certain, also remembering that he had been too tired and had closed the store at six o'clock.

No wonder everything feels so strange. I must have

been asleep at least fourteen hours straight. He yawned and stretched his arms. I might as well wait and rest in bed.

Upstairs, he checked Allan, who slept soundly, and returned to his own bed.

Farber felt something cool and soft against his cheek, like the touch of Sarah's hand to check if he had fever. Eyes opened, he saw his son wiping with a sponge. He smiled and sat up, reaching out to pat the boy's cheek.

Allan, returning the smile, thanked God.

"What do you think I am, a showcase that you have to clean?" He leaned back and changed his expression to a frown. "I feel like I had the flu or something. What time's it?"

"After nine."

"I've been here all morning?"

"You've been in bed a whole week, Dad."

Farber shook his head in disbelief. "Why didn't you wake me? I really must have been sick." He pushed Allan's hand away. "Stop washing me, will you!"

"Dr. Thompson said you were supposed to rest."

"Who's he?"

"The doctor who's taking care of you. He's coming in a few minutes. I've got to finish before he comes."

Farber grunted, taking the sponge away from Allan. He quickly ran it over the dry areas of his torso and returned it to Allan. "Okay, finished."

A knock on the door downstairs summoned Allan, who returned with Dr. Thompson.

[273]

"Feeling better, Mr. Farber?"

"Could be worse, could be worse."

"You're suffering from a little strain. Overwork. You'll be better now."

"What strain? Just a little flu. That's all."

"You've got to take it easy. Stop worrying. Everything will be all right."

Farber sat up. "Allan, get me my pants. Doctor, how much do I owe you?"

"Forget about it."

Farber nodded, pleased. "I've got to open the store. It's enough vacation already."

"Mr. Farber, you've got to stay in bed a little longer. I'll tell you the truth. You've had a nervous breakdown."

Farber laughed loudly as he swung his legs around to the side of the bed. "Look, I've got a lot of things. I'm even allergic to pork. But I'm not *mishugah.*"

Allan blushed when his father used the Yiddish word for crazy. He was glad to see Dr. Thompson smile and nod his head.

"You'll be all right, Mr. Farber. But you'll have to rest another day, at least. It's almost lunchtime and the day's almost shot for business."

"The evening's the busy time. You're the one who's crazy, doctor. I've got a living to make. Who's going to pay my bills?"

"If you open the store today, I'm going to charge you for the visits I made here. That's because I don't like to waste time on a patient who won't listen. Well, what do

[274]

you say, close up and not pay, or open and pay?"

"Okay," Farber said, lying back in bed.

In the hall, Dr. Thompson whispered to Allan. "He's far from being in the clear. It might even get worse."

Farber made up his mind to sell the store as he lay in bed waiting for the alarm clock to go off. Body aches and soreness, unmollified by the hot and humid morning, communicated themselves to his mind, now fully awake after being up only a few minutes. His decision came shortly after he cursed the electric clock whose alarm set at six his own subconscious had anticipated prematurely by waking him at five thirty.

He dreaded getting up, dressing, shaving, opening the store, and standing on his feet until ten at night. The store was his coffin, he thought, and the hours the nails for it.

It had been several weeks since his illness, and although he grudgingly accepted the diagnosis of a nervous breakdown, he dismissed the fear that the store might erode deeper into his mental health. He'd sell the store because he was tired of the work and the hazards and not because the store was no good. He was making and saving some money, but the work seemed harder.

He closed his eyes to concentrate on enjoying a cool breeze blowing lightly across his face. The night had been hot, but he had turned the electric fan off since its noise kept him awake. At three in the morning, sleep had come, late, as it had on previous evenings when there was neither heat nor the noise of the fan to keep him awake.

Who would be crazy enough to buy this store? he wondered, opening his eyes to look at the clock. Five after the hour. He must have dozed. But why hadn't the alarm gone off? He vowed that he wouldn't get out of bed until it rang.

It sounded. Farber, imbued with the thought of selling the store, got up with a faint hope stirring within him. He'd find a broker and put the store up for sale immediately.

Three hours later, the milk put away, the morning customers for breakfast foods waited on and gone, he ate a breakfast of black coffee and a slice of devil's food cake. Holding cup in one hand and cake in the other, he leaned over the counter, bracing himself on his elbows. There was little he could do to spruce up the store and make it more attractive to a buyer. The bumpy wooden floor, held together uncertainly by rotting planks and underpinnings, he'd replace by a few planks and floor braces.

He looked around at the flies dotting the air, their black specks spotting pull-down cardboard advertisements attached to strings of the fluorescent lights. On the old flypaper hanging behind the meat counter, the insects escaped entrapment by alighting on long-dead, nonsticky comrades.

The window with its multicolored crepe paper installed by a cigarette salesman reminded him of the jungle. The colors of the paper, already faded by the sun, ran in waves since being subjected to drops of rainwater dribbling from a leaky ceiling. Beneath the crepe on the sill empty soda pop bottles stood like stranded and forgotten sentries. Like tropical plants that trap and devour insects, the bottles contained dead flies stuck in a residue of syrup and live ones which futilely buzzed and bounced against their glass cages.

A large, amorphous movement flashed in front of Farber's eyes, interrupting his reverie. Mother Matthews waved and smiled at him through the window before entering. He noticed that her summery dress was cut short and tight; its front buttons straining but failing to make full connections, revealing a light brown slip. For a moment he thought, and hoped, that it was her skin that he saw.

"Mistah Simon. How're ya doin'?"

"Fine, thanks."

"Ah just came in not to really buy anything but to tell you how glad ah feel that you feel better. Ah might even give you some *free* consultation now that you old self back again." As she had once done long ago, she winked at him and made him feel an odd tingling in his body.

What did she mean by free consultation? he thought, wanting her but feeling shame for his desire. "Thank you," he said, avoiding her eyes by darting his toward the meat counter. "Nice pork today."

I'm a pork-pig. An animal. Where's my decency? Sarah will never forgive me. She's gone. Who am I kidding? What's left in this world? Unhappiness and hard work. Thievery and murder. Take what you can while you can.

"Ah think ah'll order couple-three items, after all. You been closed for a long time on top the fact that ah been tradin' somewhere's else also." She winked again and made

[277]

her way behind the counter as she usually did to help herself to the cans of sardines which were directly behind him.

"Yeah," Farber said, "I lost a lot of trade." It had been more than a month since Sarah's death, but during the two weeks the store had been closed because of the funeral and his sickness, the customers had grown accustomed to buying elsewhere. Even so, a brisk evening business of beer, soft drinks, and light summer food more than made up for the temporary loss.

"Mah larder is empty," she said as she eased in front of him, forcing him backward to the shelves. Then she pushed herself against him in order to reach behind his back for the cans. "Everthing ah own is empty."

She licked her lips and somehow emitted a strong odor of perfume which enveloped him and excited his senses. He found himself almost involuntarily sucking in short, swift sniffs to catch as much as he could of the sweet pleasure of the perfume.

Suddenly, she thrust forward again, harder this time as if losing her balance. Pinned against the shelves, he grappled with the cans to hold on to something.

No, no, he thought. She couldn't be trying to excite me, to want me. It was too soon after Sarah. Decency. Whose decency? he asked himself. Mine or Sarah's?

"Me oh mah. Mah feet's all butterfingers today."

The screen door slammed shut and a boy of about fourteen walked in, his black eyes popping at the strange arrangement behind the counter.

Mother Matthews quickly picked up her cans and re-

[278]

turned to the front counter. "Looka here, Mistah Simon. Ah got to run. But ah need a case a beer. Could you bring it on up?"

"Not now," Farber said, looking through the corner of his eye at the boy. "I'll have to do it after I close the store. Ten o'clock okay?"

The boy smirked and cleared his throat.

It's the truth, Farber wanted to tell the boy. I can't leave the store right in the middle of the day. I'd lose more customers. I'm not interested in her, now or at ten o'clock. What's the use in telling that to the boy? They know about sex and making love before they're ten years old. Look, sonny, my wife just died, he felt like saying. I'm a decent man.

"That's fine, Mistah Simon. Put it on the book."

He wanted to tell her that there was no more credit, no more book, but he could not. She left, and only because of the boy, he did everything within his power not to look at her legs and buttocks.

The boy, hanging his jaw low, turned to look at her and then tossed thirty cents on the counter. "Pack a Camels."

"You old enough to smoke?" Farber wanted to take vengeance on the boy for intruding.

"Ah'm old enough to fuck."

"Keep your filthy mouth at home!" Farber shot back, slamming the cigarettes on the counter.

"Where mah matches?"

"A penny extra for two bookmatches. They cost me money, too." A forcefulness filled him, brought on by the

[279]

visit of Mother Matthews and the obnoxiousness of the boy.

With jaw hanging lower, and brow furrowed, the boy mumbled under his breath before he spoke up. "They free in the drugstore."

"Get them free in the drugstore."

They stood staring at each other, each not giving ground. Farber's forcefulness of two mixtures now added a third, that of frankness resulting from his belief that he might not be in business much longer.

"I know what you're thinking. A cheap Jew. If I'm so cheap in asking for a penny, you're more cheap for not giving it to me."

The boy, surprised, shrugged his shoulders and left without the matches.

For the rest of the afternoon, Farber felt a sense of exhilaration. He seemed to float as he waited on customers, smiling when he wasn't whistling or humming. He felt young and energetic. The sale of the store would remove a yoke. Responsibility was being shorn away from him. And then there was Mother Matthews. Despite his efforts not to think of her, she kindled in his mind strangely, forbiddenly, tormenting him by dancing out of his reach each time his picture-mind called forth her image.

A tinge of excitement stirred in his groin and he shivered, as one does during the first few seconds in a hot shower. He perspired heavily in the hallway as he waited long minutes for Mother Matthews to answer his knocking.

Carrying the cold cardboard case of beer, now resting on the doormat, had done little to cool him.

Although intensely alert and wary as a young fox, he breathed softly as he tried to catch his breath, daring not to make sounds which would bring inquiring eyes.

What took her so long to answer?

He hoped she'd be pleased about getting the cold beer. Usually, he sold only warm beer by the case which he kept in the storeroom. Loose bottles were sold cold from the walk-in.

The door opened and she faced him squarely, cowlike. She wore a silky robe with a loosened sash which helped reveal the cleavage of her breasts and the height of her thighs.

"Ah was coolin' off in the bath. Sorry to keep you waitin' out here in the cold."

He laughed too long and loudly, eager to burn up some of his tension. "It's okay. I'm not in a hurry." He bent over and picked up the case. "Just let me bring this in. They're all ice cold."

"That's a treat. How come you so good to me?" She stepped aside to let him pass. "Right in the kitchen's all right. On the table."

An exotic but strong odor of burning wax candles and perfume served to summon an intoxication which made him enter a world different from his own; a world which could do nothing but interrupt briefly his dull and hard life.

"You gonna stay for a beer, Mistah Simon?"

[281]

What he had hoped she would say, she said, yet her words surprised him into silence. He stood, awed as if present in a holy place, wishing he had never come and that he could stay forever.

"The opener's in the sink drawer. Under the sink. Just pull out the drawer, baby. You see it."

He walked over mechanically, stopped for a moment at the sink, and turned to face her. The sash, now untied, hung loosely at her sides. The robe parted, whether by design or accident he did not know, or care.

She smiled at his expression of ardor. "Now, ah'm a bit embarrassed at you lookin' at me like that and me lookin' like this. Don't make no sense me slippin' into somethin' respectable now. You already seen me almost like ah am. Ain't got much more to show you." She smiled. "That is, if you interested in seein' more."

With shaking hands, he turned away from her, embarrassment and shame enveloping him. What did she mean? he wondered. He didn't know whether she teased him jokingly or really wanted to have intercourse with him. Nervously and noisily, he scuffled with forks and spoons as he looked for the opener, hoping to gain moments to escape her presence and thus gain his.

Suddenly, she came close up behind him and raked the front of his pants with her fingers. "Baby, you don' even got you profile yet."

He jerked his body away to escape her hand, which alternately massaged and clawed the front of his trousers.

[282]

"Careful, baby. You almost knock me over."

Farber couldn't keep his eyes away from her body, now revealed in all its tawny pudginess, purple teats, and kinky triangle. Her nonchalance surprised him more than her body; she behaved as if she wore a slip or some other garment underneath the open robe.

She took him by the hand. "C'mon, Mistah Simon. Les' go. Or do you want a beer first?"

He didn't answer or move. His heart pumped furiously and his knees felt unhinged.

"It been a long time since you had you some snatch. How long it been? Since the Missus die? Ah know it tough on you body, 'specially a man body, when the come juice don't come but stay. It build up in you and you feel like tearin' the world apart. C'mon." She pointed with her head toward her bedroom, and then walked, almost pulling him behind her.

"C'mon, baby. Take you clothes off."

"No, I want them on."

"Oh, that good. That the mark of a minute man. Some studs ride me for a hour, almost."

Her robe slipped from her body onto the floor, and she sat, naked, on the edge of the bed. Dropping his trousers and underwear down his legs until they hugged his calves and covered his shoes, he plopped next to her.

"C'mon, Mistah Simon. Get it up. The night and the mood ain't gonna last forever." She touched his penis and whispered for him to close his eyes. "Make believe ah'm Miz Simon."

[283]

"No, no!" he shouted, standing up but losing his balance because of the dropped trousers. He fell on top of her knees. The sight now of his trousers, down but not off, and his shirt still on him, gave him a feeling of being a busy and mighty ruler while she, in her demeaning, subservient nudeness, appeared as his ever-fulfilling slave. His clothes, to him, expressed masculinity against the femininity of her bare skin. He motioned her to the middle of the bed.

He pushed hard against her, trying to cause her pain, hating her for being the racial sister of the man who murdered his wife, and for leading and letting him commit an immoral act.

"You rough, Mistah Simon. But ah'm not complainin'. It feel good."

He became angrier, stronger, harder. He didn't want her to enjoy his deed of hate. A wave of relief overcame him; his hatred ebbed to indifference, boredom.

"Mah, mah," she sighed a few moments later, "you a minute man."

He pulled up and fastened his clothes. "I've got to get back." Near the door, he turned to her. "I don't have time for a beer, now. Allan will worry."

"Mistah Simon, you know ah makes a livin' from givin' advice and fortunes. But nobody around here really buyin' that now. When you poor, you don' put down that kind of money. So ah ask mah friends to help me now and then with a donation."

She flung her robe on her shoulders. "Give what you

wish. But ah wish you would give. That sort of mah motto now."

"Okay, forget about the case of beer."

"Baby, ah get five times that much for half hour of advice. You got to be kiddin'."

He knew she was a prostitute, but the realization that she was asking for money hit him hard. It was the first time he had been with a woman of her sort. If only he wouldn't have to pay, he thought. Perhaps that would lessen his sin.

"I don't have any money on me." He felt dirty, outside and inside. How many before him? How many of their crawling germs and lice were transferred to him. "How much do you want?"

"You wish is mah command."

"Let's make it that case and five dollars. I'll deduct that from your bill that you owe me."

"That all?"

"I'm sorry, Mrs. Matthews, ah, Mother Matthews."

"You son give me more than that."

"Allan?"

"Yeah. He even a better fuck than you."

After a few moments of stunning disbelief he assumed a serious expression. He left, slamming the door, not because of anger for Mother Matthews or Allan, but because of haste to see the boy. In his tired and guilt-blunted mind, he believed the woman capable of transmitting to Allan by psychic means what had happened. He had to explain to Allan, and tell him that what they had both done was not so terrible.

[285]

Allan returned home from Mother Matthews' building a few minutes before his father. He had stood outside her door listening, and forming pictures in his mind of his father's movements, much like his own had been.

His anxiety and fear of being discovered had argued against that curiosity and concern which had forced him to follow his father and to remain in the hallway with an ear pressed against the door. The fact that the apartment belonged to Mother Matthews further shocked him into espionage. From the beginning, Allan had suspected something. Before his father had left, he told Allan about a case of beer that had to be taken to a customer. What customer needed beer to be delivered at home? Allan had thought. Men could carry their own. The women? If they had husbands or male friends, the men would have picked up the case. If they were without men, and he knew that many of them were, then they were also without money and couldn't afford beer. Credit? Maybe, but his father had begun to restrict credit.

More important to Allan had been the fact that his father almost never made deliveries at night. A fear crept into his mind that someone might attack and perhaps kill his father. If he didn't follow and protect his father, he'd find him lying hurt or dead on the street.

Now he was back home, hating his father for betraying his mother, and for being with Mother Matthews. As far as the Farber family was concerned, he thought, that woman belonged to him, even though it had been a long time since he last visited her. Besides, he told himself, there was something unhealthy and dirty about father and son sharing the same woman.

Allan heard his father coming in through the side door, which he slammed and then shook by the knob to check whether it was closed. Next came the sounds of heavy footsteps on the stairs, the silence of a pause at the landing, and then the continuation of the footfalls.

Usually, Allan would have called out, "Dad?" not so much as a reassuring question, but as a greeting. Farber would then answer, "Yeah."

Both were silent now.

What could I tell him? Farber thought. That it's all right to go screw with a whore and then tell him not to go again? But what about me? How long am I supposed to mourn, a month, six months, a year? As if time made a difference.

He stopped in the doorway of Allan's room and watched him put down a book he was reading. They gazed at each other, betraying no feeling, each waiting for the other to make a confession and a plea for understanding and mercy. A fraction of a second before his father turned away, Allan picked up the book.

The broker, Abe Roth, and the prospective buyer stood for a while examining the exterior before entering. Roth, nervously scratching his chin, smiled at Farber. "Mr. Farber, I want you to meet Mr. Gondolous. Mr. Spyros Gondolous."

[287]

Gondolous, large and dark with caveman sullenness, nodded without shaking hands or saying hello. Hair covered his exposed skin like ants over a dead worm. His wrists, the back of his hands, and even the knuckles grew hair. They sprouted in waxy efflorescence from his ears, creating an ill-conceived earmuff which turned thicker and blacker near the lobes. A short but thick moustache, joined by hair wildly springing into the light from the dark of his nostrils, was guarded over by a huge nose, over the skin of which tiny, separate hairs shared space with blackheads. His eyebrows formed one continuous line, uneven only where they joined over the nose. He was completely bald.

"I was telling Mr. Gondolous here about your store," Roth continued, giggling as he tapped his breast pocket for a cigarette. "Mr. Gondolous here is looking. So naturally, I immediately thought of your store, Mr. Farber."

Gondolous nodded. "You got all nigger trade?"

Farber shuddered when he heard the spoken word, glancing out of the corners of his eyes to confirm his already absolute certainty that no customer was in the store.

"Yeah," he answered. "All colored trade."

"Good. No good white customer. Nigger customer best."

"That's what I say," Roth said, his head shaking from side to side involuntarily as he continually shifted his stance. "White shows up white on the register. That is, nothing. Black shows up black. In the black. That's a

[288]

play on words," he informed Gondolous.

Gondolous shrugged his shoulders. "Shit."

"White customers are too choosy, too know-it-all," the broker, unperturbed, continued. "Can't make any money on them. The Hershey Bars, they're the best. Give them their nookie and their bottle, that's all they care about. You can keep your elbow on the scale if you're so inclined."

Gondolous looked around the store, walked a few feet, stopped, and spread his legs apart. He began to rock on his feet, creating a squeaky, ship-on-the-sea noise. "Floor pretty bad. Shit."

Roth forced a laugh. "Forget about the floor. This is a good business. Fifteen hundred, sixteen hundred. The sky's the limit. It all depends what you want to put into it."

"Shit. What kind insurance you carry here?" Gondolous asked Farber.

"I have an application for plate glass insurance. I understand I can get it."

"How much?"

"Well," Farber said, speaking slowly to gather his facts, "the man before me, Mr. Gittelson, it cost him thirty-eight dollars a year. I let it lapse, but I'm going to renew it again." A slight blush appeared with the lie.

"What they ask you for premium now?"

"I'm not sure. I think it's about one hundred fifty, maybe one seventy-five."

"What else insurance? Break-in? Holdup?"

[289]

"Can't get those around here, Mr. Gondolous," Roth said. "This whole area's been canceled out by the companies some time ago. You should know that."

"I know. I been in business."

"Then you also ought to know that you can't get a good store unless you're willing to make sacrifices," Roth almost shouted in his enthusiasm. "So somebody makes it rough on you once in a while. So you die of cancer from smoking cigarettes, or you get hit by a car. So what?"

"I not afraid nigger holdup!" Gondolous raised his voice and Farber glanced nervously at the door. "One time one shoot me close and gunpowder make face black like him. I not afraid guns. But insurance not cover holdup, shit. I go broke."

Roth, his staccato laughter breaking a few moments of silence after Gondolous' outburst, pointed a finger at Farber. "You ask this man if he's going broke. You going broke, Mr. Farber?"

Farber shook his head. "I got fire insurance. It's the only insurance I got now."

Gondolous rocked on the floor. "Wait till you first fire and then they cancel."

"You make enough money," Roth said, "you don't worry about insurance. Everybody's worried about insurance except Mr. Farber here. To be truthful, Mr. Gondolous, we'll tell you the truth. Could I tell him the truth, Mr. Farber?"

Farber nodded.

"This man here recently had a tragic accident. He lost

[290]

his wife. He had a nervous breakdown. He now wants to retire since he feels he made enough and can retire to live a full life without working anymore but just taking it easy."

"This store going broke. It got look of bad store. Mister, I bet you best customer the rats and cocker-roach. Chain store sell stuff for what you get at cost. I bet you got someting chains ain't got. Credit." He walked over to the door. "I wait in car, Mr. Roth."

"Number one," Roth shot back, "you're making a mistake. Number two, you're being too hasty. So he's got a little credit. Select clientele, I tell you. Call his bluff on a guarantee of fourteen hundred. Put up or shut up. It's a good store."

Gondolous raised a hair-infested arm and waved it thumbs down. Then he rocked near the door, invited new squeaks, and left without saying another word.

"Lousy Greek bastard," Roth said. "This is the third store in an hour."

"All got insurance problems?"

"It ain't that so much. It's something else. You can't even give away these small stores anymore. A person's got any sense, he buys into a big shopping center. Times have changed. An agent's got any sense, he don't handle these momma-poppa stores anymore."

"So you don't want to help me sell the store?"

"It's my living," Roth said. "Shit."

The disappearance of the sun down into the horizon barely affected the high temperature and humidity which clung tenaciously to the arrival of dusk. Perspiration poured through Farber's underclothes, trousers, and shirt to soak his apron. Had he worn still another garment over the apron it would have also been dampened.

To hell with it, he said to himself, still gloomy over the visit of Gondolous and Roth hours ago. He thought of closing the store in spite of the busy in-and-out trade which emptied the soft-drink box. Only a few cases of beer remained.

I'll take Allan to a movie and get something to eat outside. I'll give him a break.

Few words had been exchanged by them since Farber had been with Mother Matthews a few days ago. Yet Farber had silently forgiven Allan the day after. He's a growing boy, he had thought, and she got him like she got me. For that I won't blame him.

He felt sorry for Allan, moping around or hanging on the radio or television, day in, day out. He had blamed Allan's behavior on Sarah's death but now realized that perhaps the boy acted the way he did because he had been forbidden to associate with his Negro friends.

It was a mistake. I should have let him alone. I'll make up to him now. Take him out. Business is slowing down and all the drinks are gone, anyway. I won't lose anything.

He had begun to put away a few of the perishables into the refrigerator when the screen door opened and shut several seconds later, telling him that more than one customer had entered. Without turning around to see who they were, he heard the sound of many feet shuffling and scraping the floor. Their bodies threw off odors of sweat that filled the store, like smoke in advance of a fire. Next, his eyes were assailed by the sight of Fat Nasty and two other youths.

"Dabba, dabba, doo, Mistah Jew. How do you do?"

"What right do you have coming here saying that?" Farber spoke with quivering lips. "Who do you think you are? Get out of here!" He despised himself for being afraid of the youths when he really shouldn't be. He knew his fear translated his face into a pallid, horror-stricken mask which encouraged his enemies.

Fat Nasty's lips, thick like a swollen piece of liver, parted. "Mothahfuck, we got a right here. Maybe we comfist-tating this here store for the black peoples."

The youth's companions laughed and shouted, "Yeah, yeah," rhythmically stamping their feet, shaking shoulders, and drumming thighs and hips with fingers and palms. All of them wore T-shirts and tight-fitting khaki trousers. Their hair, long and fuzzy, and rising high, resembled that of the pruned pompadour of a poodle. They nodded in unison and shouted support for their leader.

"Man, tell the Jew he just gotta go," said one of them.

Fat Nasty's face gleamed with animal perspiration. His round arms were the size of a normal man's thighs, and his chest heaved like a young gorilla's. "That right, mothah," he said. "But you got a chance. Pay the dues and we let you white ass stay."

"Does Tammu know about this? I want to know about that," Farber said, hoping he might talk them into leaving without trouble.

Fat Nasty shook his head and clenched his fists. "He

[293]

don' know nothin'. He desi-nate me collector, thas all. None you mothahfuck business, anyway." He came closer to where Farber stood in front of the meat showcase and raised a palm quickly, either as a sign for Farber to hand over money or as an intended blow to the grocer's midsection. Only Fat Nasty knew, since Farber interpreted the move as an attack and quickly slammed the youth's arm aside.

Fat Nasty, youth and weight on his side, lunged at Farber, pushing him against the showcase. Next he drove a huge fist all the way from his shoulder into Farber's abdomen. The grocer gasped at the pain stabbing deeply into his very being. He fought an impulse to retch as midsectional muscles and nerves reacted against the sudden, unnatural intrusion into the hallowed world they guarded. Clutching the showcase for support, Farber stood up, cold and dizzy, his heart thundering, his mind crying, Where is Allan? Where are the police?

A chopping blow downward across Farber's neck dropped the grocer again. He tried to rise but his legs were stiff and incapable of movement, like planks of wood. Helplessly, he watched as Fat Nasty kicked him, now on the hip, and then on the ribs and shoulder.

Reaching out, Farber grabbed for the ankles of the youth who screamed with delight at the prospect of having at last met opposition to make the fight interesting. The grocer ducked his chin against the youth's knees and held on desperately, not daring to let go as he tried to avoid the fists which sought his head. Fat Nasty jerked his legs free,

[294]

but at the expense of allowing Farber to scramble dizzily to his feet.

The circle of caramel-colored faces melted backward in surprise. Farber grunted, his body jerked, and with all of his strength, the muscled power earned from a lifetime of hammering nails and sawing boards, he propelled a fist upward against Fat Nasty's jaw. The youth tumbled backward. His friends scattered aside to avoid the body, which landed on its back with an arm dangled underneath.

First there was the sound of the fall, and then the sharp, splintering noise of a bone being broken before the screams of Fat Nasty began. He rolled on his abdomen, howling with pain. A piece of jagged white bone stuck out from within an oozing, bloody red and black forearm. Tears streamed from his eyes as he rose to his feet.

Farber struck the two others, stunned by the loss of their leader. They managed only to parry and ward off his blows. Like a dog attacking chickens, he hit one, then the other, and even the helpless Fat Nasty. In Farber's mind he tore at the murderer of his wife, he pounded the blubber of Tammu, and smashed the faces of Quinn, Gittelson, the lawyers, and the insurance people. He beat unmercifully at all the flesh around him. His hatreds and frustrations became living and real and wholly destructible.

Much later, after he had cleaned himself and washed Fat Nasty's blood off the floor, Mrs. Jackson came in to ask if he had heard a rumor about a grocery man who chopped up a colored boy with a meat cleaver.

[295]

The sounds of sirens came through the air and prompted Farber to think that a big fire must be burning somewhere. He listened intently for a few moments, feeling a strange, prickling apprehension down his spine.

His body ached from the blows he had received from Fat Nasty, he wheezed when he breathed, and he knew that by tomorrow he'd feel stiff all over, yet his mind felt clear and calm. It was almost as if the fight, like his encounter with Mother Matthews, had freed him of pressures and prejudices. And then he wanted to do something for Allan, and he felt an exhilaration in calling for his son.

"Let's give ourselves a break. How'd you like to go out for a movie and something to eat?"

"Okay, Dad."

"I'm closing the store now. Why don't you help me with a few chores and then we'll go. Okay?"

Allan nodded and Farber thought that he detected a pleased alertness behind the placidity of the boy's expression. He wondered how long he'd be able to contain his son. There was no reason to believe that Allan would stay with him if the store remained unsold, nor was there any doubt in his mind that Allan hated the store, and probably emulated Sarah in despising his pursuit of profit.

As they worked preparing for the next day, several customers who thought the store still open knocked but were turned away by Farber waving his arms. He knew his willpower further gratified his son, who expected him to open the door each time to gain a few more pennies.

Their work almost done, they heard a frenzied pounding on the door, as if the person making the noise had immediately decided not to waste time by knocking softly at first.

"Closed!" an arm-waving Farber shouted, but still the rapping continued.

Farber ran over and saw a youth, shirtless, with perspiration streaming on his naked torso and glistening in the reflection from the streetlamp. The boy wore a red cloth swathed like a turban around his head.

"What do you want?"

"Where Allan?"

Allan, behind his father, came up to the door. "What's the matter, James?"

"They gonna come burn you-all out. Better get out quick."

Farber shook his head. "What do you mean? What are you talking about?"

"A riot, man. That what. A white mothah chop off the arm of a black boy. And then he use a knife to cut the boy in little pieces."

James turned around, looked over his shoulder, and narrowed his eyes to see if Farber and Allan were heeding his advice in any way. Father and son, however, stood transfixed near the door. James waved his arm effortlessly as a sign of farewell to Allan and ran down the street.

"Mishugah," Farber said, his head shaking.

Moments later they heard an explosion from a few blocks away followed by a muffled rumbling and a loud crash. Outside, men and boys ran in all directions.

[297]

"They're going to kill us!" Allan whispered loudly. "We've got to get out of here."

No, it couldn't be, Farber thought. Not here and not now. It was another bad dream, another nervous breakdown. The newspapers he'd been reading didn't hint of anything. It was a mistake. Some boys were throwing stones. That's all.

"Shut up and take it easy. Just don't get excited. First of all, nobody is gonna kill nobody. Second, I'm not going to run away. My property isn't going to be turned over free to the public. I'm not running a giveaway show."

Farber felt a cold satisfaction from his words. He didn't even have to look at his son's face to know they had an impact. "You'd better go upstairs if you're scared," he added, knowing it was a cruel thing to say.

"I'll stay down here with you," Allan informed his father grimly.

Farber knew his son was determined. He thought himself a fool for saying he'd remain in the store come what may, for it made a change of decision hinge upon destruction of his word and character in the eyes of his son. He looked into Allan's eyes and saw those of Sarah. The resemblance between wife and son was heightened somehow in his mind by the exigency of the moment. Please, the eyes said, let's not go to Washington. Don't leave me in the store alone. Leave the store now before it's too late.

He had sacrificed Sarah and now it was his and Allan's turn. This god-monster of shelves and smells was going to devour all. Its appetite was never satisfied.

[298]

"Okay," he said. "We'll go upstairs together." He dashed over to the register and emptied the bills and coins into a paper sack which he then carried into the kitchen and deposited within the unused furnace. If there were any looters, he thought, they'd never look in there.

Then he turned off all of the lights, hoping that the darkness might hide the store somehow from the rioters. For a moment he thought of selectively damaging a few things, breaking one of the windows, knocking down merchandise so that the hoodlums would think that the store had already been hit, but he couldn't bring himself to destroy the big window, which he'd replaced several times already, or the shelves, so recently painted by him to improve chances of selling the store, or the goods, which cost so much money.

In the safety of Allan's bedroom they looked for a while at the people who resembled war refugees carrying their worldly goods. Laden with heavy shopping bags, they raced by, shouting, screaming, laughing.

A loud crash from the store below startled Farber and Allan.

"I'm going to see what it is."

"No," Allan protested. "You'll get killed. I'm going with you."

Downstairs, a small flame in a bushel of freshly watered lettuce caught their eyes. It burned the rag wick stuffed in the mouth of a bottle nestling in the lettuce. Not daring to move, they watched breathlessly as the wetness of the lettuce slowly extinguished the fire.

[299]

Protected by the darkness of the store, they looked out through the gaping hole in the window. The person who had thrown the bottle had merged into the flowing crowd.

Farber pulled the partially burned wick and inspected it, accidentally dripping gasoline from the bottle. "Molotov cocktail," he told Allan. He looked at the ceiling and envisioned flames leaping and lapping at it.

"Okay, Allan. Let's get the hell out of here before we burn up alive." He was glad the possibility of fire gave him a way out without losing face in front of his son.

"Where we going?"

"To Mother Matthews'," Farber replied.

They crouched by the door for a few minutes waiting for a break in the crowds of people. Finally, they slipped out as Farber closed and locked the door behind him. Edging close to the building, he thought of the loss of his store, and of the long months he had spent in building it up. What could he do to save it? You're a fool, he told himself, still worrying about money at a time like this.

"Wait, Allan. I'm going back in for a second."

He reopened the door and first went over to the bread stand from which he scattered loaves of bread on the floor. Then he took soap powder, breakfast cereal boxes, and other large items that would be easy to pick up later, and laid them near the loaves. Rioters looking through the window, he reasoned, might be satisfied. At any rate, he decided again not to destroy the store partially on the chance it wouldn't be gutted completely. If they broke in, he hoped they'd only pick up the goods from the floor.

[300]

Acrid smoke filled the hot, muggy streets. Wailing sirens managed to outshout the noise of gunfire and explosions that filtered in from surrounding blocks. In the distance above the rooftops, plumes of oil-black smoke billowed against the fading light of the evening sky.

Farber and Allan jogged from doorway to doorway, hiding and observing before stealthily advancing a few more feet. They went unnoticed by the people who rushed passed them, carrying pieces of furniture with price tags dangling wildly.

They reached Mother Matthews' apartment and both beat frantically on her door. There was no answer. A youth came in through the entrance downstairs but turned to leave when he noticed them.

"He saw us," Farber said. "We can't stay here."

Drenched with sweat, their faces flushed pink from the heat, they turned instinctively like dumb animals toward their only known shelter.

They returned to find a crowd swarming around the store. Half a block away, they watched incredulously as man after man dodged shards of glass to jump through the broken front windows and exit with bottles of beer and wine and cartons of cigarettes.

Motioning Allan to stay close to the protecting trunk of a tree, Farber cursed himself as he watched a man drop a case of bottled beer, spewing foam and liquid over the sidewalk. The drinks and cigarettes should have been the bait, he thought, not the bread and cereal boxes.

Suddenly, as if to revenge himself for dropping the

case, the man pulled out a bottle from within a nearby automobile and lit a match to a piece of cloth hanging like a tongue from the bottle's mouth. The bottle, shedding bright white and red in the night, flew through the window and exploded, spreading jellylike flame which licked the outside perimeter of the window.

The rioters, casting long fierce shadows from the firelight, retreated from the burning store in the direction of Farber and Allan.

"White mothahs!" one screamed in a throaty, angry voice.

Farber looked over his shoulder. There was no place to run. Another mob came toward them from the opposite end of the street. He thrust Allan behind him, next to the tree. For a part of a second, a picture flashed in his mind, that of seven months ago when he had pushed his son forward to avoid a boy who had wanted to carry their bags. Now Allan, however, scurried from behind his father and stood by him as the two groups advanced in a slow, menacing way.

Numbed by fear, Allan waited for the beating. He'd fight for a while, he decided, more for show than for glory or hope of winning, and then give up. There were too many of them. He and his father would get their beatings and that would be the end of it. No more. Then they'd go home. But something bothered him as he watched them approach. Would they really be satisfied just to injure or were they after more? Would they kill?

He had always seen movies or read books about a group of people who were all bad, except for one or two

[302]

individuals. The Japanese aviator who didn't gun down the parachuting American. The Indian who freed the pioneer from a burning stake. But were there any good ones around now to save him? Where were Dr. Thompson and Yolanda? Mother Matthews, even James and Ferry, were probably out in another mob like this one.

He swore to himself that he'd hate them forever and ever, and that nothing could change his mind. As individuals they had killed his mother and now, as a mob, they were going to kill his father and him.

"Smash in they white jelly faces!" Farber heard one of them cry as a lead pipe came flying out to hit him on his right shoulder. It felt as if that part of his body split off from the rest of him.

They are not going to touch Allan, he swore to himself. With one arm hanging limply from his damaged shoulder, he swung blindly in front of him with his awkward left one. A sharp stone struck the point of his chin and continued its path to hit his Adam's apple. He gagged and saw a flash in front of his eyes. Then he knew he was going to die. He hoped that his death would satisfy them enough so that they would let Allan live.

"Please," he shouted above the noise. "Let my son go."

For a moment they stopped. They remained immobile like a frieze portraying a guerrilla force armed with claw hammers, kerosine-filled bottles, knives, rifles, and iron bars.

One man, cheekbones flat like his nose, leaped in front of the others. He held a smashed bottle in front of him, like

a banderillero at a bullfight whose duty it is to simultaneously goad and weaken the bull.

"He gonna go! He gonna go next," the man with the
bottle roared. "Come on, boy. Show you daddy the color
of you blood."

Allan ordered his arms and legs to attack, but his flesh
quaked at the demand. He prayed to God to make him
Superman, Hercules, Samson, so he could rip the lamppost
from its concrete moorings and swing it like a baseball bat.

The man pressed forward, pointing with the jagged
bottom of the bottle. He jerked and waved it wildly, feign-
ing jabs as the crowd yelped with delight. Farber raised an
arm in defense. A mixture of spittle and sweat ran down the
chins of both attacker and victim.

Another man, impatient with his colleague's game
playing, entered the circle. He held a long length of chain,
one end of which he wrapped around his wrist and arm.
Twisting his body for additional force, he lashed out with
the weapon, which whistled like a menacing bird. The iron
spun around Farber's neck, knocking him to the ground.
The attacker then dragged and pulled Farber like an unwilling leashed dog.

Now the rioters' shouts turned into an almost hysteri-
cal wail which reverberated over the block, riding the
smoke-laden air along with the sounds of sirens and
gunfire. Like cheerleaders, the men clapped and goaded the
chain man on with an unintelligible chanting accusation
which served to justify for them their behavior and the
action of their protagonist.

Allan rushed toward the chain man and grappled for the weapon. The man pushed him away, freed the chain from around Farber's neck, and whipped it across the boy's midsection. The impact of the iron links against flesh and bone made a sound like that of a shovel digging into earth. Allan screamed and fell. Pain distorted his face, clamping eyes shut, disrupting his skin, and stretching his mouth. He rolled over on his knees, instinctively preferring the second blow to come on his back, and clawed for something to grasp. Near the base of the tree, he felt a large root, gnarled and charred as it lay exposed above the protection of the deep earth.

Farber tried to rise, but both attackers kicked him and, like gladiators, pointed their weapons toward the rioters in expectation of a sign. The rioters grew silent instead, listening to a whisper of a sound whose familiarity made it stand out clearly and distinctly in the neighborhood roar. All eyes turned toward Allan.

A heaving nausea overtook Allan and he gurgled. He tore at his windpipe with one hand as if to dig a hole to admit air or to permit something to escape. Vomit spewed in front of him, and at the feet of the two men, who quickly stepped backward into the mob. Although eager for the blood of their enemy to soak their clothes, they were unwilling for his sickness to smear their shoes.

Some of the men backed away, repelled by the sight of the vomit and its unmistakable odor. For the others, its humanness reduced their hatred to hesitative dismay, and they also turned away. In a matter of moments, the mob

[305]

broke up into groups of twos and threes and disappeared around a corner.

Both father and son sat up simultaneously. Expecting a trick, they looked and then listened unsuccessfully for the mob.

With a grunt, Farber rose to his feet and leaned over the boy. "Are you okay, Allan?"

"Yeah. Just a little sick in the stomach." Allan could see the rust marks from the chain on his father's neck, and a large, red bruise on his arm.

"We've got to get out, Allan. Some other maniacs might . . ."

A loud explosion cut into his words.

"The kerosine tank! The fire got to it!"

The night brightened with flames from the store shooting out streaks of black and red. Allan saw a small, dark movement emerge beneath the smoke pouring from the open door. It was Dracula, moving quickly and evenly like a rolling ball. The animal, singed fur bristling, turned its head to take a last look at the burning store before it jumped into the street. The rat ran a course along the gutter passing within inches of Farber and Allan and brushing its ponderous body against the sidewalk wall as it moved down the block.

Allan, too frightened about his own life, did not feel cheated over the escape of Dracula. He gazed unthinkingly at the rat until it became part of the darkness.

Farber looked only at the store. My god-monster is gone, he thought with a mixed feeling of relief and bitterness. Thank God, no more.

[306]

And yet he felt no release; no more freedom than he had ever known. Although the events blighted his comprehension, he realized that he never would be free, and that he had in thought committed a sin against the store, the very fiber of his being. His thoughts engendered a new emotion of bewildered guilt and emptiness.

It's a shame that I should think this way. All that I've worked for is gone.

The two stood mesmerized by the flames. For Allan, thirst suddenly became more important than the lingering pain in his midsection, than his weariness and fear.

A taxicab slowed down as it approached the corner. The driver was a burly mountain of darkness, with chest and shoulders hulking over the steering wheel. He came to a complete stop to peer at the fire.

"Mister, mister!" Farber ran over to the cab. "Please help us. Take us out of here."

The cabbie's black face, covered with a sheen of perspiration, twisted into a scowl. "Man, you got to be crazy. I'm goin' home and stayin' there till this sheet ends." He looked around apprehensively. His eyes were heavy-lidded, as though nature, resolving his fate as a cabdriver, saw to it that he would have some protection from glare and exhaust fumes.

"They'll kill us. Please, I'll give you money."

The cabbie released a rattling laugh. "Tough. They get my tail, too, luggin' you-all around."

"Then just take my boy."

The driver stared at Allan, who trembled, eyes wide in spite of smoke filling the air. Now the driver's head shook and nodded alternately. His lower lip quivered. When he spoke, his voice contained tones of both a cold snicker and a pitying sob. "Oh, sheet, man! What you wanna do that to me for?" He shook his head again. "Get in. Both of you. In the back. On the floor."

The car jumped forward. "Keep you tail down and don't look out no window," the driver ordered. "Don't lift you head or someone'll shoot it off."

The trip became a succession of sharp turns, sudden stops, squealing brakes, and shouted curses as the driver swerved to avoid hitting rubble or striking people who ran in the streets, shrieking and throwing rocks and bottles which bounced off the car.

"Blood brother, blood brother!" the driver cried out of the window every time he saw a knot of people ahead of him.

When they came to a quiet area, the driver breathed deeply and brushed his arm across his face, exchanging the perspiration on his arm for the sweat on his face. He leaned back in his seat, more at ease.

"Man, I ought to switch on the light so that my crazy brothers could see I'm black." He laughed. "We need light to see that I'm dark." Still more relaxed, he turned and looked down on his two passengers shriveled with arms clutched around their folded knees. "What you need is somethin' to black you face like commandoes." Again, he laughed.

At the next corner he slowed down, uncertain of his direction. A shot from a rifle rang out. He slammed down hard on the gas pedal but a barrier of overturned cars blocked the corner. In the briefest instant, the car was surrounded by armed black men.

General Tammu wore Mexican bandit-style ammunition belts crisscrossed over a khaki shirt and, despite the heat, an Australian soldier's wide-brimmed hat, and jodhpur breeches, clean but strangely misshapen, as though they had been stored for a long time in a trunk until they could be used for a worthy occasion. In one hand was a bugle, tarnished and dented.

He walked over to the driver's side. "What's the problem, blood?"

"I don't like being shot at."

Tammu peered inside. The ladder of his chins vibrated before the loud laugh left his throat. "Well, well! The illustrious mobile enterprise of Farber and son." He laughed again. "Out, mothahfuckers. All of you."

Tammu examined his three captives, shaking his head. "Still getting the black man to carry you on his back, eh, Farber?" He addressed the driver. "You keep 'em hidden on the floor and they'll miss the action. They won't be able to see black women and children dead out in the streets. Yeah, old whitey's moving in on the good blacks now. He doesn't know the difference between the good blacks and the bad blacks. Black's black as far as he's concerned."

Tammu looked at Allan. "Yeah, a lot of black blood's gonna be spilt tonight. Bug's black blood. Say it over and over again, real fast. Bug's black blood. You say it, Farber junior."

[309]

Allan shrugged his shoulders and kept his eyes on the ground, expecting a blow to fall from one of the blacks surrounding him.

"Say it, mothahfucker!" A thin Negro, whose high cheekbones and tight, narrow headband made him look like an Apache Indian, stepped forward to strike Allan.

Farber curled his fists. "Leave him alone, you animal!"

Tammu, his khaki shirt a vehicle of sweat, waved aside the Negro. "That's right, call us animals. That way you white mothahs won't feel too badly about shooting us up. No siree! Maybe this is what you want to finish us off once and for all."

The cabdriver cleared his throat and finally spoke. "He don't want to finish nobody off. He just want to get out a here. Can't you see they both hurt, man?"

Tammu stared for a long time at the driver, and then at Farber and Allan. He patted his bugle, tucked it under his ammunition belt, and with almost the same movement, jerked his finger. "All right, nigger. Get your white mothahs out of here." He turned toward his men, motioning as though their purpose was not to kill, but to injure, for in death the lesson would be lost. Nevertheless they slunk back, mean-faced like a tomcat that has just lost a bird through carelessness.

Minutes later, the driver pulled over. "Here you be. You could walk the rest of the way."

"What do we owe you?" asked Farber.

"Nothin'," the cabbie said, pausing to allow them to

hear the already distant sounds of the rioting. "This one's on me."

Farber nodded his appreciation, expecting to toss some money on the front seat as soon as he left the cab, but the man quickly whirled the car around and headed in the direction from which they had come.

"Thanks!" Allan managed to shout out of a parched and scratchy throat. "For the ride! For saving our lives!"

The cabbie gave no sign of acknowledgment. Allan waved frantically, bitterness growing in him that the cabbie, who had almost sacrificed himself to help them, now chose to ignore them. Of a sudden, he thought of Yolanda, ignoring him on the playground as she drew the attention of the bullies away from him.

Yolanda had saved his life. In his mind he traveled back to the playground that night and found her alone, her sobs muffled and her shoulders shaking. Yolanda, you did it for me. Death's Head and his two hulks would have stabbed me and let me bleed to death. You stopped them the only way you knew how.

Despite his realization of her sacrifice, remorse dampened his eyes. He had left her and now he would never see her again because she had spoiled her body. While he could have Mother Matthews, she who had slept with hundreds, he would not have Yolanda because he idolized her purity, which he had thought belonged only to him. He couldn't overlook or forgive her shame and defilement. She had suffered because of him—that was all the stronger reason for giving her up.

[311]

"Let's go," his father said. "We'll be here the rest of the night if we don't start moving."

Soldiers with rifles came into view. A sergeant whose thick helmet chin strap failed to conceal the fact that he had no chin approached Farber. "What are you two doing in the riot area? We've got a curfew working."

"We live here. I own a business."

The sergeant tilted his helmet back so that Farber could see his truncated face. "Probably not anymore." He shook his head. "Better keep on moving."

Farber thought as he walked. My business. Something that really belongs to me, not like a job or an apartment. It's not a bad business. It could be better, it could be worse, but it's mine. I'll go back. Collect whatever insurance there is and money the customers owe me. If the place was burned down, I'll declare bankruptcy. No one would blame me. I'll start all over again, this time with a lawyer. I'll have that bastard Gittelson over a barrel. He'll have a hard time finding someone else to rent his place. He'll just about pay me to occupy it. The customers? I don't want them to love me, and I don't want to love them. All I want is to make a living.

They came to an intersection busy with traffic, and each watched in surprised silence at the people carrying on with their daily lives while in another part of the city a battle raged.

Farber tugged at his son's elbow. "Come on. I think there's a hotel within walking distance."

Allan pointed. "There's one."

[312]

"Looks too expensive. There's a cheaper one right down the block. We're just going to stay a day or two, until things cool down. Then we'll go back and see what's what. I think the money'll still be in the furnace."

"We're not going to open again, are we?"

"I am, not you. You're going to stay with Benny and go to school in New York. That's what your mother wanted. You'll be with your own kind." And you won't get in my way and worry me to death, Farber thought.

"It's too dangerous. They'll kill you. Why can't you just go back to being a carpenter?"

"First of all, no more carpenter work for me. That's past history. I like being in business. I just have to take it easier, keep shorter hours. Maybe I'll hire some guy to be my helper and bouncer. Second of all, this *shvartzer* stuff isn't going to last. I'm not going to run away just because they want to blow off a little steam. My bet is they really like to have a few white faces in the neighborhood."

Farber paused to think. I'll take out the glass windows and put in boards. No sweat. I'm a carpenter. No, I'm not. I'm a businessman. To hell with the plate glass manufacturers and the insurance companies. I'll invest in a burglary alarm system. There's a risk in getting hurt in this business just like any other.

"I think you should open a store in the suburbs, in a white neighborhood."

"First of all," Farber replied, pleased that he knew the right answer, "going to the suburbs costs a lot of money, which I don't have. Second of all, a small man can't com-

[313]

pete with the supermarkets out there. In the city, there's still a chance. All you need is to work hard. Working in a store for me is like driving two-penny nails after you're used to spikes."

From the corner of his eye Farber caught Allan's worried expression. "You could come visit me as much as you like. I'll get a nice apartment in a good neighborhood. Just don't rush me. Give me time. I'm just learning the business. I've been in it seven months. A baby takes nine months just to be born. Give me more time."

Rain began to fall, accompanied by a cool breeze from the north. Allan flicked out a dry tongue to catch the drops.

Farber stopped and placed a hand over his son's shoulder. "This is the hotel I had in mind."